The Easy Hour

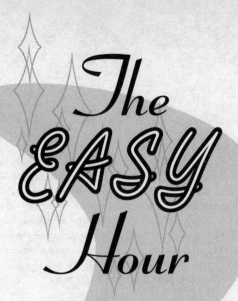

The EASY Hour

Leslie Stella

THREE RIVERS PRESS • NEW YORK

For my parents

Copyright © 2003 by Leslie Stella

Published by Three Rivers Press, New York, New York.
Member of the Crown Publishing Group, a division of Random House, Inc.
www.randomhouse.com

THREE RIVERS PRESS and Tugboat design are registered
trademarks of Random House, Inc.

Printed in the United States of America

Design by Fearn Cutler de Vicq

Library of Congress Cataloging-in-Publication Data
Stella, Leslie.
The easy hour / Leslie Stella.—1st ed.
    1. Women's clothing industry—Fiction   2. Chicago (Ill.)—Fiction.
            3. Retail trade—Fiction.   I. Title.
        PS3569.T37972 E25   2002
    813'.6—dc21   2002010522

ISBN 0-609-80972-5

10 9 8 7 6 5 4 3 2

FIRST EDITION

Chicago is an October sort of city even in spring.

—Nelson Algren

Chapter 1

*S*obriety was on me before I could get out of the way. It was the mirror's fault. I woke up with the worst hangover of the modern era but was not shocked into full equanimity until I saw that creature lurching out of the glass. What . . . what happened to me? I had worn a smock and clogs to bed—why? A cigarette butt had burrowed deep into my hair. I combed out other debris (cork remnants, a toenail, a toothpick with a bit of bacon clinging to it) and deftly applied makeup with the help of a grout bag and trowel. The phone rang.

"How horrible for you!" began Tim in a delighted voice.

"It's a bad one," I admitted. "I slept in clogs."

"Not your hangover! I'm talking about the *Chicago Society* article. What did you do to that reporter last night? He hates you."

Tim saved me the trouble of running out to the nearest newsstand in my clogs, smock, and fatback hat, and began to read aloud.

DIETRICH'S HALLOWEEN
—A HONEY OF A TIME

By Babbington Hawkes

The fabulous and salty Honey Dietrich outdid herself last night with a Halloween dual benefit for two new projects, the restaurant Nub (you know where it is) and infantile melanoma (a very sad type of cancer). Amazing to see the Daleys (cowboy and cowgirl) rubbing elbows with Dennis Farina and

Keanu Reeves (Mafia hitman and extremely cute mad scientist). Honey herself, divine in retro couture, provided an outstanding Sonoma chardonnay from her family's West Coast winery and Nub chef Pietro Bangalore offered the best of Nub's eclectic nouvelle American bistro cuisine . . .

. . . dancing to the sounds of the Weasel Walter Five were our own Roger Ebert (thumbs up on the cabbage patch, Ebes!), Judd Nelson (with new Prince Valiant coif—methinks a starring role in the next Merchant-Ivory period piece is afoot), and a certain portly weatherman from Fox News. Unfortunately, dear friends, as I was preparing to interview Chef Bangalore on upcoming menu changes, the *person* who had staked herself out at the buffet all night inhaling entire platters lurched into *moi* and yakked rumaki and Yankee pot roast tidbits all over my butter-soft Ferragamos. Perhaps certain *persons* should stick to flogging Fishman's sportswear instead of attending social functions where they are woefully outclassed, not to mention overfed . . .

No, no. I was fairly, almost 100 percent positive that that wasn't me. That didn't happen. It couldn't have. My smock was clean when I woke up. How dare he call me a "person," self-righteous queen Babbington Hawkes, society gossipmonger *snob*. How did he know who I was? I've only encountered him once or twice in the past, and I'm sure I just stood there hangdog and speechless as usual.

"Have to get back to the reference desk now, old trout," said Tim. "Call me later."

I threw on clothes and made it to Fishman's with five minutes to spare. My work friends soothed me with home remedies. Nan from Hosiery brought me cheesecloth stuffed with rice that she'd heated up in the staff microwave. I held it to the base of my throbbing skull and ignored customers. My senior, Mrs. Lubbeth, always hogged everybody who walked into Women's Wear anyway and only threw me the BOBs (in retail parlance that's "biddies on budgets"). But she did allow me a really long coffee break when I came in, then pulled some cotton balls and a bottle of witch hazel out of her purse so that I might dab some under my eyes. I should carry cotton balls around in my purse, but there's only room for a credit card and one key.

"What's her majesty's first name?" asked Nan, crouching down behind the counter. The executives frowned on fraternization between departments. Divide and conquer and so on.

"Who knows? She's been here eight hundred years, and no one's ever called her anything except 'Mrs. Lubbeth.'"

Nan said, "Except Bernie from Admin. He calls her 'Mrs. L.'"

I was terrifyingly close to hurling Starbucks all over the watchband rotisserie. The mention of freakish Bernie had dredged up some flickering memory from last night. His hair, yes, that was it. Plenty sickening in its usual "party fro" state (business in the front—party in the back), it had been lacquered with sparkly orange hair spray. Halloween, right . . . he was a spaceman. What had I been? Something in a smock. Suddenly, I felt very cold.

I said, "Nan, I found a toenail and bacon fat in my hair this morning."

"Again?" she sympathized.

Mrs. Lubbeth, unwise to my new hiding place under the counter, walked around the department looking for me. With her way-bleached Angie Dickinson hair and Pucci caftan, Mrs. Lubbeth was a harsh visual dose that morning. She was sort of motherly, in an Endora-from-*Bewitched* way. Quite unpredictable, she'd bring doughnuts and cookies for us in Women's Wear, then without warning, start goose-stepping around the atrium, howling about sales figures. Sometimes I thought she was putting a curse on me, mushing her lips around and squinting, but usually it turned out that a caraway seed had simply slipped under her partial.

Fishman's had put up a huge sign at the designer boutique, proclaiming, WE NOW STOCK SIZE 0! I know it's something to shoot for, but I think it would feel anticlimactic to try on clothes and whisper to the mirror, *I've done it. I'm finally a zero.* Frankly, I *have* said that, in the usual sense of zero, and it's not so thrilling.

Nan popped her head over the counter, keeping watch for the return of her manager. We saw a tiny woman milling about the designer boutique, which was a corner of our women's wear department. It was partially cordoned off with tall chinoiserie screens to keep regular people out. Mrs. Consolo headed this Fishman's subdepartment, as she was the only one of us sleek enough to wear designer originals and smooth enough to convince sixty-year-old dowagers they looked fabulous in knit Galliano.

The shopper approached Mrs. Consolo with a dress and said, "Do you have this in a zero?"

We couldn't hear Mrs. Consolo's response, but the small customer said loudly, "No, no, a *zero.* The two just hangs on me." We exchanged glances. Mrs. Consolo disappeared into the back room. Perhaps she was pawing through discarded scraps of fabric under the seamstress's chair, looking for one that was small enough.

If it were me, I'd ask for the zero in a soft, modest voice, implying that I had simply been *born* a zero, not that I had clawed and murdered my way *into* zero.

Nan leaned into the countertop mirror and made infinitesimal adjustments to her long red hair and cute Edith Head bangs. She wore one of our new pink cashmere sweater vests over her bare chest, just flat enough to get away with it. I tried that last week, and my right breast made an unfortunate appearance when I smacked the cash register during a voided transaction.

"Oopsie!" I had said, tucking it back in.

The customer, a middle-aged doughboy buying women's panties, had said, "It's not subtle, but it works."

Nan saw her manager advancing. "Better go, see you later. What are you staring at me for?" She looked down at her vest. "It's not a zero, if that's what you're thinking. But cashmere, cashmere . . . isn't it to die for?"

More coffee and more hiding from customers lifted some of the migraine, depuffed my swollen-udder eye bags, and generally reduced me to my normal witlessness. Sobriety gained on my hangover and with it brought full memory of the previous evening.

It had begun in my apartment with Tim disparaging my Halloween costume.

"Is that the best you could do?" he asked. Deep, disappointed frown lines settled into their usual locations.

After a lifetime of hearing those words on thousands of occasions, I had always hoped I could come up with something better than my standard "Uh-huh" or "I guess not." Decades of practice should have supplied me with some clever, cutting rejoinder.

"I don't know," I replied doubtfully, looking down at my costume.

"A ghost? A ghost?" asked Tim. "This is a *Honey Dietrich* event, Lisa. Do you know who's going to be there? Oprah. Maggie Daley. Judd Nelson."

"From *Taxi*?"

"Don't be an idiot," said Tim, roughly pushing me into my dressing area, or closet. "You need to be seen, recognized, if you want to get invited anywhere around here." I liked to think of Tim as my annoying yet slightly loveable gay sidekick, but in truth he was more like a highly strung marine sergeant with a fondness for tiny pastel cigarettes and haute couture.

I was glad I'd been invited to the party, though everyone who worked at Fishman's had been invited. Socialite Honey Dietrich liked us because we never blabbed to the press that she bought half-price irregulars in our designer boutique. It seemed strange to me that the heiress to the Dietrich salt fortune would be so frugal.

She always said, "It comes from living through the *war*, sugar." Quick subtraction on the store calculator provided no clue as to which war Honey could have lived through. Even if she had had as much plastic surgery as was popularly surmised, she could not have meant World War II; she was in that nebulous late-forties/early-fifties range. Then what? The Korean War? Not exactly a time of famine, unless you were Korean. The war on drugs seemed a more likely possibility, what with the government cracking down on unnecessary refills of Nembutal and Valium and everything.

"You look like a floppy Klansman," said Tim, pulling at the peak atop my head.

I said, "They only had fitted sheets at the thrift."

"You really went all out for this party, didn't you? Sheets at the thrift!"

I make $208.25 a week after taxes. I buy the sheets for my bed at the thrift.

"All *you're* wearing is a black polyester suit and giant googly-eyed glasses."

He dusted off invisible lint from his cuff and smirked. "I'm Alan Greenspan."

I thought he was the lady from the Old Navy commercials.

Tim cut a huge hole out of my sheet and yanked it down over my head. Then he put my hair in big Farrah curlers and said this was all he could come up with. When asked, I was to say that I was a beauty client of Bumble and Bumble.

"But I don't want to be a customer of Bumble and Bumble," I said. "It's ridiculous."

"No one says 'customer' anymore, and it's not ridiculous, it's New *York*. You need some kind of clout in Chicago."

He then tried to get me into a cat suit, but I explained that cat suits looked lousy on my saddlebags. He said I needed fashionable ankles and shoes to stick out below my beauty-client smock. He asked for Blahnik stilettos. I gave him Birkenstock clogs.

I was desperate for a cig, but we were late.

We hailed a cab at Division and Ashland. All sorts of witches and zombies were fighting over cabs at the corner, but Tim barreled through shouting, "I'm Alan Greenspan, goddammit! I'm Alan Greenspan!" and the crowds parted like the Red Sea. No one even wants to get *close* to an economist these days.

We reached the Gold Coast in half an hour. We could have just taken the El, but you can't show up at a Honey Dietrich event on public transportation.

Tim said, "No one must know how poor we are. And for God's sake, don't mention you grew up in Bridgeport, not that everyone won't guess the moment you open your mouth." Tim had no idea how hard it was to eradicate Thirty-first Street from speech. I still lapsed into its flat vowels and lockjaw cadence, particularly when I was starving for Polish "sahh-sidge" or criticizing "da Mare," Richard Daley.

Mike Royko put it best: Bridgeport is a community that drinks out of the beer pail and eats out of the lunch bucket. We are hard-wired for mustaches and Chess King sweaters, for tailgating, for public nuisance. Like a town of relief pitchers, the men are broad in the beam and have strange facial-hair configurations. The women are dwarfed by their coifs. Bridgeport is the South Side— "dese-dem-and-doze" Italian, lace-curtain Polack, bog Irish, blue-collar, stockyards, sluggers, the Daley empire, hog butchers, wheat stackers, builders, and wreckers. Doughnuts can be purchased at any moment of any day. The White Sox–Cubs game is known as the "War of Northern Aggression." I've tried to exorcise my background, but I'm second-generation Bridgeport, and its stains and scars have marked me for life.

Honey's Halloween party was held in one of those cramped, fashionable restaurants that pop up every few minutes in Chicago. They have unappetizing names like Yanal or Flem's. This one, Nub, was Honey's present darling but was expected to cave when she grew bored of it in six months.

Anxiety dawned upon me. "Tim," I said, "I forgot my cigs."

He dragged me past the Nub doorman, a fifteen-year-old boy in pink marabou who informed me, "We have a no-smoking policy, ma'am."

Before Tim had butchered it, my ghost costume had had a perfect little O cut out at mouth level, just the right size for a Kool or a cocktail straw. Without the restrictive O, I would probably eat food and drink beer, two habits that have recently eclipsed smoking, my primary vice.

"Oh, hell," I said. "A buffet."

Tim steered me away from a massive cheese sculpture and into the arms of Honey Dietrich, who was surrounded by a gaggle of dowagers and pretty socialites and young artists. She was dressed in vintage black satin Pauline Trigère, all blond finger waves and red lips. Her triangular nostrils flared hungrily at my friend, hazel-eyed long drink of water that he is. She kissed me forcefully on the mouth.

"I don't believe in air kissing," she said, her eyes never leaving Tim. "So false."

"Honey Dietrich, this is my friend Tim Gideon," I said.

"Oh? Are you the one always leaving those Bibles for me in the hotel?" she murmured, batting three feet of eyelash at him. He smiled stiffly, as though he hadn't heard the Bible joke for the last thirty years.

We discussed our costumes. Honey laughed uproariously at witty Greenspan, and proclaimed my Bumble client garb to be "too, too sick-making." Tim gave me a surreptitious thumbs up, as this was an accolade of high praise currently in vogue. I guessed that she was Veronica Lake, but she shook her head and told me to guess again.

"I'm really not good at guessing," I said.

"Guess!" she ordered.

"Um, okay. . . ." I tried to think of other beautiful blond actresses that would flatter her. "Grace Kelly?"

"No, guess!"

Despairing, I said, "RuPaul?"

She blanched, but assumed I was not clever or daring enough to poke fun at her, and let it slide. "No, darling, I am *last season*!"

The tension had built up, and somehow a laugh quite unlike my own escaped me. It was high-pitched and abrasive and psychotic. What was she talking about? Everyone knew I had no idea.

Tim stepped up to the plate and rescued me. "Oh, right! Fall 1999 retro forties! Very good, Ms. Dietrich. Lisa has *tons* of last season in her closet, so she would know!" It was sort of a rescue, in that now they all pitied me for my outdated wardrobe instead of detesting me for my ignorance.

Afterward I slumped against Tim. "She makes me nervous."

He patted my rollers kindly and led me to the bar. I eyed the taps lustily.

"Go easy," warned Tim. "And *please,* no Old Style. If you must, have an expensive Belgian beer."

"Rum and coke," I requested.

"My God!" howled Tim. "Are we at a sorority picnic?" He asked the bartender for two vodka tonics. Humbly, I sipped mine.

"How's work?" I asked.

"Sucks. Frigging playpen. I told the director, if I can't stage the puppet shows my way, there's no point in my being there at all. That set her teeth on edge, little prig bureaucrat." Tim is a children's librarian. He's stormed out of so many staff meetings, the library director now holds them in a locked room.

"You?" he asked.

"It's okay . . ." My voice trailed off and my eyes clouded over, reflecting on my career.

"See that?" Tim pointed at a man in full Kabuki array. "That's my next boyfriend. His father owned a tart shop and was killed by an employee."

"Just tarts? It seems incredible that one could sell only tarts and remain solvent, especially in such a nontart city as Chicago," I said.

"I *know*! But it was very successful."

Before I could stop him, Tim slithered away toward the Kabuki tart orphan. Oh, God, alone. I downed my vodka and turned back to the bar. Suddenly hordes of Fishman people bellied up—demanding drinks, and laughing. We were all out of place at this kind of party, with its opera benefactors and botanic-garden patrons. It was obvious that Honey was just buying our silence about her designer irregulars. But with an open bar and tables of free food, I, for one, was not about to talk.

Tim was right. I was going nowhere by socializing only with Nan from Hosiery, Jesus from Sporting Goods, Philomena from China, Hui from Men's Wear (also from China—actually, Hong Kong). I needed new acquaintances, but first I needed a drink, and to get it I had to remain in the beer line with the assembled geniuses from Fishman's.

"Old Style," I ordered.

"Hey!" shouted Bernie from Admin. His hair . . . ugh, it was responsible for the resurfacing of my entire memory of the party. "Another Old Style drinker! 'Member that commercial? 'It's our great beer and they can't have it.'"

I smiled weakly and made a break for it. Bernie—ordinarily barely tolerable—was unendurable right then. The party fro, the ill-fitting spaceman costume . . . it all threatened to drag me down to Fishman's level—Fishman's *Admin* level—here at Honey Dietrich's.

An hour passed. A man dressed as a licorice whip made me dance the electric slide with him. It was okay; my smock flared out in kind of a cute way. Licorice Whip tried to get it on with me, but I wasn't having it. I escaped to the bar, grabbed an econo-sized Old Style, and wandered over to the buffet table. Everyone had eaten the Cajun catfish squares with peach chutney, so I nibbled on rumaki and clods of meat straight from the serving platter.

Again, wretched Bernie materialized as I shoveled in the last bite. He really loved catching me scarfing, the little jag-off.

"Boy! You really like beer!" he said. "You're my kind of woman."

"It helps me get through social situations," I said, shooting the tankard in one gulp.

He looked concerned. "So you use alcohol as a crutch?"

These days, I use it as a wheelchair.

I moved away from Bernie back toward the monument of meat. Little pot-roast squares had been stacked in the shape of the Sears Tower, which I managed to convert into a mid-rise apartment building in five minutes. I paused in my grazing, or rather my razing of Chicago landmarks; the pot roast and rumaki weren't getting along in their tub of Old Style and stomach acid. God, it's *their* great beer and they can *have* it. I held on to the table as the room swung about, as a mincing little man in shiny shoes looked on in abject horror. . . .

At some point thereafter, Tim Gideon Bible finally showed up and yanked me away. He clamped a petite blue cig between his lips.

"I really appreciate being deserted," I said. "You wouldn't even be here at this party if it wasn't for me." He looked contrite and handed me the little blue bone. I cast about for the marabou cig police, then inhaled. Decent . . . Sobranie. Tim said Sobranies were no longer exported to the United States, but he had a connection in duty-free Germany.

I exhaled and looked around. "Where's Kabuki Tart?"

Tim adjusted his tie, a sad expression playing at the corners of his mouth. "He thinks he's not gay."

"Oh."

"I told him none of my boyfriends are gay."

I hugged him sloppily. "He'll come around if he's drunk enough."

Tim smiled gently and removed my arms from his waist. "Well, this won't help."

No one could be more pathetic than I. Drunk at Honey Dietrich's Halloween party, in front of society. In front of that mincing little man, that reporter from *Chicago Society* who was furiously scribbling in his notepad while a flunky scrubbed his shoes.

It had been a really long time since either Tim or I had a boyfriend. Well, there *was* a stranger at a Cubs game last summer who grabbed me and slobbered on my neck—which constitutes a date, I suppose, by Cubs fans' standards—but it lacked the emotional intimacy of a mature relationship.

"Let's walk off your drunk," suggested Tim. We didn't walk off "drunkenness," as that implied escaping from temporary inebriation, but rather walked off "drunks": wobbly, blotto companions who shadowed us at parties, embarrassing us and making us sick. We walked off drunks the way others tried to lose geeks and infatuated freshmen and licorice whips.

We went a few blocks over to the lake and sat on the cold flat stones of the jetty behind the Mag Mile. We watched the waves break down the shore, watched the gambling dinner boats cruise by. I went riverboat gambling last year and won twenty-five bucks. I'd shouted, "I have the loosest slots in Joliet!" and security was alerted to my presence.

I have had celibacy and poverty thrust upon me like a medicine ball.

My drunk, my evil twin, my Mr. Hyde, liked this train of thought. She could always sense the slightest bit of melancholy coming on and turn it into a full-blown assault upon me, which I was powerless to refute. She told me to take a powder while she took over my speech. "Tim, some people are born for the poor celibate life, while others have the poor celibate life thrust upon them. Neither are bound for sobriety."

"Is that an excerpt from your speech to the graduates?"

My drunk continued. "One cannot be celibate *and* poor *and* sober."

"No, indeed."

My drunk sighed. God, she sounded pathetic and ridiculous. "Tim, old sock, if I have to be poor and celibate, I refuse to be sober. It's the one thing I can control."

He pulled me up and handed me a little gold box of Sobranies from his suit coat pocket. "I don't blame you, old trout. Here, have a smoke. I got them from the doorman."

"The doorman is your German duty-free connection?"

"Only *one* of my connections."

Ha, "no-smoking policy," eh, little pink doorboy? God, I love Sobranies, their pastel shades are so calming.

We caught a taxi finally. My $650-a-month studio rehab is only four blocks from Tim's flophouse $425 one-bedroom. My building is on the verge of co-op; his remains smack in the middle of Latin Kings territory. He admits it's the ghetto, but rent and lives are cheap, so it's okay.

He blew me a kiss out the cab window as I turned toward my building.

"Bye, old Tim, old Gideon Bible!" my drunk called out. Ooh, the Bible joke is a big no-no, she *knows* that. But he just flipped me off good-naturedly as the cab sped off. He let me get away with it because, as names go, I have it worse.

My name is Lisa Galisa.

Chapter 2

*B*y noon, the cheesecloth-rice sack had given out. Migraine crept back, stomach started churning. I may have had my own unique drunk, but I got the same hangover as everyone else.

We at Fishman's were told to ambush our customers as they emerged from the fitting rooms, and say, "That looks great!" or "Pretty skirt." Usually I tried to hide in the handicapped dressing room to sneak a cig, but if a lady ran into me and asked if her suit fit well, I'd say, "Oh, yeah." It's not like I didn't try. But Mrs. Lubbeth was unimpressed with my enthusiasm. She said if I would just apply myself, I might one day receive the coveted brown name tag that senior salesladies wore. Until then, I had to wear the white one that signaled to shoppers how lousy I was at my job.

"Hon, you've got to say they look beautiful, make them want to buy it," she said. "That's the only way you'll make a good commission." That, and not getting shoved into the clearance rack by Lubbeth as she stampeded toward old-money hags.

A shaky elderly lady pirouetted in front of our three-way mirror as I smiled glassily at her. She studied every thread of the black, conservative Chanel suit, murmuring, "Gee, I don't know. What do *you* think?" What was there not to know? If I could afford Chanel, I would just buy it and dispense with the questions.

I tried to look enthused, as Lubbeth spied around the corner. "Oh, it's to die for," I gushed.

The old lady met my gaze in the mirror and said coolly, "How nice. It's for a funeral." Mrs. Lubbeth told me to take a lunch break while she homed in on my commission.

I sat in the commissary and ate half a grapefruit and a boiled egg. The cafeteria worker who slops things on trays for us cautioned me against the bagels in the basket on top of the counter.

"Dirty," she said quietly, shaking her head. "No good." She looked around nervously. Would the cafeteria manager burst out from behind the swinging doors, telling everyone to calm down, that the bagels were in fact *not* dirty and perfectly acceptable for eating? Would the worker lose her job? Would I, if I refused the bagel? And if it was dirty, how did it get that way? Did it fall on the floor or in the toilet? Bugs, was it bugs? Was it just stale? Stale was okay. Or did the baker have oozing pustules on his hands when he kneaded the dough?

"Thanks," I said. I slid my tray along toward the cashier, who rang up my order and said it was nice to see someone *finally* eating those boiled eggs.

I sat down at a far table and dialed Tim on my cell. He used to take calls on his cell phone all the time while at work, until the library director begged him to leave it at home. The constant ringing was distracting to the patrons. I called him directly at the reference desk.

"Reference! Hello!" he shouted.

"It's me."

"Uh-huh, hold on," he said, then shouted some distance away from the phone, "They're arranged alphabetically by author's last name. Do you know the alphabet?"

I said, "My head hurts."

"*Tell* me about it. What did they make those V&Ts with, Wolfschmidt?"

We talked about the party. It turned out Licorice Whip was Roger Ebert's personal assistant. He scheduled all of Ebert's in-town appearances and booked his dinner reservations. Roger Ebert was Chicago's own Renaissance man. At parties, it was rumored that guests would shout out topics upon which he would extemporize at length: botany, French literature, the Lake poets, the nicest rest room in a five-block radius, cheapest francheezie, no category too obscure or too mundane. He knew famous people and fawned like a teenage girl around them. He obviously appreciated our many fine restaurants and seemed like the type of man who would not mock your ignorance of wine. He was supposed to be a very good dancer and had a friendly sense of humor. Everyone liked his special editorial pieces in the *Sun-Times* where he complained about politics. His two-part series on the fate of the University of Illinois's mascot, Chief Illiniwek, also met with huge favor, particularly since he took both sides of the argument. First he said Illiniwek was *not* a racist figure and everyone should just settle down. Then he said, hey, if some people are offended, then maybe it *is* racist. At some point, everyone was happy. So along with being an expert on film, politics, and pop culture, he has mastered race relations. Damn, I should've gotten down with Licorice Whip. Then I could've made friends with Ebert—platonic, unless he felt attracted to me. I am not a stickler for looks, and anyway I've heard that Ebert has a beautiful penthouse overlooking Lake Michigan and a superb collection of Modiglianis. Ebert could teach me about movies and art, and I could try to do something with his hair and get him into Joseph Abboud. Ebert has this sort of dumpy, everyman quality about him; you look at him and say, "Big deal. I could find one of these anywhere." But then he opens his mouth, and you find yourself transfixed by every lament, anecdote, and flaring imbecility that issues forth. You feel like congratulating yourself for discovering the remarkable human beneath the maroon sweater.

Tim said, "I see Licorice Whip at Ed's Warped Records on North Avenue all the time. Maybe I can set something up." Then he screamed, "I'm sorry, you can't sleep in the library! Wake up and walk around! Wake up!"

"I gotta go," I said. "I need to sneak a smoke outside, and I want to pick up a *Chicago Society*. Is it raining in Uptown? It was supposed to rain here, and I don't want my Sobranie getting soggy."

"Yeah, it's raining. Why do you want to read that thing? I already read you the gossip column on the phone this morning."

"I need to see it myself." I hung up, ran outdoors and down the block to the newsstand, and grabbed *Chicago Society* out of the freebie pile. I lit my cig and walked back to the building, reading.

Well, there it was. My first appearance in the society pages had been a blow-by-blow account of my reign of revulsion and depravity. The rain soaked me and my cig gave out. At least Babbington—ruiner of lives, chronicler of nausea—didn't use my name, and with two dozen Fishman floggers there, only a few people might recognize me in his description. God, please don't let anyone know it was me. This was not the type of publicity Roger Ebert would appreciate. My mascara was all smudged; I could see it in the Fishman display window. I rubbed it off as best I could. Damn you, Babbington. The window dresser changing the mannequins looked down at me and smiled. I smiled back. Oh, new Miu Miu. Cute.

Chapter 3

*M*y dad had a dress shop in Bridgeport from 1965 until it tanked in 1993. It was called Leisure Lady and Daddy marketed to women who were too old for the Limited, but too poor for decent department stores. Although he remodeled several times, he always kept the red shag carpeting.

"I like it," he said. "It's bright and lively." In truth, it was uncomfortably arterial and provoked aggressive outbursts from everyone who came in the store.

My brother, sister, and I worked weekends and sometimes after school, taking inventory, hanging up clothing the customers had thrown on the floor. When I was in high school, Daddy occasionally let me stand behind the schlock-jewelry counter and peddle, but his main idea (rightly so) was to keep the workforce out of sight. My brother wasn't even allowed to walk in the front door of Leisure Lady, his very presence so upset the ladies. He had to come in the delivery door by the Dumpsters. Then he'd sit and pick his nose, quietly singing REO Speedwagon ballads while pretending to restock leatherette belts. Such was his personality.

On Thirty-first Street, Leisure Lady sat amidst a long line of liquor stores, bars, and doughnut shops. On the way to work in the morning, my dad usually found broken forty-ouncers and taco-riddled vomit on the sidewalk outside the store. He'd hose it across the street, where it would splatter across the door of Mikolajczak, Polish Butcher and Baker. Sometimes the butcher would come out and stare at my dad, or nudge the puke away with his toe. But he didn't speak English, so he never said anything about it, presumably accepting it as part of American life.

That was Bridgeport. My parents have never really forgiven me for moving to the North Side.

Daddy likes to say, "I suppose now you go to Cubs games," as though my northward immigration was just a ruse to sit in a more comfortable stadium with aging frat boys. White Sox fans, cozy in the flying saucer that is Comiskey Park, fireworks whizzing by their ears, hate not the Cubs so much as Cubs *fans*. Hate the friendly confines of Wrigley, hate the ivy, hate the rooftop scammers atop nearby three-flats, hate the Old Style vendors, hate the beer-bong lunatics bleeding red and blue all over the cheesy bars on Clark Street. But I must admit, enduring a Cubs game is nothing like enduring normal baseball. No one expects them to win, and by the time the game's over, you're too sloshed to mind. Tim and I take in a few games every summer, usually sitting by a guy with one tooth who shouts "Woo!" every five seconds.

Daddy also warned me about a life in "retail hell," as he put it, but clothes are the only thing I like, even if I suck at selling them. He and Ma have given up on my doing anything worthwhile. I have so successfully lowered their expectations that they whooped with delight when I finally bought a bed.

"Stell, Stell!" screamed Daddy the day I called to tell him about the bed. "Get on the extension. Lisa bought a bed!"

Ma clicked on. "Oh, my God, you're not sleeping on that photon anymore? Box spring, too? Frame? Sal, she got a frame to put the bed on!"

"I know," he said happily.

My pre-owned sheets insult my sixteen-hundred-dollar mattress/ art deco burnished-metal headboard set, but there you have it. I dropped my whole savings from eight years following around Mrs. Lubbeth. I'll probably buy some new sheets in January when Fishman's has their white sale and I can use my staff discount.

. . .

I visit my family every Sunday even though taking the Ashland bus south is a giant pain in my ass. Ever since they messed up the route of the Dan Ryan El, I don't feel comfortable switching over in the Loop. My only consolation this Sunday was that *Chicago Society* is not a very popular paper down in Bridgeport. My parents have no illusions about me, but why throw that in their faces?

I walked down Morgan Street toward their bungalow. From a block away I could see Ma's rear end sticking out of the yew hedge. Sometime in the eighties, the advent of jewel-toned silky warm-up suits dawned, and Ma has never looked back.

"Hi, Ma," I said. My mother backed inelegantly out of the yew and stood up.

She gave me the once-over and said, "Is that what they're wearing these days?"

"Bye, Ma," I said, walking into the house.

My dad was sitting in his recliner, watching the Bears game on TV. I kissed him on top of his toupee, and it shifted.

"Would you be careful? I'm out of glue." He sighed and turned off the game. "I suppose you heard the Sox didn't win the pennant this year."

I sat down on the loveseat and said, "I heard. But there's always next year, right?"

He sat there glumly ruminating over the Sox's failure. "The Cubs didn't win theirs, either. They never win *anything*," he said defensively, as though I was in the habit of lording the Cubs' 65–97 record over him.

We sat quietly in our living room. The floral sofa sagged miserably in the middle cushion. A needlepoint pillow that read "Born to Shop" was tucked amongst other sofa pillows. The mantel clock chimed the quarter hour, surrounded by high-school senior photos of me and my siblings. A red braided rug, still matted with the hair of our dead dog, had faded in the square of sunlight that moved across it each afternoon. My dad wore those leather scuff-slippers that retired men like, gray flannel trousers, and an orange sweater. His toupee was the sandy brown color of his youth, even though his sideburns and remaining hair had turned gray. His old, eighties-era toupee had been the same color, but much longer and fluffier—not really a good look for a man, even in 1985.

"Well," he'd said back then, showing me a page from *People,* "this is really what I'm going for."

It was a picture of Jon Bon Jovi.

Strangely enough, in 1985 my dad did in fact resemble a grandpa-ish version of the pop star. Even without his wig, he still sort of looked like Bon Jovi, but favored Conrad Bain.

"Are you taking karate?" he asked suddenly.

"No. . . ," I said, wondering if he was having one of his senile moments. He was staring at my outfit.

"Oh! This is just a new thing we got in at Fishman's," I said. "It's the Japanese look. Very spare, yet flowing. Do you like it?"

He nodded. "I think so. The pants are so short. Like clam diggers, kind of."

They were so *not* clam diggers. They were spare, flowing dojo trousers. They were reckless and wide-legged. They cost $240. True, I was tired of the wraparound surgeon's top with six-inch sash and weird clogs, but nothing else went with dojo trousers.

I said, "Daddy, they're reckless and wide-legged."

A voice called out, "Just like you," from the kitchen. Daddy turned the Bears game back on while his disappointment of a son sacked the refrigerator.

Chip stood at the counter arranging various cold cuts and condiments. I joined him, as it had been a long time since breakfast. No matter what my parents may think of me and my retail hell and empty savings account, at least I had moved out of their home, which is more than can be said for my brother and sister, ages twenty-five and twenty-seven, respectively. Chip's room, a testament to a lifetime of pot and complaint, housed his most cherished items: a mercury glass bong, Morrissey CDs, and a small shelf displaying tattered copies of *Reveille for Radicals, Catcher in the Rye,* and five books by Noam Chomsky. Gina's room had also remained virtually unchanged since childhood, with its posters of puppies and horses and a bulletin-board collection of religious postcards.

Of the three of us, I was the big loser in the Galisa name nightmare. Ma claimed a rhyming name was "goddamn-knockout gorgeous." I disagreed.

Gina—short for "Virgina"—silently endured her unusual and provocative Christian name, along with Ma's flimsy inspiration: "It's more original than Virginia. You'll thank me one day."

Chip was the only Chip in Bridgeport, as far as we knew. It wasn't a common name in our circle. Shriek "Jim-John-Joe" out the window, and eventually some skid would amble out, looking around, but Chips were rare and elusive. My brother's proper name, Charles, was marginally better, though infrequently used. It was saved for showing off in front of strangers ("Charles just loves shopping with his mommy"), yet even then it was mauled by Ma's shrill South Side accent. It came out in two harsh syllables: *Char-ulls.* It sounded like a skin disorder or a parasitic infestation: *Sorry, Chip can't come out, he picked up some char-ulls in the woods, and we're trying to burn them off.*

Chip—the once-heir to the Leisure Lady empire until its miserable ruin, the boy who wept during his own renditions of "I Honestly Love You" and other Olivia Newton-John hits, the jobless man with a penchant for chess—lived at home with his parents and hadn't dated since the prom.

We made ourselves hoagies and sat at the sparkly boomerang-patterned kitchen table. Chip said he and his friends were thinking about starting an underground magazine.

"Why don't you run it out of Ma and Daddy's basement?" I suggested. "That's underground."

Instead of scowling into his salami and cursing, he simply stared at me with an expression of joyful surprise. "That's a *great* idea! Why didn't I think of it before? We knew we couldn't afford to rent an office anywhere." I will probably be blamed for what was really just a sarcastic jab on my part.

I said, "You know, Chip, I've been thinking. We have had poverty and celibacy thrust upon us like medicine balls, haven't we?"

"Speak for yourself," he said. "This underground magazine is going to be my ticket to the big time."

"Oh, yeah, do-it-yourself publishing is a real cash cow."

Chip shrugged. "Shows what *you* know."

"I know enough to move out of my parents' house."

He plowed ahead. "People will pay to read insightful writing on interesting topics."

"But nobody wants another Sal Mineo fanzine."

We were interrupted by our mother, who had come in to wash off the garden dirt.

After she'd dried her hands, she gently grasped Chip's face and said, "My son, my son." Then she screamed, "Hi-*yah*!" and gave me a judo chop in the Adam's apple.

Every Sunday, Gina filled in her calendar with tasks for the coming week. Each square detailed her work schedule as well as private goals and leisure activities.

"I'm ready for this week," she said after I came in her room and sat down on the bed. I had recovered from Ma's throat assault ("I thought you were taking karate") with a hit of my brother's pot and needed to rest. I stretched out with my head on the pillow as Gina tacked the calendar to her bulletin board, its reminders to "clean grease trap at work" and "buy get-well card for fry-cook" nestled in among "take two-mile walk past pet cemetery," "look at leaves," and "prepare for future."

She stood considering her handiwork, perhaps envisioning the long week of introspection interrupted by shifts at the deep fryer. An anxious expression crossed her face, and she said it was just possible for her to rearrange her schedule that moment if I wanted to take the two-mile stroll with her to visit our dead dog's burial site.

"No, thanks," I said. "Your schedule's all done. Let's not mess it up."

"I can take it down right now," she said, her hand poised at the thumbtack, sheets of legal paper and Magic Markers at the ready. "We can take the walk today, and I can switch it with raking the leaves and sock repair."

I confessed that I really had no desire to visit the dog's grave. It was a fine dog, one of those brown ones, but it was time to move on.

"I can't," Gina said. "I miss her." The death of our dog years ago was not only sad, but also puzzling and disturbing. It appeared to all witnesses that the dog had committed suicide.

"Maybe you should get another dog."

"Ma won't let me," said my twenty-seven-year-old sister.

I'd asked her to move in with me several times, though I didn't really have room for her working-farm model or thousand back issues of *Dog Fancy*. But she said she wasn't ready to move out on her own yet. Not while Ma cooked three meals a day and vacuumed her room every Friday.

I yawned and looked up at the ceiling. She still had those glow-in-the-dark stars up there. She replicated only constellations that were animals, like Leo and Canis Major and Ursa Minor. While I was debating whether or not to offer her my conjectures about celibacy and poverty, she asked what I did on Halloween.

I told her about the party, skipping the climactic event detailed in the press. Gina had helped Chip hand out candy at the front door.

"I was a ghost," she said.

Chip had worn Gina's McDonald's uniform, which had evidently been too tight, as he kept sticking out one leg and pulling at his crotch all evening. Mothers plucked their children from the doorway all night, glaring at my brother and his lewd dance.

I said, "I might go out with this licorice whip."

She asked what his name was.

I said, "He's Roger Ebert's personal assistant."

"Oh, it was so sad when the bald guy died. That guy who looked like Henry Mancini."

I said, "You know, he's dead, too, Mancini." We sat there awhile, thinking about the dead and the bald in respectful silence.

"Guess who else was at the party?" I said suddenly. "Judd Hirsch!"

From the living room, through onion-skin walls, our dad shouted, "The second most annoying man on earth."

"No, wait," I said, "it was Judd Nelson." Our dad appeared in Gina's doorway then.

"Not the second most annoying man on earth?" he asked, disappointed. I shrugged—it was a matter of opinion.

He said, "Number one, of course—"

Gina shouted, "Alan Alda!"

"Close third?" he asked.

"Hal Linden," I sighed.

Our father, satisfied that he had instilled some of his values in us, turned back toward the living room, toward his friend the television.

Daddy was ordinarily a mild man, a man who blushed at his own vulgarity when he called Pol Pot a "stinking rat." His ire was raised only by television celebrities of middling appeal.

"Hey," said Gina, "I'm going on a date, too. This man asked me out at work."

"You shouldn't date coworkers," I said, reflecting on possible dalliances with hideous Bernie from Admin.

"I'm not. It's a customer."

"Wait a minute. You mean to say that some . . . some *person* walks into McDonald's, sees you flogging fries under a heat lamp, wearing your hairnet and uniform, and he asks you for a date?"

"Yep," she said. "Our eyes met across the Ray Kroc death mask."

I stood up abruptly. "I gotta go. I forgot something. I gotta go."

"What's wrong? Where are you going?" she asked, following me out of her room.

Chip cackled as he passed us in the hallway. "To get that big medicine ball out of her gut."

I walked back down the street. At the corner was Wysocki's Tavern, which was run by our neighbors, a Polish-Korean family who seriously overestimated the racial tolerance of Bridgeport. I saw my old friend Fred Wysocki at work behind the taps, so I stopped in for a little Old Style.

"Hey," he said, setting down the glass in front of me. "Visiting the asylum?"

After five more glasses, my skull released its hold and sunk comfortably into the bar. Fred warned me not to rest my head there, as the oak slab was pitted and defiled by a generation of chaw-spewing longshoremen, but my drunk waved away his advice. Such things didn't bother her, nor, for that matter, me: the lifelong clerk, the celibate fool in the ladies' department. The thing was, I didn't object to my job at all. It was my inability to succeed at it, or at basic social interaction. Even Tim, an anomaly himself as the angry children's librarian, realized that I fit nowhere, that I could not be depended on to behave or control myself or even to dress appropriately for a Halloween party; that I was, in every sense, more comfortable as a ghost, hidden from sight, than as a human. I was not even a good ghost, and Bumble and Bumble would never agree to fix my awful Art Garfunkel perm. Only my drunk accepted me. I was, as Babbington Hawkes put it, just a person, and a chunky South Sider at that.

A toothless elderly fellow bought my drunk another Old Style. I would never have accepted a drink from one of these Wysocki's losers, but my drunk was in charge tonight, and she took on all comers, the little strumpet. So it was really *her* rear end that he massaged with an arthritic hand. She slapped his claw away with a giggle. The two of them made me ill.

"Lisa, I could call you a cab," said Fred. His mother, affectionately known as the Dragon Lady in our youth, stood glaring at me from the other end of the room. Everyone knew she governed Wysocki's like a tyrannical abbess at a monastic convent and permitted no disgusting behavior in her bar.

"Get lost, kid," said my drunk's friend to Fred.

"Hey, man," said Fred, "why don't you leave her alone and go on home?" I wished my drunk would listen to Fred. She was making a spectacle of me.

The old guy snarled, "Get lost, kid!"

Fred leaned over the bar and grabbed him by his collar, which, I had just noticed, was yards too big for this season. He shouted, "I'm thirty-two and I said *go home*!"

The old man stood up shakily and said, "Aw, all you chinks look like you're twelve years old." He stumbled out of the tavern as the Dragon Lady advanced.

"I'm calling you a cab," said Fred firmly.

"Okay," I said. My dojo trousers, reckless, wide, had twisted themselves all around my crotch and were now covered in greasy fingerprints. I stood up to fix them and suddenly my vision narrowed to a single pinpoint; everything faded from my sight except the image of a lonely salami hoagie, and my drunk threw up all over Fred and his bar.

He cleaned me up and put me in the taxi. The Dragon Lady said she was telling my mother. Fred said not to worry, just to get home and sleep it off. I nodded and Fred shut the car door.

Fred Wysocki was the first human being who had been kind to me in weeks, and I had rewarded him with vomit.

I clamped my hands around my ears to keep my brain from leaking out and whimpered silently, *Oh, Babbington Hawkes, what have you wrought? Everything was great, just frigging fabulous before you insulted me in your paper.* Well, not fabulous, okay, not *good*, all right? But at least I had never thought to be dissatisfied with my life, meaningless void that it was, before now. I didn't need a great life. I was okay with not-horrible, not-wretched. For me, if things were indeterminate, neutral, it was almost like life being good.

Twenty bucks later, the cab pulled up in front of my building. The driver made sympathetic comments about getting his own ass kicked in tae kwon do. As I got out, the rest of my cash fell out of my dojos into the car. I left it as the tip. I made it okay to the door, but my drunk tripped me in the entryway. I thought that was a pretty lousy thing to do, and tears swam in my eyes. *Oh God,* she sneered, *are you gonna cry?* I said no, and put my key in the door. *You're not gonna dump me just because of tonight, are you? Because I'll tell you something, sister, I'm your only friend in town.*

Chapter 4

S ome of the marketing people at work came up with this new ploy. Every few weeks, the entire store would have a new theme, and all the departments would have to decorate and modify their appearances to fit in. Now that Halloween was over, we had time for just one theme before Christmas (which apparently would remain just "Christmas"). Today marked the start of "the Greek Islands." Some executive said November is the most popular month for the jet set to cruise the Aegean. We were to appeal to the wealthy Chicagoan's need to escape our country and embrace Hellenistic decadence in the form of better sportswear and home furnishings made in Taiwan.

Mrs. Lubbeth, the two other juniors in our department, and I sat down to have a little brainstorm with the rest of Women's Wear. Mrs. Consolo and her assistant, a sulky Russian girl, from the designer boutique came, along with Nan and her manager, the shoe people, and Doris Mingle from Irregulars.

Mrs. Lubbeth consulted her clipboard. "All right, ladies. Table-top is redoing their department in lots of blues and white, like a seaside Greek café. They're going to have demonstrations downstairs in Cookware every Wednesday at noon with the chef from Odysseus, plus they are featuring sales on all Greek-inspired flatware.

"Our friends in Men's Wear are trying to appeal to . . . what does it say? Oh, yes, the 'shipping magnate in all men.' Simply put, more luxury items, higher prices. Lizard and croc wallets instead of cowhide. Suspenders with silver clasps, cruisewear. It looks like

Hui has his work cut out for him." Everyone knew Mrs. Lubbeth's dislike for the head of Men's Wear; she felt his window dressings were in poor taste, and five years ago he had made contemptuous remarks about the success of her eye job.

She continued. "Junior Miss, taking their cue from Men's Wear, is putting emphasis on luxury for today's teen. We're talking yachting, we're talking Athens discotheques, we're talking school holidays in Gibraltar and Tangier."

We're talking Christina Onassis, before all the booze and diet pills. We're talking marketing people too lazy to come up with a set of guidelines that would eliminate all this foolish guesswork on behalf of each department.

We in Women's Wear could not agree on the route we should take. Irregular Doris Mingle wanted to toe the party line on cruisewear so that we could dump last season's dismal sarong shipment. I wanted to take a completely different tack and do up the department in Helen of Troy, complete with Trojan Horse and staged confrontations between King Menelaus and Paris.

Mrs. Lubbeth vetoed the Trojan War. "I'm not putting up a bunch of messy friezes and turning the central atrium into ancient Sparta, nope, forget it. That's no way to unload tweed skirts, I can tell you."

Mrs. Consolo said, "I must agree. We have to stay within the confines of the luxury theme. It's the only way to sell John Galliano." The Russian girl stamped her foot and refused to promote Greece on political grounds.

"We're not asking you to participate in Romania Days," retorted Mrs. Lubbeth. "Get a hold of yourself."

Nobody even bothered addressing my cojuniors in Women's Wear, who suggested we do "Greek Week" with *Animal House* decor and ritual hazing. Silent moments ticked by.

"Hmm," said Mrs. Lubbeth.

"What?" Everyone looked at her expectantly.

"Well, if the junior miss department wants to do young Christina Onassis, and Men's Wear wants to inspire the 'Aristotle Onassis in everyman,' I think Women's Wear should do Maria Callas."

"Maria Callas," said Nan thoughtfully.

"Maria Callas," said Mrs. Lubbeth. "Yes, 'The Diva in You' slant. Nights at La Scala. Her opulent Ritz apartment."

"The torrid affair with Onassis," I said, warming to the idea. "Satin gowns, neat Dior suits, and, naturally, cruisewear for sailing on the *Christina* in the early 1960s."

"Excellent!" cried Mrs. Consolo. "How else could we feature Pucci print swimwear and Missoni wool coatdresses and Prada fur tippets in one collection?"

We congratulated Mrs. Lubbeth, who reminded me sotto voce that *that* was why she had been head of Women's Wear for eight hundred years. Nan said nothing, but merely stared at me with a curious expression. I asked her what was wrong.

She said, "Nothing's wrong. It's just that . . . well, you really resemble Maria Callas yourself."

Everyone turned to me. Doris Mingle asked what Maria Callas looked like.

"Like that," said Nan, pointing at me. "Maybe thinner around the middle, at least in 1959."

Mrs. Lubbeth peered closely at me. She pushed my hair around and moved my face from profile to profile. "I see it," she said slowly. "I see it. The pointed nose. The small teeth. The dark eyes and hair, minus Lisa's disastrous perm. Even the abundant hips, the long hands. Yes. We may make something of this yet."

Nan and I planned to go to lunch at the Cheesecake Factory. All that talk of the Greek Islands and seaside cafés had made us hungry. We were getting our coats on at the staff closet in the back room when I noticed Irregular Doris Mingle hanging around, pretending to read the emergency–fire exit poster. Doris Mingle, six foot two, bamboo-cane thin, all sebaceousy with enormous toucan nose and mouth too large for her head, boobless and penguin-footed, all witchy dishwater hair and furry arms. Doris Mingle, of the irregulars—not even Honey Dietrich–sanctioned designer irregulars, but mere ordinary irregulars . . . hanging hems, wrinkled seams, dye stains, broken zippers.

"Hi," she said suddenly. Her voice sounded like it came from under her tongue.

"Ick," murmured Nan, pulling me out of the back room.

I looked back with a twinge of guilt. "Bye, Doris," I said.

Nan and I walked down Michigan Avenue toward the Cheesecake Factory. Once inside, she took off her carmine mohair beret and shook out her silky red hair. I took off my leather dude cap (à la Brian Johnson from AC/DC) and tried to shake out my hair, but it didn't move. Okay, the perm was a bad idea, but at the beginning of summer I looked fantastic, like Diana Ross except fat and white.

"Well, we just couldn't have," said Nan, checking her watch.

"No," I said, "I suppose not."

We sat at a table near the far window. Tacitly, we agreed; no matter how cold-hearted it was, we could not have asked Doris Mingle to lunch.

"I don't know about you," said Nan, "but I need my lunch hour to *unwind,* not to make idle chitchat with a tongue-tied freak."

It would have been boring and painful, sitting here while she gawked at us. Nor would she have enjoyed it. So it was really the kindest thing to do.

"Not that I'm trying to be *mean,*" she said.

"Me either," I replied. "But some things are just not meant to be."

To think on Halloween I'd been considering throwing over Nan for the Honey Dietrich contingent. That crowd would never have me. Nan and I were shaped by the same mold.

Maybe I would have a little wine with my pasta. But first a new green Sobranie.

"Ooh, where'd you get those?" Nan squealed. "I love, love, love them. So cute and little, like green Capris."

I exhaled. "They're not anything like Capris. They're Sobranies; they come in a slim flat gold box, in various pastel shades, and they are expensive. You can get them from only an unscrupulous duty-free German, not Walgreen's."

"Babe," she said, snatching a cig from my box, "I remember going to Walgreen's with you after you dug change out of the lounge couch for a pack of Kools. *Kools,* darling, prison cigarettes. So don't pull that bullshit with me."

Two white wines later, I enjoyed a pink Sobranie outside Fishman's. Nan went straight in, presumably to throw up her lunch before the break was over. Just guessing, but nobody stays that thin on pasta primavera in the middle of the goddamn day. I dialed up Tim at the reference desk.

"Ye-es," came the greeting, drawn out and irritable.

"Guess who's coming to dinner, old sock."

He answered, "Sidney Poitier?"

"No. Maria Callas."

He paused. "Really. *Really.* That *is* good. Lisa, that's what you should have been on Halloween. Did you just think of it now?"

I told him about the Fishman's marketing campaign, and La Lubbeth's mysterious allusions to making something of me.

"Hmph," he said, at a loss for derision. "You do look like the diva. You even have the same pale olive skin and wide-set Anne Bancroft eyes"—then, into the distance he shouted, "Dewey decimal system! Can you count? Do you know what 'six hundred' looks like? Well, it's between five hundred and seven hundred. Six-*oh-oh.* Look, just go ask one of the kindergartners over there"—"Anyway," he resumed, "guess who else is meeting us for dinner."

"Aristotle Onassis?"

"Good one. No, Licorice Whip!" he exclaimed. "Now, before you get all worked up, he doesn't know I'm trying to trick him into meeting you. He thinks I'm fishing for info about—guess!"

"I don't know, let's see . . ."

He shouted, "Kabuki Tart! Kabuki Tart! You see, it turns out that Licorice Whip (being Ebert's assistant) attended a screening of *Gladiator* at that theater across from the tart shop the same night—"

"—Kabuki Tart's father was killed by an employee!" I finished.

"Right! So they kinda know each other. Licorice Whip had been standing outside on the sidewalk, making notes for Ebert on the many historical inaccuracies of the film, when the police pulled up. He practically saw the whole thing. Apparently, there were pastries *everywhere*," he said. "He delivered a funeral wreath there from the *Sun-Times* afterward, and got to talking with Kabuki Tart."

The dinner plans were set. Pacific Café, eight o'clock ("Licorice Whip just *loves* Vietnamese noodle dishes"). I hated stamping out the butt of my Sobranie, but I'd smoked it all down, and my break was over. It was still a cute little pink stub; I wished I could just put it in my pocket so that it would never have to touch the ground.

I snapped my phone shut, then opened it up again. Fred deserved an apology and a thank-you call. What was his number? Hmm, information calls are expensive on the cell phone. I closed it.

By the time I clocked out, Mrs. Lubbeth was still drawing up her plans for the Greecification of Women's Wear. I tried to peek over her shoulder at her notes, but she covered them with her bosom.

"Mustn't peek, Lisa! I'll let everyone know their tasks tomorrow. We have to shake a leg because Men's Wear has just put in a requisition to Maintenance for the construction of a giant ship's wheel, and I believe we are going to need a lot of help from Maintenance ourselves."

Mrs. Consolo directed the Russian girl, who staggered around the main display platform with armloads of clothing, muttering words somber and Cyrillic. Ah, changing the mannequins. Mrs. Consolo waved to me and smiled. She was on the fabulous side, for a matron. Very tiny, very tan, very Dolce & Gabbana. While Mrs. Lubbeth was kind of maternal, she was also prone to screaming fits and stomping around. Mrs. Consolo was maternal, too, but in a soft-spoken and calm way, like a cool aunt. Technically she was subordinate to Mrs. Lubbeth, but she commanded the same amount of respect, and Lubbeth treated her as an equal. The ladies' department was like a well-run socialist state. Families— governments—should model themselves on our infrastructure. But then there would be no men.

"Look at this blouse," remarked Mrs. Consolo. "Look! Have you ever seen anything so gorgeous?" Chartreuse with little white polka dots, side wrap, flouncy sleeves. Usually that type of thing didn't appeal to me, looking all tea partyish and Junior League, but somehow with Mrs. Consolo beaming at me and Russian Girl scowling under the weight of several wool suits, it suddenly looked very beautiful.

"I'll take it," I said. Just the thing to wear to Pacific Café, feminine and chic, yet subtle. Licorice Whip struck me as the type of man who appreciated subtlety, drunken groping and electric slide notwithstanding.

Mrs. Consolo ordered Russian Girl to set down the wardrobe and ring me up. Then she asked what I would wear with it, suggesting a gray tweed skirt and fishnets. That was popular about two seasons ago, but I didn't like it even then. I had tried the fishnets numerous times, but they made me look like sausage casing.

"Three hundred twenty-three dollars and sixteen cents," droned Russian Girl.

"You forgot my staff discount," I said.

She said, "That is with staff discount."

I swallowed with difficulty. Mrs. Consolo seemed so happy with my purchase. I handed over my credit card.

"Thanks, Nastassja," I said, picking up the bag.

"Anna," she said.

I had to hurry home in time to shower, change, and cab it over to Pacific Café. Buttoning up my jacket at the store's exit, I saw, reflected in the glass door, Doris Mingle, watching me from behind a tower of irregular underwear.

Chapter 5

Why did I do my apartment in all white? Why, why? Everything was filthy, and so dated. I hated that I'd decorated in an all-white Moroccan textile–marketplace theme. Nobody does that anymore. Chocolate is where it's at. Hell, I hoped Licorice Whip would not be coming home with me tonight. It was impossible to clean house *and* get ready in forty minutes. Clothes were all over the floor, except, thank God, my lingerie, which had been neatly folded into the thirty extremely small drawers of a pharmacist's cabinet. A saucepan, dried with some opaque substance, sat in the middle of the kitchen table. Three white coffee mugs with dingy rings waited patiently on the floor beside my bed. I kicked them under it. I tore through pile after pile of clothing, looking for that short black taffeta skirt and motorcycle boots. Finally found them, but the skirt smelled funny. It had been trapped under my old workout clothes, back when I belonged to Bally's. I sprayed it with air freshener.

I arrived at the restaurant just five minutes late. Tim sat alone at a table by the front window. He was still in his library clothes, conservative button-down shirt and corduroys. He'd ordered us two Kirins and I sat down heavily, regaining my breath.

"Where is he? Where's Licorice Whip?" I asked.

"He'll be here, he'll be here," he said. "Now don't ask him about Ebert. I've heard he's very sensitive about mentioning his boss. He never does, in fact; considers it a breach of privacy."

"Okay," I said.

"And try not to get ripped and hurl all over him, will you?"

I recalled suddenly, painfully, my night at Wysocki's. "Hey," I said, "don't tell Licorice Whip what Babbington Hawkes wrote, okay?" Tim looked at me blankly.

"You know, the gossip columnist who said I . . . uh, about . . . the hurling."

His eyes lit up. "Oh, right, right! Poor thing."

"Thanks," I said quietly.

"Not you; *him*! Do you know how much Ferragamo costs? Bile will just eat those little slippers right up. Anyway, don't worry about him anymore; he's got bigger problems."

Tim took the latest *Chicago Society* out of his briefcase and laid it on the table, opened to the "Letters to the Editor" page.

FARINA *NOT* IN COSTUME

To the editor:

I read with interest your November 1 article on Honey Dietrich's Nub benefit. I would like to clear up a glaring error made by Mr. Hawkes. As Dennis Farina's personal stylist, I can assure you he was not, in fact, costumed as a Mafia hitman, but had just come from the Palmer House (where he dined with family) dressed in a $1,200 Valentino suit. Mr. Hawkes had better check his sources, or his eyeglasses, more carefully the next time. Although with the unfortunate incident he described involving his shoes, one can almost understand his befuddlement. *Almost.*

Sincerely,
Greg Y. Loomis
Personal stylist to Dennis Farina and others

"I'm not sure this makes me feel any better," I said. "Now Babbington will blame me for confusing him about Dennis Farina."

"Look!" whispered Tim. "It's Licorice Whip! He's coming in."
Tim waved him over.

"What's his real name?" I whispered back.

We stared at each other in dumb befuddlement.

Two Kirins later, I loosened up. Licorice Whip introduced himself to me as Luke Sheehy; I introduced myself, then endured the
audience's customary giggle fit. Though Tim and I had been friends
for several years, he always acted as if he had never before heard
my full name. I tried to toss in a few Gideon Bible jokes, but they
had begun discussing Kabuki Tart and proceeded to ignore me for
the next half hour.

"I love Japanese beer," I said, trying to participate. "It's so . . .
spare . . ." My voice trailed off as the men examined their Kirins
for spareness.

The waitron took our orders. I went right to the sushi page and
chose the spider roll. It's classy to eat just a simple roll of seafood
while others are wolfing gigantic mouthfuls of soba.

I asked Luke if he liked working at the *Sun-Times*. Tim flashed
me a horrified look, but I wasn't asking about Ebert, just his gen-
eral work environment.

"It's a good place," said Luke cautiously. He was a handsome
man in a lean-jawed way. I preferred a good lantern jaw, like
Fabio's, but society does not permit me to prefer Fabio over anything, at least not out loud. At Tim's insistence, I buried a lot of my
natural inclinations, like my origins, accent, and predilection for
swaggering Italians. He slapped me whenever I said "Sout' Side"
instead of "South Side," although frankly he begged me not to say
the words at all. In a perfect world, perhaps the world in which a
Fabio-inspired romance was set, friends would not make such
demands, but Tim only wanted me to succeed in the life I desired.
Why object?

When our food came, I saw that the spider roll was neither
simple nor spare. What kind of Japanese food was this? The

monstrosity before me resembled an Asian Dagwood sandwich. I could dislocate my jaw by taking one bite. It would have been impossible to cut, even had I been ridiculous enough to request occidental flatware when my friends were using chopsticks. I tried to bite the first slice in half. The seaweed refused to sever and all the soy sauce–soaked rice tumbled into my three-hundred-dollar blouse. Like a Ubangi lip, the mangled spider roll hung from my mouth as I ground my teeth into the filament of tough seaweed. Finally after a brief struggle, the slice capitulated and I shoveled the remains into my mouth with my hands.

"Bravo," said Luke, smiling. At least he had a sense of humor and was not completely horrified by my eating habits. Tim massaged his temples as though in pain. Maybe I would try not to bite the next slice, but just bulldoze the whole thing in and deal with it.

As it turned out, there was not much need for me to be mindful of my table manners. The boys were too engrossed with the topic of Kabuki Tart and his obvious, if not admitted, gayness. Like a couple of magpies, they scrutinized and deconstructed his entire character and personality. I was sort of swept along with it, too. I wondered if people discussed my sexuality over bok choy and wasabi. If so, they would probably comment on how long it had been since I was seen in the company of a straight man, and how lonely, desperate, and horny I must be. The magpies would be right. Luke seemed like a nice enough fellow. He certainly enjoyed gossiping, always a plus. It would be fun to spend time with a good-looking guy who could maybe introduce me to Ebert one day. As an experiment, I slid my leg between Luke's knees. His obsession with Kabuki Tart's sexual orientation had me thinking that perhaps he was rooting for the other team. However, his sudden changed expression and mechanical responses to Tim indicated we were both sitting on the same side of the stadium.

"Well!" shouted Luke, when Tim paused a moment in his monologue, "shall we go?" He looked at me hopefully.

Tim was a good sport and knew when he was beaten. Mankind's most sparkling conversationalist does not stand a chance against a tipsy, loose woman. Always on the lookout for me, he whispered as we stepped outside into the chilly air, "If he makes it upstairs to your apartment tonight, you will never see him again. And you'll never meet Ebert. Get it?"

We three walked together. When we reached Ashland, I turned abruptly, waved good-bye, and left lean-jawed, slack-jawed Luke alone with smirking Tim Gideon.

At home I waded through piles of debris from door to bedroom. Issues of *Harper's Bazaar, Marie Claire, Metropolitan Home,* and stacks of CDs covered the floor and the white tuxedo-back sofa. A bolt of fabric for some forgotten project was shoved in the corner. The framed photos that normally sat on my end table had been vacated to make room for dirty dishes and now lay facedown on the floor. I picked up a small one—me and Gina in a photo booth last year—and an old one—Gina gluing cotton balls to the face of young Chip. No messages blinked on my answering machine. I considered calling Fred Wysocki with my apology. It was after ten, though, so the rates were higher. And I shouldn't rack up unnecessary cell-phone charges. I looked all over for my regular phone. Finally found it on the bathroom floor under a black silk slip, but by that time it was too late.

Chapter 6

*M*rs. Lubbeth spent all day ordering around the maintenance crew. Other departments had the men build a display or two, or they petitioned Admin for petty cash to buy theme-centered decorations, but only Women's Wear asked the men to construct palazzos and balcony facades and a miniature of the stage at Covent Garden. Maintenance put together a lousy reproduction of Maria's Ritz apartment and a shoebox-sized diorama of Covent Garden, but claimed they would need overtime pay for the palazzos, etc. Mrs. Lubbeth said Marketing would be loath to hand over that kind of cash. We in Women's Wear became rather dejected after that. I sat for a few dreadful photographs, hair and makeup courtesy of Nan and Mrs. Lubbeth, that were going to be framed and hung discreetly around the department. They had dressed me in weird robes (supposedly inspired by Callas's actual backstage silk dressing gowns) that were more suited to a nursing-home grandma. Unfortunately, what little resemblance I bore to Maria in real life translated to film as only a lazy eye and giant Barbra Streisand nose. They kept two of the photos, and hung one in the rest room and one in front of the cash register. These were taken down immediately after customers congratulated me on making Employee of the Month.

Mrs. Lubbeth and I shared dirty bagels from the commissary when she broke the news to me. "I guess it's not going to work out," she said in between mouthfuls. "I had high hopes for you, too." It was nice, I guess, that someone had high hopes for me, but I had never given her any indication that I could succeed at anything. She had no business staking hope on me. She should have guessed that I had no hidden talents or qualities that would stand me out from others. She should have been able to predict that, in addition to my everyday-reality failures, I would also fail at pretending. Mrs. Lubbeth sighed with profound disappointment, looking me over. Then she either put the kibosh on me, or else a poppy seed had worked its way under her denture.

She said, "Now, Lisa dear, you'll just have to work harder at selling clothes." Perhaps she just didn't realize that she hoarded all of our customers. Perhaps I was somehow invisible to her the moment a wealthy matron with money to burn strolled into the department. Perhaps the truth was I inspired customers not to spend money on clingy knit dresses, but rather to flee to Jesus in the sporting-goods department for shapeless sweatsuits. That's me: in the world of haute couture, I am sweatpants.

People looked at me and gave up. My appearance, my demeanor discouraged them, they appraised me and concluded, *Why bother? Look what could happen.*

When I was fourteen, my dad asked my opinion on what young people were wearing. He was in the process of deciding what to buy for the following spring and thought to extend his customer base to include females under forty.

"I don't know," I'd said. To get involved in the operations of Leisure Lady was to endure hour-long discussions on whether Ma should be allowed to smoke in the store or why Chip would bury himself under chiffon scarves and pretend to be entombed in the stockroom. Nobody with sense wanted to become part of that environment.

"Now I don't want to drive away my ladies," Daddy had said, "but I'd like to add something a bit more youthful, daring, to drum up some younger customers." Then we went through my closet article by article while he took notes.

"What about this? What is it? Is it popular?" he'd asked, holding up a feathered roach clip.

"Very popular," I assured him. "Hair clip," he wrote down. He examined my wavy-soled black suede G.A.S.S. shoes from Thom McAn, my flared Wranglers, my many velour items, my fringed leather vest. I never claimed to be the barometer by which to judge teenage style; I was simply an insecure pothead with a fear of pegged pants. Needless to say, spring 1983 brought a reduced profit margin to Leisure Lady, which featured a collection of clothing that looked like a cross between Talbot's and the concession stand at a sold-out Styx concert.

After lunch, I walked through Men's Wear to see how their end of Greek opulence was coming along. The massive ship's wheel had been mounted on a pedestal surrounded by smaller pedestals offering Armani ready-to-wear, Coach key chains, and linen handkerchiefs embroidered with *A.O.* monograms (Aristotle Onassis?) in block letters. Hui, only thirty-three and already head of Men's Wear, was deep in conference with two maintenance workers. It was impossible to ignore that money changed hands.

"All right, Monday morning," said one of the workers, pocketing the bills. "See you then, Huey."

Hui scowled at their retreating forms. "Not Huey, not a giant infant duck; it is pronounced 'Hwee.' *Hwee!*"

He rolled up a blueprint copy they had been studying at one of the display tables and muttered, "Idiot inferior white thing—ah, Lisa! How good to see you."

I said, "The wheel looks nice."

"Oh, yes, that. We're expanding that idea, except the fools in Maintenance need me to hold their hands the entire time. My wife—who is a bedridden imbecile—could work faster and with less supervision."

I told him we were still struggling in Women's Wear to focus our ideas.

He smiled sadly. "It is not particularly Greek, 'Night at the Opera.' Too bad we are not doing Florence or Milan. You must be having a difficult time." I refrained from telling him about the Maria Callas failure.

I asked him about the blueprint. He lifted his eyebrows.

"Come on, Hui, I won't blab to anyone," I said. "What are you planning to do?"

Hui, immensely proud of all his ideas and his swift ascent in the Fishman hierarchy, did not like to keep his genius to himself. "All right, I will tell you, but only because you always appreciate my creative vision." This meant that I was the only person who didn't object to last summer's undressed mannequins crouched on hands and knees in his window display. Hui explained that he was simply trying to move vast unsold shipments of men's black berets, and decided to go with a militaristic exhibit. The mannequins, jaunty berets tipped down over one ear, were surrounded with a ring of barbed wire, upon which hung shreds of the American flag. The display had been bolstered with a sign that read RESISTANCE ON ALL FOURS.

He unrolled the blueprint. "We are going to recreate part of the *Christina* around the ship's wheel. You saw the maintenance fool tagging behind the older idiot? You noticed undoubtedly his resemblance to young Aristotle Onassis. He is going to come up to Men's Wear each day at noon, dressed as the celebrated tycoon himself, and sit on the *Christina*'s bridge, inspiring our customers to greatness."

A young Onassis . . . yes, the barrel chest, the low brow, the bronze skin, the beaked nose. Even his hairline, which rose barely two inches from his eyebrows, matched the tycoon's, and the dark hair streaked with gray could be combed back, magnate-style.

"Hui," I said, "you are a genius. There is no other word for it."

He lifted his shoulders in a parody of self-deprecation. "I assure you, in Hong Kong I am quite ordinary."

Once out of Hui's sight, I ran all the way to Women's Wear. Breathlessly, I whispered his secret to Mrs. Lubbeth, who enveloped me in her caftan with a suffocating hug.

"Do you know what this means?" she cried. "If Maintenance is building him the bridge of a yacht, then they cannot deny us a few requests—especially if we threaten to expose their financial arrangement to Mr. Fishman. We *will* have you as Maria Callas, taking your rightful place up at the balcony—once it is built—throwing kisses to the customers, your adoring public. Bouquets of roses will be tossed at your feet as you sweep through Women's Wear in Givenchy. We will play the recording of *Medea* each day at noon as you make your rounds."

"Me, Maria Callas," I said wistfully.

"That's right, you just leave it all up to me. We'll stick it to Men's Wear, mark my words. Their janitor Aristotle won't hold a candle to our diva," she said. "Lisa, darling, darling girl, you have done a brilliant thing!"

Apparently brilliance can be classified as wheedling information out of a colleague with promises of secrecy, and then revealing the plans to his rival. Clearly I had never shown business savvy before, not when I influenced the burnout line in Daddy's store, nor when I gave my approval to the garment that brought about his ruin: the one-legged pantsuit. Certainly neither my wisdom nor compassion was evident when Leisure Lady shut its doors for good and I pretended my dad didn't lie on the couch for six months paralyzed with melancholia. I am like everyone else in Bridgeport, quite ordinary.

Chapter 7

I spent three hours cleaning my studio apartment after work. I hoped Licorice Luke would call, and I needed to occupy myself with busy work. There was not enough room in my closet for my clothes, even with my summer things in storage. I thought maybe I would give Gina some of the things I was less fond of, but what was the point? I am a size twelve, and she could only be a six at her fattest. I thought about giving some things to the Salvation Army, but do they really have use for resurrected Gucci or bias-cut cocktail dresses? They wanted Irish fisherman's sweaters, and wool suits, things schoolteachers needed for work. But I decided I could donate my old Birkenstocks. I bought them five years ago during feng shui–mania, when I thought they could provide the same balance and perfect harmony for my hammer-toes that pushing chairs against the north wall did for my inner *chi*. However, my theory about harmony and Birkenstocks yielded to my theory about mixing better sportswear with cork-soled Lord-boards, and they became things to wear when taking trash to the incinerator room.

I'd never cultivated a proper shoe fetish. Shoes tend to draw attention to the calves and thighs, and when yours resemble broken elephant legs, you concentrate on using garments to conceal. Maxiskirts and big bells obscured my legs; grotesque hats and my monstrous perm drew the eye away from the rest of me. But I couldn't continue to let motorcycle boots dominate my wardrobe. They distracted from the clothing, which after all was where my money was going. I would have to make room in the closet for more shoes, that was all there was to it. And I would need to buy a new armoire to accommodate my excess wardrobe, at least until Gina gained weight.

At nine o'clock the phone rang. Hoped it was Luke.

"Hey, Lisa?" The voice, male, harried, vaguely Bridgeportian, nearly drowned out by the blaring of television and shouting customers, was not Luke's. Oh, Fred. Oh, shit, *Fred*.

"Hi, Fred," I responded. "I was gonna call to thank you, I mean to apologize, but I've been swamped at work and . . ." I trailed off waiting for him to jump in and take the burden of embarrassment from me. He didn't.

I continued. "And, well, I'm sorry about the other night, is all."

"That's okay," he said. "Worse things have happened in this bar. Mom and Dad expect me to take it over completely when they retire, so I've been ordering sick sand in bulk."

"God, Fred. I'm an idiot."

"So you're all right now? Good. Hey, I'm starting a new thing here on Sundays: Fred's Easy Electronica Hour. I'll be spinning Burt Bachrach, Serge Gainsbourg, Brigitte Bardot, and Gilberto Gil mixed in with the James Taylor Quartet, the Elevators, Portis-head, and Stereolab. Come next week, okay?"

I said, "It's been done to death."

He said, "Not at Wysocki's Tavern."

I tried to picture his usual customers, the over-fifty stevedore, bricklayer, meatpacker crowd, bobbing their grizzled heads to easy electronica music, swilling Old Style and double bourbons. I couldn't. Would they give up their jukebox (George Jones, Hank Williams, Jr., and Elvis) for even an hour? But after hurling all over Fred, I was in no position to refuse any requests.

"I know Fred's Easy Electronica Hour will be shocking for some of the old guys here," he admitted, "but I'm trying to attract a younger clientele."

I've heard those words before. I recalled the image of Daddy prostrate on our floral sofa after the one-legged pantsuit debacle. His head looked so small and round without his Bon Jovi toupee. I've seen what happens when I offer my opinions on what modern kids are into, and I vowed to keep my mouth shut this time.

By ten-thirty, Luke still had not called. I would never break out of involuntary celibacy at this rate. I called Gina, hoping Ma would not pick up the phone. But she did.

She shrieked for ten minutes about a horrible story the Dragon Lady had told her. At the diatribe's end, I made out that Ma had understood every word the Dragon Lady said, except that the drunk whore who threw up in the bar was me.

"That's terrible, Ma," I said. "What kind of people are tramping around the neighborhood?"

"I don't know, maybe all the hookers they kicked off North Avenue in your neck of the woods came down here. You better be careful when you come visit next time; it's not safe like it was in the old days. We didn't know how good we had it."

In the good old days, all we had to worry about were racially motivated beatings and a corrupt police force.

Finally she put my sister on the phone. Gina agreed to come with me to Fred's Easy Electronica Hour Sunday night, as long as she had finished rearranging her religious postcard board by then. She had exchanged 3-D Christ for the Black Madonna and now had mixed feelings. The Black Madonna was beautiful, but Gina missed how Christ's eyes followed her around the room, and how his Sacred Heart leapt out at her. My sister drifted about in a blissful world populated with talking animals, superhero-like saints, and a hip, wise-cracking Jesus. She conducted lengthy conversations with Saint Francis as well as with neighborhood pets—and not just dogs and cats, but goldfish, hamsters. I think she yearned to start a church for animals, but marketplace demand for such things was unreliable.

Before I hung up I asked her if she ever read *Chicago Society*. She said no; between McDonald's and struggling through family dinners each night and watching *Columbo* with Daddy, she didn't have time to read the society columns. I wondered if my sister could be growing cynical and bitter. Perhaps there was hope for her after all.

Chapter 8

Doris Mingle had been saddled with the unthinkable. She was assigned to showcase new designer irregulars to Honey Dietrich. Mrs. Consolo was in conference with Fishman's buyer all morning; Gulag Anna (formerly Russian Girl) could not defer properly to Honey; and Mrs. Lubbeth was busy preparing me for my maiden role as Maria Callas. That left Doris as the only choice, as she at least was familiar with irregular craftsmanship. She dutifully led Honey to the private showroom, in the corner of which was a small alcove. Mrs. Lubbeth and I sat in the alcove applying my makeup, preparing my wardrobe, and softly playing Verdi's *Aida* on the portable stereo for inspiration. This meant we witnessed every painful, pitiful exchange between the queen and her gangly knave.

Honey began. "Let me tell you a little something, what is it—Doris? What a darling name; that's what they named girls in *my* day, sugar. Look at what I'm wearing right now. Go ahead. I won't bite, you can touch me. This is a one-of-a-kind Halston from 1977. I'm not ashamed, Doris, to tell you I picked it up for a song from a little secondhand shop in New York on Orchard Street. These shoes? Jimmy Choo, half price from a sample sale. I paid a third of what my winter coat is worth, simply because the lining had been sewn in sloppily. My Chinatown tailor fixed it in no time. What I'm trying to say is that I wear only the best and I never pay retail. Now show me what you have."

Doris, quaking in her sensible, size-thirteen Cobbie Cuddlers from the Big-n-Tall Gal shop, silently combed through the rack she had assembled that morning. It couldn't have been easy, with Honey tapping her foot and humming "The Girl from Ipanema" and Mrs. Lubbeth and me watching her out of the corners of our eyes.

"This is nice," said Doris, holding up a candy-colored number.

"Is it?" asked Honey. "Why is it nice?"

Doris stared hard at the dress. "It's red?"

"What makes it a nice red dress?"

Doris said, "Christmas?"

Honey sighed. Mrs. Lubbeth made attempts to abandon me in the alcove. Did she want to rescue Doris from Honey's inquisition, or save Honey from Doris's ineptitude—and garner herself a fat chunk of Honey Dietrich commission? I didn't know, but I held fast to her wrist.

"Doris has to learn," I whispered. My hair looked like a towering medieval headdress, and I wasn't releasing Lubbeth until it was fixed.

"All right, Doris," said Honey. "First off, who made the dress?"

Doris consulted the tag. "Anne Klein."

"Then that's all you need to say. I can see that it's red, and I can judge for myself if it's nice. It's not. Next!"

When giving customers like Honey a private showing, one had to be supremely self-confident and insist that a garment was fabulous and that some celebrity adored the designer. People like Honey needed to be bullied; there was no room for chatting, for mild suggestions. Lubbeth and Consolo could talk customers into almost anything. I couldn't; Doris couldn't.

However, one needed to have some idea of the type of thing that would appeal to Honey. It was a waste of time showing her anything conservative, understated, or modest. Even slipping a few dignified items onto the rack tended to darken Honey's whole view of the collection.

At Fishman's, nothing reflected more poorly on an associate than the failure to close one sale with a customer who had intended to lay down hundreds or thousands of dollars at a private showing. Of course, Doris failed.

Honey wrapped herself up in her trademark assemblage of honey-colored doohickeys, scarves, tippets, and cashmere wraps, slung a camel-hair handbag with luggage-leather trim over her shoulder, and drifted away from Doris without saying good-bye. She shot a meaningful glance at Mrs. Lubbeth, who was calming my schizoid coif.

"Tut-tut, girls, priorities," she said, peeved that we hadn't rushed out to salvage the private showing, and waltzed off.

It was difficult for Mrs. Lubbeth to deal with the lost sale as well as Honey's condescension, as though she was a teen caught skipping study hall to smoke in the john. As for myself, I was used to Honey's haughtiness and was grateful she had not mentioned Babbington Hawkes's column.

Mrs. Lubbeth barked at Doris to hang up the rejects and go back on the floor. I snuck in a cig and dragged happily until she came back and slapped it out of my mouth.

"I used a full can of Aqua Net on you," she said. "Do you want to go up in flames?"

It was almost noon, time for me to parade around Women's Wear, but Mrs. Lubbeth was having trouble getting the zipper of my gown to comply. The gown was not Givenchy, as had been promised, but the sort of floaty voile popular with mothers-of-the-groom. I braced myself against the wall, trying to narrow my rib cage by an extra millimeter while Lubbeth commanded, "Suck it in, suck it in!" Maybe I could have the last rib on both sides of me removed, just like Cher. They were just taking up room. What good were they doing where they were? None.

"Outstanding," said Mrs. Lubbeth as she finally got the zipper up. "Now you look fit for a Hellenic cruise aboard the *Christina*." I regarded my reflection doubtfully. Perhaps they could find some role for me aboard a yacht, but likely it would be as ballast.

"Does this have to be sleeveless?" I asked, holding my arms out on either side.

She sighed. "I just spent ten minutes getting you into it, and now you want out. What's wrong with sleeveless?"

I flailed my arms, watching the atrophied triceps flop around. "My bat wings. I look like I'm wearing a flesh cape."

"Oh, nonsense," she said, pushing me out onto the floor. She ordered me to dazzle and took away my cigs.

My first day as Maria Callas will be remembered as a horrendous flop. I stumbled around in Lucite-heeled pumps and said, "Hey, how ya doin'?" to customers while Nan, Lubbeth, and company looked on in horror.

"Imperious!" hissed Lubbeth. "Be imperious!" I changed my greeting to a stentorian "How *do* you do?" and wondered when lunch was. This didn't seem fair, being Maria Callas on my own lunch hour. When would I get time for a sandwich? It made me irritable instead of imperious.

For a while I sat on a red velvet throne the maintenance guys put on the display in our central atrium. It was the same throne used for the Fishman Santa during Christmas and had stains on the seat cushion. The display was supposed to look like Maria's opulent Ritz suite, but more resembled the set from a high-school production of *The King and I*.

A child, convinced I was one of those living mannequins, came up and poked me. Its mother yanked it away, admonishing it not to talk to "the nasty man." Another kid came up and said, "Hi, Mister Lady. When will Santa be here?"

I said, "How should I know?"

Mrs. Consolo came by. The meeting with the buyer had not gone well; she could not dump the new shipment of tweed A-line skirts—nothing Greek or luxurious about *those*—and she was mad.

She said Mrs. Lubbeth, after watching me swagger around the department like a dock loader in drag, had come down with a migraine and had gone to lie down in the back room. Mrs. Consolo suggested I assume various regal poses until the hour was up and they could discuss what it was I ought to be doing out here.

"Did you have to get me the Santa throne?" I whispered. "Why isn't anyone throwing roses at me?" She said our budget couldn't afford roses and that all the good display furniture had been snapped up by Men's Wear. When she was out of sight, I skipped out on my throne duties to see what the hell was going on in Hui's department on the fourth floor.

In the elevator, people stared at my Persian-deity eye makeup and stomach-squashing bodice.

"How ya doin'?" I said.

In Men's Wear, Hui ignored me. He was still mad that I divulged his secret plans to transform the junior janitor into Aristotle Onassis. I hid behind a rack of leather coats and spied on the men's display.

They had created a beautiful mahogany bridge to surround the ship's wheel, complete with canvas umbrellas and leather-cushioned benches, chrome ship railings, tables of Baccarat tumblers, Louis Vuitton valises spilling over with gold pocket watches, the linen *A. O.* handkerchiefs, casually placed Gucci slippers, silk cravats. Set off to the side were leather club chairs, oriental rugs, and green baize-covered tables strewn with poker chips, playing cards, and cigars—presumably Aristotle's private smoking room. Throughout the department, one could hear from the stereo system the soft crowing of seabirds, the crash of waves, the distant clanging of a buoy. Customers crowded around the display, stood three-deep at the cash registers, fought over silk ties and gold fobs.

Suddenly I became aware of a presence behind me. I whirled around and came face to face with young Aristotle. He wore a crisp white shirt with French cuffs, khakis, and the same Gucci slippers that I'd seen on deck. Clouds of dark hair sprang from the V exposed by three unfastened shirt buttons. His face had the deeply tanned, craggy character lines of a senior shipping magnate. Everything about him was square, from his head to his torso to his fingertips. His lips were suspiciously sensual. His black hair was slicked back from his forehead, and he wore a pair of large dark sunglasses with small gold interlocked *G*s on the arms.

"Good afternoon," he said seriously. "I am Aristotle Onassis."

"Good afternoon," said I. "I am Maria Callas."

He lifted his sunglasses briefly, revealing eyes as black as the midnight sky over the Acropolis. "But you can call me Ray," he said.

"And you can call me Miss Callas," I replied imperiously, and flounced out of Men's Wear.

As I waited for the elevator, I peeked back over my shoulder. Young Ari stood watching me with a bemused expression from the bridge of the *Christina.*

When the lift came, I hurried in and pushed the basement button. It was obvious that I was a failure as the diva and no one was going to bring me lunch. The basement was full of Fishman floggers. I waited in line at the deli counter like any other schmo.

"Ham on rye," I ordered, sliding my tray along the counter. At the end of the line, when the cashier demanded payment, it suddenly hit me.

"No pockets," I said, futilely patting down the mother-of-the-groom gown. And my purse was up in my staff locker. "No money," I clarified. I asked if it could be put on my tab.

"Your tab?" screeched the cashier. "What do you think this is?" She began to draw my tray away. The ham on rye was as tantalizingly out of my reach as a bag of cash on a Brink's truck, as a respectable job with a diversified 401K, as a life imbued with meaning.

"Please," I said. "I'm so hungry." I made sad sounds. She grinned—it was an evil moss-toothed troll's smile—and slowly shook her head. Where was my savior—the dirty-bagel counselor, Mrs. Lubbeth, anyone?

"I've got it," said a voice behind me.

Aristotle Onassis drew $5.75 in singles and change out of his immaculate khaki trousers and handed it to the cashier. I looked up at him in gratitude.

"Don't worry about it," he said. "Tips."

I said, "You get tips?"

He escorted me to a table in the back. I thanked him and he waved my words away.

"It's the least I could do after our pleasant meeting in Men's Wear," he said.

I smiled crookedly and sat down. Then I quickly stood up.

"What's the matter?" he asked.

"Nothing."

"Why are you standing?"

"No reason. Just like standing." My God, the stomach-squashing bodice had rendered me totally incapable of sitting in the god-damn cafeteria chairs. I had definitely felt something snap when I sat down; whether it was a clothing hook or one of my useless ribs, I did not know. Beads of sweat broke out on my forehead, and my stomach rumbled as I stared forlornly at the sandwich, still sitting on the table beyond my reach. Aristotle looked at me questioningly. Oh, what the hell, it was too much to hope I could ever appear in public as anything less than a complete moron.

"Actually," I whispered, "I can't sit down. This . . . this iron maiden of a corset is too tight."

"Hmm," he said, "I like standing, too," and he stood up, handed me my sandwich, and lit a Chesterfield in full view of the nonsmoking citizenry.

There we stood: I, happily devouring ham on rye; he, with his cigarette and abundant chest hair. It was not too bad looking like a witless idiot, standing erect as a beefeater, shoveling in food while wearing a dress my grandmother would not be caught dead in, as long as someone stood with me.

I hardly noticed the stares of those around us, hardly noticed Hui watching from behind the colonnade at the cafeteria entrance.

Back in my own department, I passed the throne display with its schlocky fake window and chintz draperies, the four-poster bed made up with dudsville polyester (no longer needed in the bedding department, as a child had thrown up on it last spring), and went straight into the back room to see Mrs. Lubbeth. She lay rigid on a cot and held a cold washcloth to her forehead. Her blue paisley caftan hung down over the edges of the cot, giving her the appearance of a giant floating beanbag. Her wild Angie Dickinson hair was spread out on the white pillow like a tarnished halo.

"It's not you, it's me," she said weakly. "Maybe the days of achieving excellence in window dressing and storewide pageantry are dead. Now it's all about music videos and standing around meekly while customers refuse our help. I shouldn't have shoved you into the Maria Callas role. You were happier as an anonymous junior saleslady."

But I wasn't. I thought I was, but now that I'd seen the possibilities for Women's Wear and, let's face it, myself, in Fishman's Greek Islands wonderland, I couldn't go back to sneaking cigs in the handicapped dressing room and alienating customers. I saw a chance for greatness, and Mrs. Lubbeth was not going to back out on me now.

I told her all that I had seen in Men's Wear, the extraordinary measures Hui had taken to create the popular public ideal of Onassis, and how male customers waited in line to buy alligator poker-chip cases, distressed-leather steamer trunks, and sterling-silver flasks; how women flocked around young Aristotle the janitor, taking inventory of his wardrobe, his toiletries, his many beautiful useless accessories—hoping perhaps to transform their own dull husbands into worldly men of substance. The flurry of buying and selling going on in Men's Wear would have stunned even the most mercenary broker at the Board of Trade.

Mrs. Lubbeth propped herself up on an elbow. "Do you really think we can compete with Hui? He's merciless and inhuman—absolutely the best salesman Men's Wear has ever had."

"We have to be tough with Maintenance," I said. "That's the real key to success around here. With a junior maintenance man in the Aristotle role, the other janitors will naturally give him first dibs on the choice display stuff. You *know* how strong the ties are for the Chicago custodial union. And with Hui padding his gratitude with cash, the janitors will build him anything, provide him with whatever he asks, and give us the dregs. Although why Hui would want to deny us equal access to the janitors is a mystery to me."

Mrs. Lubbeth sat all the way up and tossed her cold compress in the corner. "You know why: he's ruthless and set on being the most successful manager in Fishman's history. Believe me, hon, I've sat through a decade's worth of marketing meetings where Mr. Fishman practically wet himself when announcing quarterly sales stats. 'Oh, a big round of applause for Mr. Zhang in Men's Wear, who exceeded all expectations *again* with a sales increase of seventy-five percent!' I'm sick about it. The next thing you know, they'll shove all of Women's Wear into a broom closet so that Hui can have the whole building."

"Thank you, Greek chorus," said a voice from the doorway. There stood Hui, hostile, arrogant, and awesome in well-cut Issey Miyake.

He spoke coldly, staring at Mrs. Lubbeth. "I have stopped by to insist that you cease spying on my display and stealing my highly original creative ideas." Pointing at me, he continued, "Also, I demand that your shroud-wrapped clerk stop annoying my Aristotle. He is a sensitive janitor-cum-magnate and does not need the menacing obsession of this . . . this one-woman goon squad."

"I was hungry," I said.

"Get out of here, Hui!" shouted Mrs. Lubbeth. The rising voices brought Nan, Mrs. Consolo, and Doris Mingle into the back room.

"Gladly," replied Hui. "Shall I pass on any message to the boys and girls asking for the 'fairy man' outside Santa's workshop?" Turning again to me, he said, "And may I add, in the spirit of kindness, that you have neither the figure nor the poise to portray Maria Callas, nor even the dubious carriage needed to wear that ridiculous washerwoman's housecoat. Perhaps your senior will do you the favor of cloistering you in the stockroom, where your presence will not offend shoppers nor frighten babies."

With that, he stomped off.

The women immediately fussed over me. They all said Hui, master of psychological intimidation, was just trying to destroy my confidence and scare Mrs. Lubbeth into altering her marketing plan.

Mrs. Consolo said, "He must be very worried about your potential success; why else these dramatics?"

"That's right," said Mrs. Lubbeth, squeezing Mrs. Consolo's hand. "Thank you, dear. He's just trying to unnerve us. Lisa, I promise we will do whatever it takes to make you comfortable and successful as Maria Callas. Please don't listen to Hui." All the ladies agreed to help. Mrs. Lubbeth vowed that our marketing scheme would succeed and that with a lot of hard work and makeup and spandex, I would look fabulous.

Doris Mingle said quietly, "I think she looks nice just the way she is."

"Please, Doris," said Mrs. Lubbeth, "we all know what kind of weight 'nice' pulls around here." Doris faded into the wallpaper.

"Do I look like a transvestite?" I asked the ladies.

"Not in a bad way," said Nan.

Chapter 9

*B*y Friday evening, Mrs. Lubbeth informed me that she had wrangled a substantial check from the marketing department for the construction of a decent Ritz suite as well as a balcony facade that I could access by an extension ladder in the stockroom. She decided to scrap the Covent Garden diorama and asked for a large reproduction of the Rome Opera House, done up exactly as it was in 1950 for Callas's much-loved performance of *Aida*. Mrs. Lubbeth had finally called in eight hundred years' worth of favors from the executives.

"You don't work here as long as *I* have without building a little clout for yourself," she said. "Plus Mr. Fishman has come to rely heavily on my advice and support over the last few decades and wouldn't deny me anything, if I asked in the right way."

Mr. Fishman, a handsome fellow of eighty-five with the body of a polio victim, had always liked Mrs. Lubbeth, though everyone knew he was a real tightwad. I hoped that her "asking in the right way" did not mean she had to see him naked or touch his weird, withered bod. But maybe she liked that look. Who was I to judge? I was designing myself to be Mrs. Ebert.

She continued. "And guess what else? I've arranged for you to spend the evening and Saturday at Crump's Spa and Salon, all on the Fishman tab. Photos of Maria Callas have already been sent ahead, and they know what they have to do, darling. You just relax and enjoy." She patted my cheek and said my driver was waiting outside to whisk me away.

Crump's! *Only* the most exclusive spa in all of Chicago. Honey Dietrich went there for long weekends of detoxification and kelp wraps. Princess Diana had visited the salon for highlights in 1996. Visiting dignitaries came for the chemical peels, and stayed for the juicy gossip and unsupervised midnight whirlpool sessions. Crump's soothed everything from overtweezed brows to misunderstood wives. So they had a little scandal with their shiatsu masseur and the daughter of an Argentinean ambassador; so what? Scandal just added to the Crump mystique.

She said I should just go straight to the spa from work; there was no time for me to go home first. The car waiting for me wasn't a very impressive type of vehicle, but I made a big production of getting in the backseat so that others leaving Fishman's would see me being chauffeured.

"I'm ready, driver," I said.

"OK, Lisa," said a familiar, tongue-trapped voice.

"Doris! What are you doing here?"

She sent the seat flying backward about ten feet to accommodate her giraffe legs and said, "I'm driving you to the spa. Mrs. Lubbeth promised me overtime."

"Oh," I said. "Do you think I'll get paid overtime to *go* to the spa? After all, it's on my own personal time."

She didn't know. Oh, well. I took out my cell phone and called Nan on hers.

"Hey," I said, "guess where I am."

She said, "Still with that tired old cell-phone line? Nobody says that anymore."

I ignored that. "I'm on my way for a session at Crump's!"

When I told her the whole story, she couldn't believe it. She kept saying, "No way" and "Why you?" Why? Because I'm Maria-goddamn-Callas, that's why. Was it so hard to imagine me luxuriating at *the* spa for socialites and celebrities and that Fishman's was willing to foot the bill? I'd hoped Nan would be glad and excited about my trip to Crump's, but she just sounded envious, which I guess is better than nothing.

People like Nan will never be happy for someone who is on the threshold of fabulousness. I snapped the phone shut and stared at it. It was sleek and violet, but not the smallest version available. I had to upgrade it; only losers and Ameritech repairmen carried fat phones anymore. Then I called my machine at home. Excellent, Luke Sheehy had finally called, though it was to ask me out for that very night. That just wasn't right. Everyone knew it was unwise to accept a date without at least four days' notice. He left his phone number, and I was happy to be able to return the call and report that, no, I could not see him tonight; I was going to Crump's.

"You are?" he said with obvious surprise. He *must* know that a full Crump package costs hundreds of dollars. "My boss goes there sometimes."

"Really? He does? Will he be there now?" I asked. Oh, to meet Ebert at Crump's . . .

"I don't think so," he said. "Well, let's get together some other time then."

"Right," I said, waiting for the other time to be duly requested, but he just hung up. I jabbed more numbers on the keypad. Tim Gideon should be on his way home, too.

"Reference!" he shouted. "Oh shit, I mean, hello?"

I gave him the rundown on my assignment.

He screamed with delight. "I hate you! You are so lucky . . . gee, all this because of dressing up like Maria Callas at a department store? It's so unbelievable. Can you get some free samples, like aftershave lotion or something for me? Tell me everything, everything that happens. Then I can feel like I was there, too."

I told him to meet me at Wysocki's Tavern on Sunday night. Tim complained about going all the way to the South Side, but he liked Fred Wysocki and was a huge Brigitte Bardot fan. Anyway he would be dying to hear how my session went.

"Have fun, old trout," he said, "and whatever you do, don't talk about yourself or your life to the other clients, unless you're going to lie. Use this trip to network, to climb that ladder."

I made a mental note not to be myself.

I took out my biography of Maria Callas and read for awhile as Doris drove like a senior citizen down Oak Street.

Finally I could take it no longer. "Can you speed it up?" I asked.

Doris replied, "The pedestrian has the right of way in a marked or an unmarked crosswalk, Lisa."

"Do you see this?" I shoved the book in her face. "I have to transform myself from worthless salesclerk into the brilliant, beautiful diva, and I don't have time to fool around. Get it in gear, Mingle! Move, move!"

She sped up to seven miles an hour. "You're not worthless."

I turned a page. "Did you know Maria Callas saved her family from starvation during World War Two, when the British prevented food from coming into Greece? I wouldn't last two seconds during a trade embargo. If a bunch of Englishmen kept food from coming into *my* town, I'd have a mental breakdown and drag everyone down with me."

"No, you wouldn't!"

"Yeah, I would. I don't have an ounce of her courage."

Doris said, "You have pounds and pounds of courage." I looked at her. She said, "That didn't come out the way I meant."

When we reached the spa (secret location in the Gold Coast neighborhood, penthouse suite plus two floors atop an ordinary building), Doris put the car in Park and turned around to face me.

"I hope you have a good time," she said, "and here, I got you this because I think they deprive you of such things at the spa." She handed me a Hershey bar.

I looked at it. "Candy? Jesus, Doris, it's not a weight-loss clinic. Is that what you think Crump's is, that I'm going to be a fat-farm inmate and I need to smuggle in junk food? Thanks a lot."

"I'm sorry," she said. "You're not fat, I'm dumb. I don't know anything."

"Just forget it," I said, opening the door.

She sat there miserably picking at her cuticles as I exited the car.

The doorman looked up my name and waved me in toward the elevator. I couldn't believe how natural it felt to command the elevator operator, just as if I visited Crump's all the time. Was I supposed to tip him? I couldn't afford it, and anyway he was just standing there pushing buttons. *I* could do that.

When the doors slid open, I floated into a world of gold leaf and purple velvet. At the reception desk stood a gorgeous man wearing a headset with a small microphone. A young woman in a white terry-cloth robe stood talking to him. She twirled her sash and tugged open the front of her robe when he wasn't looking, unfurling her cleavage all over the desk.

"Can I help you?" asked the man. He wore a black cashmere turtleneck and black wool trousers, and the tips of his otherwise brown hair were dyed platinum.

"Lisa Galisa?"

He said, "Are you asking me or telling me?"

"Lisa Galisa," I told him.

The terry-cloth woman gasped, "Oh, my God, is that really your name?"

So much for not being myself. He consulted the book in front of him, confirmed the appointment through his headset to an unseen entity, and smiled at me.

Then he said, "*I'll* take that," and snatched the Hershey bar out of my hand.

They put me in some kind of interrogation room. I think they called it "the bullpen." A small, vaguely sinister woman came in with a clipboard and pencil. Nervous and deprived of my standard

Friday Happy Hour, I thought she was a waitron of some sort and blurted out, "Do you have any Belgian beer on tap?"

"There's no alcohol here!" she exclaimed. My drunk said she'd see me at Fred's on Sunday and took off.

The woman ordered me out of my clothes, tossing an extremely soft terry robe and terry slippers onto my lap. I asked for a bathroom to change in, and she said I was to undress in front of her so that she could judge the natural movements of my muscles and my overall physique while I was engaged in normal day-to-day activities. Could it be that Crump's was just a beard for pervs to get free shows? She'd change that tune when faced with my struggle to emerge from control-top panty hose. Anyway, she didn't appear to be lusting after me at all as she made carping *harrumph* noises and marked up her clipboard.

I thought I was ready, but she told me I had to take off my underpants, too. I was given to understand that *no* underpants were allowed, as *it* needed to "breathe."

"Put your robe on now and come with me, please," she barked. She actually snapped her fingers. I followed her down the hall, meekly scuffing along in my terry slippers. The hall looked like a corridor in any fancy hotel with its Regency stripe wallpaper, silk-brocade armchairs near the elevator, and fake verdigris pots of fig trees by the windows. But there were no ashtrays, and I felt vulnerable.

We took the elevator up one floor and exited into an all-white corridor that led into an all-white room. Not all white as in passé white wool textiles from a Moroccan open-air market, but all white as in the chic cold white and chrome of a doctor's office. So much better than my apartment. White was not so bad after all—if it was hospital-dispensary antiseptic white. Anyway, the room had a few Danish modern pieces, a scale, a white enamel glass-fronted supply cabinet, and a small white-tiled pool.

The Littlest SS Guard, as I'd come to think of her, told me to remove my robe while she poked me with styptic pencils and pinched me with fat calipers and assessed my body-lard ratio by strapping me into an S & M–looking harness and dunking me in the pool. She weighed me and measured me and slapped my thighs, timing how long it took them to stop jiggling and settle down. She examined my face with a jeweler's loupe and yanked several strands of hair out of my head for later study under the microscope.

Finally she said, "I will have the specific results after the tests come back from our lab, but right now I can tell you this: you have the skin of a thirty-two-year-old."

That's terrible, I thought in despair, *I* am *thirty-two.*

She looked up from her clipboard briefly and said, "Your measurements are thirty-seven–thirty–forty. Three inches must be eliminated from your waist and hips to have an hourglass figure—luckily for you, hourglass is currently 'in,' and, lollipop head, big breasts on a stick are 'out.'"

"Can't I just gain three inches in my bust?" I asked.

The frau-guard jerked her head up and narrowed her eyes at me. "Who sent you?" she demanded, as though I had claimed to be a long-lost Romanov searching for crown jewels.

"Fishman's," I said.

A nasty look transformed her features. "Ah-ha. So you have won some type of store freebie?"

I explained my Maria Callas role and suggested she consult her little list there. She didn't seem to care for my tone, but she did refer to my file, which apparently explained everything.

Slightly mollified, she said, "I see, yes. I had not been informed by Joaquin at the desk. He will be fired shortly. Your Mr. Fishman has been a wonderful patron and has sent us many . . . *persons* . . . in need of our expertise. I am glad to help him whenever I can. So what we will attempt here is not an overhaul of your body-care routine, but rather a 'quick fix' to start you on the road, yes?"

I stretched back in one of the Danish modern chairs, my hands clasped behind my head. Obviously we now knew who was working for whom here. "Whatever you say," I replied.

A sudden sharp crack spliced the air, and I jumped out of my seat. The chair back, made of some cheap material no doubt, had split right down the center.

The guard smiled thinly and said, "Unfortunately, those chairs cannot handle the *bigger* girls." She offered me a white beanbag chair in the corner, assured that it would not burst under my heft.

After my physical assessment, the guard sent me to the Crump café. It was strange to think of all these spa clients at candlelit tables set with real silver, sitting in their white bathrobes and not wearing underpants. Some people ate alone, as I did, others sat at tables of two or three. Very intimate. We were not given menus, but rather were told to hand bar-coded cards to the waitrons, who then scanned them for our personal stats and dietary requirements. I was impressed that the frau-guard had tallied up my meals and caloric needs in the short time I had been abused by her.

The waitron returned with a plate of shelled peas, a flimsy sliver of fish, three cubes of cheese, and three grapes. I was told to eat everything in a certain sequence to optimize the healthfulness. I went out of order (don't like Muenster) and got in trouble. At first I thought they'd try to throw me out, but then I realized that since Mr. Fishman paid a lot of money for me to be there, they weren't allowed to expel me. Money had saved many American asses before mine—the youthful high-jinks of the Skakel kids in the seventies came to mind.

I wished the waitron would turn into a friendly sommelier. But bottled water, vintage year 2000, was, I supposed, the perfect accompaniment for rubbery fish. I felt exhausted, and all I'd done was submit to an evaluation and eat dinner. I scanned the room for interesting people. No Ebert, but there, at the back of the room, sat Honey Dietrich dining with Babbington Hawkes.

After dinner, I was sent for a dunk in the sensory-deprivation tank. They told me to think about the sound of one hand clapping. Thought about food, comfortable underwear, the taste of ice-cold Old Style, the loud music and hacking complaints at Wysocki's Tavern, a blue silk mandarin-collar Prada jacket that ought to be marked down at the store by Christmas.

At six-thirty I got a half-hearted massage from a grumpy Swedish lady who refused to take off her rings before kneading my flesh. Welts rose on my shoulders. The Littlest SS Guard barged in and dumped my purse on an empty massage table.

"Contraband," she announced, poking through my Sobranies, bubble gum, Now and Laters, and biography of Maria Callas.

"Hey, at least leave the cigarettes!" I protested.

She stared as though I was mad. *Duh,* I thought, *they're* Sobranies. *Not cheap prisoner cigs.*

The guard paused and thumbed through my book. She said she'd always had a soft spot in her heart for the woman who had been usurped by Jacqueline Kennedy. Her eyes traveled from the dust jacket to my face and back again.

"Hmmm," she said, "I can see it."

She kept her gaze on me. It was truly kind of pervy, with her staring at me, standing there in her uniform and tool belt hung with tape measures and fat tongs.

She said, "But you're too thick around the waist," and left.

I'd assumed that spas were all about decadence and sleeping in, but at seven A.M. a big man with a bald head opened my door without knocking and shouted, "Arise!"

He left a clean robe for me in the closet, and small bottles of Crump's shampoo and Crump's body wash on the sink, then told me to "await further instructions by the potted palm beside the elevator." What was going to happen by the potted palm? It sounded

Inspector Clouseau–like. I had a vision of Kato jumping out from behind the corner and throwing me down a flight of stairs, where I would be kicked to death. I showered, then remembered I didn't have my Frizz-Ease hair-calming gel. With a blow dryer and plenty of goop I can tame my hair into almost lying flat to the center of my back. My cig craving had kicked in along with a nagging ache for caffeine. Way crabby, I roughly towel-dried my hair, multiplying tenfold the amount of snarls and knots. I wanted to just walk around with a towel wrapped turban-style around my head, but my contact at the potted palm took me back to my room.

She said, "Crump's does not allow towels to be worn about the head because the scalp needs to—"

I interrupted, "Breathe?"

She smiled frostily. She was the kind of woman who wears small barrettes an inch back from her hairline, a sure sign of trouble.

My hair began to frizz up. I could feel it boinging just below my shoulders, curling and shrinking up more every second. I reached for my comb to try to stanch the oncoming fro, but the good-looking young woman grabbed my wrist and said, "No outside combs, please. Come with me."

She released me on my own recognizance into the dining room. After breakfast (one scrambled egg white with tons of asparagus), my contact ushered me into the kelp room, where I was swaddled in seaweed and left to contemplate my own existence for forty-five minutes. Then they hosed me down like a dehydrating porpoise and let me put on a clean robe.

"Am I thinner?" I asked.

The kelp master said I might have lost a tenth of a pound of dead skin cells.

My hair was now in full poof mode, bobbling an inch or two above my shoulders and bursting out a good twelve inches from the sides of my head. On my way to the salon, I heard a voice down the hall shout, "Mr. Kot-*ter*!" I looked, but saw no one.

My contact met me at the salon doors. She did a double take, then made notes on her clipboard that read, "Rethink head-towel rule."

I asked, "Are we going to do my hair first?"

"Noooo," she said. I discerned disappointment in her voice. "First mud pack and facial, followed by tweezing. Then we will address the situation with your . . ." (She vaguely gestured at my head.) "Prepare for several hours of work. At noon we will give the stylists a break." Not "We will give *you* a break," but the *stylists*, who—after battling with my hair—presumably will need electroshock therapy to jolt them back into competency.

At the mud-pack station, I finally got a chance to talk to other spa customers. I reclined in a dentist's chair while a handsome Trinidadian slathered me with a special charcoal-and-seeds mud mix. I sat right next to Honey, and two unidentified women sat to my right. In spite of the mud, the only reason I recognized Honey was that with all her plastic surgery, her face still bore the expression of a woman caught in a wind tunnel.

"Darling!" she exclaimed. "How *are* you, and *what* are you doing here?"

I gave her a brief summary of the Greek Islands experiment at Fishman's before my mask hardened. She declared Maria Callas to be too, too sick-making.

"Too," agreed the woman to my immediate right.

"Absolutely," agreed the third.

"Will you come see us at the store this week?" I asked. "We're planning lots of pageantry." Honey said she would definitely make it, then mused on how she could get Mrs. Lubbeth to do away with that horrible scarecrow who tried to sell her a red dress. My mask had hardened completely by that time, rendering me mute. My eyes swept across the ladies to my right. The one next to me had fallen asleep and snored through two perfect nostril holes. The third—writing furiously in a notebook propped up on her knees—was not a woman after all, but the womanly gossipmonger-spy Babbington Hawkes.

Finally they chiseled off my charcoal mask. I felt my face gingerly and remarked that it did feel softer.

"Don't touch it!" shouted the Trinidadian mud chiseler, Phranque. "You will ruin all my hard work with one touch of those nicotine-stained fingers." I looked at my fingertips. The little pads were all yellow and smelt of burnt popcorn. A morning without cigs had opened my eyes to the more-disgusting side effects of my habit.

I exited the mud-pack station with Phranque, who led me into a large airy room with a vaulted ceiling and marble floors. Again all was white and chrome and square. Through the skylights I saw patches of pure blue sky, and shafts of bright light streamed in through the windows. It would have been a perfect day to sit at the lakefront with a giant latte, wearing a red leather Balenciaga jacket, smoking sky-blue Sobranies, and reading Maria's biography. In bright sunlight, I would hardly notice my stained fingertips and could continue smoking in peace.

Phranque seated me near the east windows and handed the facialist my file. Words were exchanged, and I thought I saw Phranque gesture toward me while pinching closed the end of his nose.

The facialist approached me with clipboard in hand. She had startlingly white skin and white-gold hair, eyes of a hue she probably called violet, and wispy brows. She wore a white lab coat over a black turtleneck and scribbled things into my file.

"Alcohol?" she asked.

"Sure, whatever you have," I said.

She glanced at me. "Do you drink alcohol?"

"Oh. Yes."

"Smoke cigarettes?"

"Yes."

"Wear sunscreen? Avoid the sun?"

"No. No."

I also flunked the rest of the questions regarding caffeine, sugar, red meat, and white flour. She anointed me with rose water and tea-tree oil and said nothing aged you more than the Big Three: sun, alcohol, and smoking. Her tone implied that well-adjusted people don't burn themselves into leathery hides while sucking down double bourbons and chain-smoking cigarettes. I kept silent about my real problems—poverty and unwilling celibacy.

The eyebrow expert came in then. He argued with the facialist about the future for my brows. He wanted to shape them into something more current, softer. She wanted to wax the hell out of them, and shrink them into razor-thin brush strokes.

The expert said, "The no-eyebrow look is hot for West Coast Internet types, but not for this client." I reminded them that Maria Callas had brows like mine, thick and overly arched. The expert yanked out a few hairs, vigorously brushed my brows, and said, "Voilà." They looked the same to me, but I guess it would be hard to train them into a softer shape. I have had naturally mean eyebrows since junior high.

It took thirty minutes to wash and condition my hair. The stylist got cramps in her thumbs, so we adjourned for lunch.

By four P.M., they had mastered my hair. Six inches had been cut off (or "removed," according to the stylist, as though she had excised a diseased organ), and most of the perm was gone. I felt very fragile and empty and flat without it.

When the last lock fell to the floor, the stylist said, "Hello, Maria Callas. Good-bye, Big Ragu!" Everyone laughed.

She teased it bubble-style and swept up the front into a tiny black velvet bow, as seen in the 1959 photo of Maria's *La Bohème*—that's the one I like best, sort of Mary Tyler Moore, sort of *That Girl,* sort of shih tzu. She showed me how to create girlish peasant curls for *Tosca,* and most strangely for me, how to slick it down with a center part for a classic and subtle *La Traviata* chignon. Easiest of all was the playful ponytail-atop-head seen in photos of a hot, bikini-clad Maria aboard the *Christina* in 1964.

"You won't really be wearing a bikini in the store, will you?" asked the stylist, frightened.

Everybody in the salon clapped when the stylist finally announced she was done. I stared at the unfamiliar babe in the mirror and the stylist soaked her hands in a bucket of Ben-Gay.

Before my makeup session, I went back to my room and called Gina.

"Got a fantastic new haircut," I said. "Can't wait for you to see it tomorrow."

"I know I'll love it," she said. "Can't wait to tell you about my date."

"You went already? Was it horrible?"

"No! But I'll tell you all about it later. Gotta go now. I'm scheduled for watching cloud formations this morning, followed by vole tracking with Daddy in the backyard."

I love my sister. I wish she wasn't insane.

During the makeup clinic, the facialist painted my lips with beautiful, Leisure Lady shag rug–red lipstick and outlined my eyes in smoky kohl eyeliner—less Persian deity, more catlike. Then she gave me free samples! It was totally worth coming here! I really got Mr. Fishman's money's worth. Tim would be so happy when I gave him the little packets of ginger mousse shaving cream and peach aftershave and two men's facial toners. One was scented "Life-Affirming," the other was "Anti-Depression."

The Littlest SS Guard came into my room to return my candy and cigs. She said she hoped I would not overindulge in them. I said of course not. I planned to mitigate their effect with alternate doses of Old Style, in particular progression.

Chapter 10

$\mathcal{F}$red had hung a hand-lettered sign in Wysocki's front window. It read **SUNDAY NIGHTS—FRED'S EASY HOUR—MIXING ELECTRONICA, EASY, LOUNGE, BOSSA NOVA, SOME HAWAIIAN. DOLLAR TAPPERS!** The tavern looked the same as always except for multicolored Christmas lights strung up over the bar. They looked pretty, reflecting in the mirror behind the top-shelf liquors. The usual Bridgeport pre-Alzheimer's, liver-disease crowd was there. The TV in the upper corner showed mute reruns of *MacGyver* while South American crooner Chris Montez warbled "Call Me" from the stereo. Fred had dressed for the occasion in a thrift-store polyester shirt with giant swooping stripes of purple and brown, epaulets in matching material, and flyaway collar. Fred had worn hideous polyester for a full decade before Prada launched their tacky-chic line in 1995, and even though pop culture had sampled it and moved on, Fred refused to budge out of his poly world.

"Hey, man!" he said, setting down a glass of Old Style in front of me. "Your hair looks awesome! Cool dress. Did you do all this for my Easy Hour?"

I explained that Fishman's Greek Islands theme was responsible. Fred poked my hair gently.

"It's like a helmet," he said admiringly. I had teased it up into a bubble-flip, just as Crump's instructed me, and stuck in that cute little shih-tzu bow on top. My new dress (vintage Alaïa from Snooky's consignment shop) complemented my new hair—thick, scratchy white poly with center stripes of red running vertically and horizontally, like a big scarlet cross on my front. Very appropriate for the Easy Hour, with its 1960s naughty-choir-girl-at-Easter-dinner feel.

I asked, "So it's not the Easy Electronica Hour anymore? Just the Easy Hour? That's much better."

"Yeah, all the guys here thought 'easy electronica' meant I was offering free tutorials in TV/VCR repair. Anyway I'm trying to promote the culture of Easy. It's what everyone wants: the jet-set lifestyle . . . glamour, money, impractical clothes, deceivingly vapid music. Brazil. Smoking with Algerian writers. Bad health. Laissez-faire politics. Filet mignon. Crème fraîche. Midnight travel." He said this as he pocketed the nickel tip from a machinist with only nine fingers.

"That's just what we're trying to promote at Fishman's with Greek decadence and Onassis excess. As in 'the shipping magnate in all men.'"

"That's excellent," he said, mopping up spilled beer on the old oak bar.

The Dragon Lady sat on a stool at the end, scribbling into a large ledger. She appeared to be balancing the books for the tavern. Fred's dad stood behind her with his hand on her shoulder, staring up at *MacGyver*.

Everyone knew that when his army unit left Inchon, Mr. Wysocki brought his immigrant wife home to Bridgeport. Nobody used her first name, but instead called her Lee, her family's name. Everybody considered Fred's dad to be a successful small-business man, running his tavern for over forty years with his helpful wife. He owned a home and the bar's building; he rented out the apartments overhead; he had a son, kind of lazy, but nevertheless a son who would one day run the tavern. In truth, Fred's dad was a depressed alcoholic, and it was the Dragon Lady who had been in charge of the bar, the business loans, refinancing the mortgage, and Fred's education. No one credited her. Fred said she didn't care. She worked hard, hoping to save enough money to go back home. Fred said when he was a child, he and his mother used to sit near the shore at Promontory Point in Hyde Park and watch the waves break on the beach. The Point, the stretch of lakefront that juts out from Fifty-fifth Street, is a beautiful spot and took her mind off of life in Bridgeport. She told her son stories of Inchon. She talked about her father, the farm, the Yoshino cherry trees. He said she gazed longingly over Lake Michigan, as if just beyond its dark waters lay Korea.

The tavern door swung open, and in came my sister and brother. Gina sat next to me while Chip greeted Fred.

I said, "Why is *he* here?"

She said, "He wanted to come. I couldn't stop him."

"You *must* stop him. The next thing you know, our parents will want to come out with you."

She smiled weakly. A moment later the door swung open again, and Ma and Daddy waltzed in, rubbing their hands to banish the cold November air. I stared at Gina in shock. Barhopping with the Galisas is definitely *not* Easy.

"I couldn't help it," she protested. "Everybody asks where I'm going, and then they tag along."

Ma and Daddy walked right by me and said hello to the Wysockis. Ma, autumnal in a warm-up suit of gold silk, ordered blackberry schnapps and peeped into the Dragon Lady's accounts ledger. Daddy, dejected Bears fan in a shrunken blue sweater and orange slacks, stood staring at *MacGyver* and sipped his Old Style.

"They must not have recognized you," said Gina. "You look great."

She ordered a ginger ale. Fred looked expectantly at Chip, who said, "I'll have what my mom's having."

When Ma finally recognized me, she started screaming, "Sal! Sal! Look at your daughter!" Then they rushed over to touch my hair and mess up my makeup. Ma insisted that she always told me

I'd look better with a short flip. Chip hid beer nuts in my hair, but Ma slapped his hands away.

"Maybe I should run home and get my camera," said Daddy.

At that moment Tim Gideon sauntered in, and the stereo erupted with the sound of a bunch of Brazilians singing "Más Que Nada."

Tim, for some reason a real favorite with my parents, came up and hugged Ma and told Daddy what beautiful daughters he had. Gina, in ponytails and shapeless overalls, blushed. Tim threw his arm around Ma's shoulders and grinned at me. Chip rolled his eyes.

Ma called to Fred, "Another blackberry schnapps for our friend!"

Tim touched my black velvet hair bow and said, "Well, you are absolutely stunning. You are *very* Maria Callas."

Happily I drank more beer. I was right to spend four hundred dollars on an impractical choir-girl dress.

The Wysockis seemed pleased at the modest success of Fred's Easy Hour. The regulars watched us with amused detachment. I watched myself in the mirror.

A young guy walked in and sat next to Chip, one of his old friends from high school. All Chip's friends were cut from the same cloth, whiny intellectuals obsessed with chess and Wilhelm Reich. This particular one, Bruce, a beefy slump-shouldered artist with a ruff of clownish red curls, had been hanging around our house for years. He, too, was a native Bridgeporter; worse, in fact— he was a graduate of the School of the Art Institute of Chicago and lived in his parents' rec room.

"Guess what, Lisa," said Chip. "Bruce and I were talking about that idea you had, you know, about us starting our underground magazine in the basement? And we asked Ma and she said we could do it!"

"My idea? It was my idea to ask Mommy if you and your little friend were allowed to play in the basement?"

Ma heard us and came by to squeeze Chip's cheeks. "Anything to help my son, my son." Her son, her son, twenty-five and living at home, would soon turn her basement into an activists' hideout where unemployed Bolsheviks would come to complain and listen to old Smiths CDs.

Tim squeezed in next to me. "Hey, Baby Chip is looking mighty grown-up these days."

"That?" I asked. "You can't mean to imply that you think Chip is attractive. Anyway, he's not gay."

Tim lifted an eyebrow.

"I know, I know," I said, "none of your boyfriends are gay. But neither man nor woman could regard Chip as a potential . . . ugh, I can't even think about it. Anyway, if you want to picture Chip in a few years, take a good look over there." I directed his gaze to my father, who adjusted his toupee in the bar mirror, the outline of his truss sadly peeking through the gap between his sweater and Sansabelt waistline.

Ma stole up and put her arms around our shoulders. "Say, you two. When are you finally going to get together?"

Tim smiled and said, "We were just talking about that."

While Tim tried to make time with my brother, Gina filled me in on the details of her date. I expected a rundown of the fast-food customer's possessions, appearance, car model, etc., but instead listened to a tribute to the man's dog.

"But what about the guy?" I asked. "What about the date?"

She said, "He's a nice person. He lives on Halsted in a condo. Anyway, after the movie we went back to his place—"

"Ah, yes, this is where it gets good," I said.

"I'll say! So we get there, and that's when I met his Labrador. Lisa, something very profound happened to me as I sat on the floor petting Satchmo." She paused, building the suspense, her ponytails quivering in anticipation. I waited, thinking, *Please don't let her say she's in love with the dog. Please.* Gina looked at me, perhaps judging whether or not I could handle what she was about to reveal.

"I realized," she said slowly, "that I can communicate psychically with animals."

I exhaled in relief. Thank God it was nothing more perverse than boring, New Age sensitivity to living creatures.

She said, "I was just sitting there, right? Petting and petting, and suddenly I had this image in my mind of chasing a purple tennis ball. So I said to the guy, 'Hey, I think Satchmo wants to chase a purple tennis ball.' And the guy flips out! Satchmo *does* have a purple tennis ball, and he *does* love to play fetch with it!"

I said, "All Labradors like to fetch tennis balls."

"But purple? Remember, I said *purple*—"

"Yeah, yeah, you said 'purple,'" I replied. Gina waited for me to respond more enthusiastically. "Maybe you're psychic. Sure, why not?" I asked Fred for another Old Style with a little blackberry schnapps on the side.

She smiled with an expression of contentment I had not seen since before the suicide of our dog.

I raised my shot glass to her, toasting the greatest success of her twenty-seven years on the planet.

"Hey," she said, eyes wide, pointing to my schnapps, "purple."

By eleven-thirty I was exhausted. It was hard watching my dad swing Ma around the tavern, dancing to the exotic Hawaiian strings of Martin Denny. She kept saying, "This is *our* kind of music, easy listening!" A cloud of doubt passed overhead. How successful can the Easy Hour be if Ma likes it?

Fred threw some Crystal Method on the stereo. The dancing stopped. Daddy looked confused and conflicted. He felt, I thought, opposed to the mad throbbing thumping, yet resigned to the modern world laying siege to the things from his past that he loved.

At evening's end, we all walked out together. Chip and Bruce discussed plans for their 'zine. From what I could discern, they hoped to attract a readership of young men interested in obscure labor history, flying saucers, and grape pop.

Daddy took me aside as we walked toward Morgan Street, asking if Tim and I were dating now. We held hands, poor Daddy.

I said, "We aren't dating. We are . . . too different. We sit on opposite sides of the stadium."

He said, "What's that mean? Just sit together."

It wasn't my job to out Tim to my parents, though how anyone could not tell was beyond me. "It's like this: Tim sits in a franchise owner–quality loge with an open bar and steak dinner, and I'm a bleacher bum."

He said despondently, "I *knew* you were a Cubs fan."

The Galisas and clownish Bruce turned down the street toward home. Tim and I walked around for a while, looking for a cab. Leaves blew down the street with a cold wind hinting of harsher weather to come.

Suddenly he said, "How come you've never gone out with Fred?"

"Are you crazy? He's my friend. It would ruin everything. Anyway, I just don't feel that way about him."

"Well, I would if I were you. Look, I know his hair is probably putting you off. Jesus, what grown man wears a bowl cut and short bangs these days? And those tinted Jim Jones glasses make him look psychotic, but he's a decent person and your families know each other. Plus he's half Korean. That is *very* in now. Half of something," he explained.

"Nope," I said, "he's my oldest friend and fellow burnout from St. Barbara's, but that's it."

"I didn't know there were Asian burnouts."

"You forget," I said. "He's only *half* Asian."

"So do you have *any* date prospects? You're kind of a hot commodity in your little choir girl dress, there."

"I'm still aiming for Licorice Luke. Or, of course, Ebert."

"Yes, Ebert," sighed Tim. "That would be fantastic."

I was cold. Tim gallantly leant me his wool overcoat. My choir-girl dress could not hold up to autumn nights in Bridgeport. I suggested taking a taxi all the way down to Fifty-fifth Street to look at the lake, maybe pick up a little bottle of something to warm us as we sat in the cold shelter of the Point's WPA park. But Tim said it was too late and anyway we both had to work the next morning.

We found a cab finally and rode northbound on the Kennedy toward home. I really wished we could have gone out to the Point. I often thought about the Dragon Lady sitting out there with little Fred all those years ago. It seemed so like those final days of Leisure Lady, when my father stared out the shop's front windows, as if his whole life's purpose had disintegrated, burned down to the ash and vanished into the Bridgeport streets. The way Fred's mom longed for Korea and the home she had left reminded me of how Daddy felt all those years, like his future was now in the past, a glimmering dream that had ended.

"I *love* Easy," declared Tim.

"It's the way of the future," I said. "Fred's right. To be Easy is to see the stars from a private plane bound for Biarritz, a flute of Roederer Cristal at your elbow, a White Russian emissary to your left, and a high-rolling Monegasque to your right. It's about owning an old Pablo Picasso Blue Period canvas as well as a new Paloma Picasso Tiffany pendant; it's about moving forward. Easy uses the past as adornment, but it rockets to the future."

He said, "You've given this a lot of thought, haven't you?"

About thirty-two years' worth. I passed Tim the little bag of goodies I got from Crump's. He asked how it went.

"Great," I said. "Anything with free samples is all right by me."

He said, "I hope you remembered every single wonderful, pampered moment."

I hesitated. "I remember every moment perfectly. They treated me like a princess," I said. I had been planning to tell him the truth: how in the midst of wealth and beauty and Babbington and physical perfection, I was all Doris Mingley. But I lied. It was easy.

Chapter 11

$\mathcal{I}$ arrived at work before eight. Mrs. Lubbeth needed extra time to properly outfit me and do my makeup before the hordes expecting Greek opulence bum-rushed the store at nine o'clock. We were trying to stay one step ahead of Hui by keeping me in Maria-mode all day long instead of just at lunchtime. I still had to attend to most of my menial duties like inventory and helping people, but I got to wear a vintage Givenchy gown—authentic this time—while doing so. I'd hoped maybe customers would be intimidated by my glamour and leave me alone.

Mrs. Lubbeth was the best. She piped in *Medea* throughout our department over the sound system (everyone felt the tragedy in the air) and then draped me in the Givenchy ivory silk Ionic-column sheath. It took us ten minutes to stuff me into the body slimmer (okay, girdle), but at least my saddlebags didn't poke out. I loved the Greek-goddess finger waves in my newly sleek hair. Mrs. Lubbeth planned to dress me each day in a gown inspired by the opera playing over the sound system. I was supposed to "be" the characters, while still encouraging customers to fork over cash.

By ten o'clock I had made a few circuits of the department, inclining my head imperiously (as instructed) to the customers. I also had to hand out little engraved cards listing the various gowns we carry that resemble the Givenchy model, including price. It seemed to me unregal for Medea to hawk women's wear, but I had to remember that in truth I was just the oldest junior saleslady at Fishman's.

The shoe people provided me with four-inch strappy stilettos in ivory peau de soie (Marc Jacobs—nice). At five-seven, on just my bare fallen arches, I towered above the customers in my new shoes. It was incredible gliding around so much bigger and more glamorous than everyone else. I felt that I could pound anybody. But the shoes were death after ten minutes, and I headed to the throne for a break. In gray janitorial coveralls, a boxy rear end stuck out from behind the red velvet chair. It shocked me to see young Ari on hands and knees with a bright yellow bucket, scrubbing the floor.

"What's going on?"

He sat back on his haunches and wiped his brow with the back of his hand. "Vomit patrol."

"But I didn't do anything!"

"Who said you did?" He looked at me curiously. He had no clue, of course, that in my personal life I probably required my own vomit patrol. "Mothers shouldn't let little kids climb on the throne so soon after breakfast. I mixed up a batch of heavy-duty sick sand, though; that seems to do the trick."

"Well, that's something," I said, "but there's still a big stain on the throne's seat."

He studied the cushion, shrugged, and turned it over. I guess science can't take care of everything.

He said he had to hurry up; he was supposed to be in Onassis garb by now. He griped, "It's hard going from junior janitor to senior shipping magnate without any change in salary."

I was dying to know what Men's Wear had cooked up, but Ari wasn't talking. Hui had sworn him to secrecy. Ari looked pretty miserable there, scrubbing away, though he really filled out those coveralls nicely. I thought of the ham-on-rye episode and gave him the Sobranie I had hidden in my bra for later. It was in pretty good shape despite being trapped between walls of flesh and steel underwire.

"Thanks," he said. He glanced about warily, then lit it. A pale green vapor rose from the floor, and the faint smell of coal tar lingered in the air.

"That's an interesting reaction," he said. "Better step away, though, in case this bucket blows."

I went to prepare for the mini-showing of my costume and accoutrements at eleven. Mrs. Lubbeth promised me a big commission on all the Maria Callas–type garments we sold. She intimated that this could spell out big bucks for me. How much commission could the junior janitor make peddling linen hankies and silk cravats? One three-thousand-dollar Gaultier dress, and I was set.

Once she deemed me presentable, Lubbeth sent me off to the cosmetics department for a facial transformation. In exchange for the free makeup session, I helped them unveil their new promotional line, "Makeup of the Goddess." I was the goddess.

The mini-showing proved to be both profitable and humiliating. We made many sales based on my costume: twelve dresses, one tiara, twenty upper-arm bracelets, eight pairs of shoes, and countless pairs of stockings. But we made our biggest sales based on a second, private showing I had to give in the handicapped dressing room, displaying our line of "firming undergarments." Ladies got to see me in my undies with girdle and, unfortunately, without. Mrs. Lubbeth used a pointer such as you see in med-school operating theaters and jabbed me repeatedly in the saddlebags.

"Note," she said, "the cottage-cheeselike formations on the outer thigh. The sheer organza of the Givenchy would only accentuate such malformations. Mere girdles of industrial-strength nylon and rubber would show through the gown's filmy material. What can the lady of ample proportions do? Lisa, don the body slimmer." Donning the body slimmer while twenty-five pairs of eyes were glued to my saddlebags, no mean feat, showed the ladies exactly what kind of miracles to expect.

Exclamations of "She's not bulbous anymore" and "I can't see where the fat went, can you?" echoed throughout Women's Wear.

Mrs. Lubbeth invited the customers to touch me, to confirm for themselves that my jiggly fat bubbles had disappeared. We sold out of all our firming undergarments, and I made a commission of four hundred dollars.

"Just think," said Nan, "if you didn't have all that cellulite, you would never have made any money." It was a shocking thought indeed.

The afternoon brought turmoil to Women's Wear. At lunchtime I toured the other departments while a hired group of fans followed, tossing silk roses at my feet. (The fake-flower department is capitalizing on my success. I should receive a commission on all the silk roses people are now buying.) I went to Stationery and Silver Gifts first. They had replaced the photos of pretend happy people in the picture frames with photos of Maria Callas, Aristotle Onassis, and various Greek beaches.

I said to the head of Stationery, "You know, you really should have checked with my agent Mrs. Lubbeth before using my likeness in your picture frames."

The head of Stationery frowned, and said, "You know, you're not *really* Maria Callas."

I said, "I am representing Miss Callas for Fishman's Department Store, and so it is my duty to see that her image is reproduced responsibly. At least put the pictures in expensive mother-of-pearl frames instead of those hokey cherry-veneer ones." When I walked away, she mumbled that I might not be Maria Callas, but I was just as big a bitch.

To the turmoil: nobody until now had bothered to see what Crystal and Fine China were doing for the Greek Islands theme. I guess we just assumed that since Tabletop was doing their department up like a Greek café, their fancier counterpart would do the same. Wrong! I walked into the department to see, seated regally on a rose brocade settee and reaching for a Waterford champagne flute from a nearby ebony table, Jacqueline Kennedy Onassis.

A crowd had gathered to gape at "Jackie" (the Fine China junior saleslady) in her navy blue Oleg Cassini–type suit and non-saddlebags.

"Hello, everybody, I'm so glad you could come," she said in the same baby voice as the former first lady. On the side table next to her was a photo of Jackie and Aristotle. She sipped from her flute. Was it real champagne? I wasn't even allowed a *cig* break, and Washington's trollop was getting sloshed on Fishman's time.

I stalked off to find the manager, Philomena, who was hiding behind an enormous Swarovski crystal panda.

"How could you do this?" I demanded, stamping my foot. "How could you let *her* be your mascot, knowing everything Ari and I have been through?" First the doomed love affair ruined by Jackie, then the trials of ham, cigs, and child vomit.

Philomena stepped from behind the panda and said, "I knew you would be upset, but it wasn't my idea."

"How could it not be your idea? It's your department!"

"Mr. Fishman asked me to install a Jackie Onassis. Who am I to argue with the boss?"

Philomena was kind of a rogue fine-china saleslady. She once made a sale to Honey Dietrich's socialite archnemesis, Sugar Rautbord—something everybody else at Fishman's had always been afraid to do. The story goes that both Sugar and Honey were prowling for flatware from the coronation of King George V, and Philomena, once securing the pieces, contacted both socialites and sold out to the highest bidder (Sugar). At any rate, Honey complained to Mr. Fishman, who thereafter always kept a short leash on Philomena.

Philomena said, "If you don't mind, Jackie's giving a tour of the replica of her Manhattan apartment—the one where she and Ari shared so many happy memories. Your presence would only complicate things."

I stomped off in anger. Why would Mr. Fishman give these orders? He was too senile to come up with this ridiculous Jackie idea all by himself. This left the question: who would ask him to order the installation of Jackie O? Who was so important to the store that Mr. Fishman would risk offending Mrs. Lubbeth? Then it came to me, in one long drawn-out, ordinary Hong Kong syllable.

Hui.

I took a cig break in the stockroom, ruminating over this development. The lilac Sobranie, though luscious, was not doing much to calm me. I'd been conserving them and only had two left in my slim gold box. I didn't know any duty-free Germans. Would I be back to Kools? I was sick over it.

Once I composed myself, I made up my mind to barge into Hui's department and see for myself what he had planned. If Men's Wear and Fine China were conspiring to oust me from Aristotle's love life, women's wear sales—and my commissions— would drop like a medicine ball out of the sky. Nobody wants to buy clothes inspired by the loser.

Men's Wear was much more crowded than our department. How many plush terry robes and alligator belts do men need? I pushed my way through the crowd toward the bridge of the *Christina*. I've never been one for high drama, preferring a lifetime of sullen glumness to making scenes, but I felt, perhaps, a bit of Maria's rage sparking within me. At the helm stood the junior janitor, sans coveralls and bucket. He was dressed in a wheat-colored linen suit with white linen shirt and no tie. Their customers could *not* be buying linen suits in November. Young Ari gripped the ship's wheel and made casual conversation with the customers (who were kept back, I noticed, by a red velvet rope—I should have asked Lubbeth for one of those. . . . Why did I have to endure matrons grabbing my bat wings and squeezing my saddlebags?). On his gaming tables were three silver-framed photographs: his wife, Tina, Maria Callas, and Jackie.

I tried to slip under the velvet barriers but a bodyguard gently pushed me back. Aristotle saw, and said, "Ah, my good friend, Maria Callas. Let her up, Niko." Niko, who bore a strong resemblance to the senior underwear salesman, lifted the rope and permitted me to walk up onto the bridge. The crowd grew silent, watching.

"You look lovely, my dear," said Ari. "*Medea* this time, eh? Which performance?"

I swallowed nervously. "My first *Medea*, May 1953, Florence."

He smiled in response. I began to relax. I sat on the leather-covered bench to his left. He said my gown was exquisite and to tell him all about it.

What was going on? He was going to let me talk up Women's Wear here? But I took my opportunity and extolled the nuances and virtues not only of the Givenchy but of our other goddess gowns, particularly the three-thousand-dollar Gaultier. I twirled and the crowd applauded politely.

"Why not tell us about what's *under* your garment?" A voice, amplified by a lapel microphone and ten years of unchallenged Men's Wear superiority, rang out. The crowd parted to let Hui stride through.

"I beg your pardon?" I asked, stalling for time.

Hui slowly walked up onto the bridge, appraising me. He smiled ingratiatingly and said, "I believe Maria Callas had to wear girdles when her weight ballooned after World War Two. Tell us about the one *you* have on." He lifted his eyebrows and raised his hands palms up, as though to say, *Shocking. But what can you do?* He definitely had a rapport with the gawking customers, treating them like close friends with whom he shared a bit of shop gossip.

This was just cruel. It was one thing to steal ideas for a store display, another to humiliate someone in front of customers and Fake Ari. I looked down at my dress and felt Maria's shit-kicking hauteur seeping away.

Aristotle cleared his throat and stepped forward. "Girdle, truss, body slimmer. Call it what you may. There's no shame in wearing one. Why, we've all worn something to flatter our God-given figures at one time or another, haven't we? I know I have." He unbuttoned his shirt and held it open. Around his middle was a sleek little body slimmer. A man-girdle! He stared at us—*challenged* us to find him anything less than virile and sexy. He stopped steering the yacht, probably sending us into the boat-dashing rocks off Crete. I held my breath. Then someone in the crowd whistled; others applauded.

The scene was getting away from Hui. He looked panic-stricken at the sight of his Aristotle standing proud and begirdled, and held up his hands, as if to show he was unarmed. "No disrespect intended, I assure you! I was simply curious about Maria's massive weight gain after the war and her cache of body armor."

Everyone waited for what I would say next. I opened my mouth but no sound came out.

Then a voice spoke up from the crowd. "Yes, Maria. Please tell us about yourself and World War Two." We all looked at the speaker, who stood a head above the masses. It was Doris Mingle.

I cleared my throat and recalled all that I could from the biography I'd brought to Crump's. "Well, when the British prevented food from coming into Greece, Maria and her family, like thousands of others, began to starve. Rations ran out. Maria became thin and sickly. But she discovered a way to keep her family alive by making an imitation ice cream out of rotten vegetables and pig fat." Doris smiled and I gained steam.

"So the way I see it, after all that, she *deserved* to eat well. I celebrate the woman whose ingenuity saved herself and others from certain extinction. I celebrate every extra pound and curve as a testament to the artist who brought joy and brilliance to the music world, the likes of which we may never see again. Oh, she slimmed down a bit of course by the late fifties, but inside, I believe she was always a woman of huge heart, generosity, and strength."

The customers wiped tears from their eyes, nodding in agreement. Hui tried to make pig-fat jokes, but the crowd wanted to sympathize with the tender, dewy-eyed diva smiling at them from the bridge of the *Christina*.

Afterward, I went back to Women's Wear to find Doris. By then all the ladies had heard what happened with Hui and had gathered around me in the stockroom, wanting to talk.

"Please, I'm looking for Doris," I said.

"I'll find her," promised Mrs. Consolo, and went onto the floor.

"What do you want *her* for?" asked Nan scornfully.

I wanted to say it, really I did. I wanted to say, "I have to thank her for saving my ass." But when I looked at Nan, knowing how we had both mocked the tongue-tied freak not so long ago, my mouth dried up, and I just said, "I'm starving and my firming garments are cutting off the blood flow to my legs. Could you please run down to the cafeteria and get me a sandwich?"

She said, "You're really taking this diva thing too seriously, you know that?" and returned to Hosiery.

Just as Mrs. Consolo returned with Doris, Mrs. Lubbeth appeared and hugged me tightly. She'd overheard my request for food and said, "Oh, good, Doris, you're here. Go down to the cafeteria and get Lisa some lunch, will you?" Doris obeyed immediately. It must suck to be accustomed to instant summonses for petty tasks.

Mrs. Lubbeth said, "Hon, I just heard what you did in Men's Wear. I'm so proud of you! How did you learn so much about Maria?"

I said, "I read a lot at Crump's." Mrs. Lubbeth said she hoped I'd had a good time at the spa. She was beginning to look less Endora-ish and more motherly.

"It was fine," I said, "except they made me feel like—"

Just then Doris burst in with a meatball sub dripping in mozzarella. "Hi, Lisa," she said shyly.

Mrs. Lubbeth took the sub sandwich from her and said, "Careful, you're spilling!" Then she ordered her back into Irregulars.

"Wait, Doris," I said as she opened the stockroom door. "I just . . . I just wanted to say thanks."

Mrs. Lubbeth said, "*I* paid for it!" But Doris knew what I meant.

My senior said if I dripped one spot on the Givenchy, she'd brain me, and what was it I'd been babbling about Crump's, where Mr. Fishman had so generously sent me.

"Nothing," I said, carefully taking a bite.

At four-thirty I was allowed to get out of my costume and wash my face. At first I thought I wanted to keep my makeup on all day and night, but when I checked myself in the bathroom mirror, I saw a rather rough-looking Greek whore staring back at me. When had *that* happened? Must have been the fluorescent lights.

Out of the firming garments, my legs assumed their normal jellied state, except now with masses of tiny broken blood vessels.

Chapter 12

*O*n the train, crammed into a seat with gum stuck on it, I opened up *Chicago Society* and went straight to Babbington Hawkes. Now that he had seen me at Crump's, he would have to accept me as part of the scene.

GET OUT OF OUR SCENE

By Babbington Hawkes

Tsk, tsk, tsk. Apparently, some people have confused the exclusive celeb spa Crump's with a rehab clinic. Saturday at the mud room, luxuriating in the capable hands of Phranque, Honey Dietrich and I traded horror stories about paraffin waxes and loofah rubdowns that had gone awry. Suddenly, a certain fright-wigged saleslady (who shall remain nameless, if not shameless) plopped down nearby and pleaded with us to come visit her at her little sales counter at her little job, so bored was she. Okay, why should I withhold information from you, dearest friends? It was the bloated hag who vomited all over my butter-soft Ferragamos on Halloween. (Let me interject thanks to my readers who sent in donations toward the purchase of my new shoes. I *did* get a new pair and they *do* look fabulous!) It was so sad how she begged us to come watch her dress up as opera star Maria Callas during Fishman's much-touted Greek Islands promotional days. I can think of no one who less resembles the dynamic diva, either in looks or manner. But, dearests, if the sideshow freaks haven't made it to your town this year, head on over to Fishman's to watch lumpy persons swagger about in couture. It promises to be too, too sick-making.

I folded up the paper and stared out the window. It was dark out and there was nothing to see.

A familiar voice called, "Hello," and its owner sat down next to me. I turned to face Aristotle Onassis, who was wearing a green turtleneck sweater and gray wool trousers. His neck was so squat that the turtleneck covered the tip of his chin and cradled his chubby earlobes.

"Watch out for the gum," I said. He lifted his leg gingerly, but it was too late.

He said, "We've never been properly introduced. Your name is Lisa, right?"

I held up my hand, putting the flow of information in check. "We better not get too chummy, Ari. Hui is now the sworn enemy of Women's Wear, and you are his deputy."

"Nope," he said, grinning. He wore large rectangular horn-rimmed glasses with extremely wide arms and his black-and-silver hair fell straight and thick across his forehead. "I'm nobody's deputy. I may be a junior janitor, but I am beholden to no one."

I knew I was supposed to pretend to be imperious, but I just couldn't muster up the energy. Besides, it's hard to feel superior when gossip columnists ream you out in the society pages.

"Well, I'm just a junior saleslady, and I'm beholden to Mrs. Lubbeth."

Ari looked at me for a second. There was certainly something custodial yet suave about my train partner. His dark eyes seemed to search my face, then he said, "The truth is, I'm really a science teacher, but since the Chicago teachers' union has been on strike for the last month, I'm now a full-time junior janitor."

"You people are always on strike," I said.

He shrugged and removed a pack of Chesterfields from his black bowling-bag satchel. He offered me one. We didn't smoke our cigs, just sat with them dangling from our lips for the next few stops. It was a comforting feeling.

Finally, as we were nearing my stop at Division Street and I got up to leave, I said I still wasn't sure if we ought to be fraternizing. After all, now that Jackie was part of our landscape, it would only be a matter of time before he dumped me, married her, and drained Women's Wear of its good publicity. Who can hold up next to Jacqueline Kennedy?

"That bag of bones? Don't be too sure, baby, that you and I can't rewrite history," said Ari as I stepped out of the train.

I stood in surprise on the platform as the sliding doors of the El closed, my mouth a shocking-pink ring around my unlit Chesterfield. The train pulled away and I saw him light his cig right there in the car as others turned to look at him in outrage. Who *was* this science teacher masquerading as a custodian masquerading as the great shipping tycoon? Who was this rank-and-file striker with the square head and bowling bag, this smoker on public transportation, this ersatz janitor with the stubborn face of a little black bull and the body of a Kaiser roll? The mystery closed itself around me, like cobwebs, and I walked in clouded thought toward my apartment. Stars shone brightly in the velvet sky above, the same stars that pierced their diamond light over Skorpios, private island of the Onassis family. The question hammered in my brain: Who *are* you, young Aristotle? I had to know.

In the doorway of my building stood a young woman with ponytails whipping about in the chill November air.

"Gina?" I called to the figure. She waved. "What are you doing here?"

She said she had borrowed our dad's car and wanted me to run a secret errand with her. After my astounding performance as

Maria Callas, the altercation with Mrs. Kennedy, and the subway cigarette shared with Onassis, I was prepared for anything.

She drove the '77 Thunderbird at a paraplegic pace northbound on Ashland. We headed toward Oz Park, site of comical yuppie basketball games and a dog-frolic enclosure. In the old days, Gina, Chip, and I would spend lazy afternoons smoking pot in Daddy's car and drive around the North Side (Chip's dealer lived in Lakeview), taking our old dog to various parks. We'd stop at Vienna Beef stands (there used to be one on every corner) and chomp down Polish after Polish as the dog snored under park benches.

"Get up!" we'd say to it. "Time to frolic." It would amble over to other dogs, then collapse in the shade of a sparse urban tree, where we fed it hamburgers as big as its head. Day's end found us at the Zephyr ice-cream parlor way up on Wilson, where one last hit from Chip's travel bong allowed us to squeeze in forty-eight-ounce butterscotch shakes or confectionery models of the *Edmund Fitzgerald* made from five scoops of coconut ice cream with Pirouette cookies for smoke stacks. The dog, bloated and immovable, lay down in the backseat, lapping melted vanilla from a paper plate.

"What are we doing here?" I asked. Gina parked the car and handed me a notebook and pen. She said we were conducting a psychic experiment.

"I can't work at McDonald's my whole life," she said as we advanced to the dog enclosure. That was true. She'd wanted to be a veterinarian when she was a kid, but our parents discouraged her because she wasn't smart enough. Yet what did the need to escape a lifetime of burger flogging have to do with us standing in Oz Park in the dog enclosure?

"Duh," she replied, exasperated. "If I'm as psychic as I think I am, I can have a new career as an animal communicator. People will pay big bucks to know what's going on in their pets' heads."

My brother, indie 'zine publisher, and my sister the pet psychic apparently stood on the cusp of incredible fortune while I, employed person, wallowed in poverty.

Gina said, "They always say, 'Do what you love, and the money will come.'"

"Someone better tell the Chicago teachers' union."

So I followed Gina around the dog enclosure. I had to make a list of the dogs in attendance and her subsequent "readings." My job was to chat with the owners, noting dog personality traits and physical ailments (thankfully dog owners are always eager to divulge the particulars of their pets' digestive habits, etc.). Gina knelt down with a German shepherd, gazing like Bela Lugosi into its eyes, gently petting it. I made conversation with the owner and wrote in my notebook:

Physical health—hip dysplasia
Personality—hates other females
Toy—big yellow Kong

Gina came over to me after a few minutes. I told her I'd found the dog version of Ma.

She said, "Okay, this is what I got: I asked the dog how she was feeling, and suddenly I got an ache in my hips. I felt that she only liked the male dogs around us and that she wanted to play fetch with her bouncy Kong toy." She read over my notes and squealed with joy.

"Big deal," I said. "All German shepherds' hips hurt, and every dog likes that stupid Kong."

"You don't believe I'm psychic," she replied in a small voice, crossing her arms over her chest.

"How do you know what it's saying? Does it start complaining like Ma— 'Jesus Christ, I pinched a nerve'—or what?"

"Not in words. In feelings and images."

I watched her pet more dogs. I petted some, too, for the hell of it.

I had to admit, after an hour's tests, she had many accurate readings. We sat on the park bench and discussed our findings. I asked her if she was just psychic with dogs, or with other animals as well.

She said, "Huh. That's a good question. Do you know any cats?"

"Just Tim Gideon. I mean, Tim has a cat."

"Great!" she said. "Can we go over there?"

If I called him first and asked if I could stop by with my sister so that we could perform an experiment with his cat, he'd hang up the phone and lock his doors. Tim, though misanthropic, adores his kitty. It was better to arrive unannounced.

We headed toward Wicker Park, passed my building, and drove south to Tim's gangland apartment. Gina couldn't believe the difference a few blocks made. Where my neighborhood had achieved the pastel, prefab blandness of gentrification, his boasted the patina that came with age, filth, and violent crime.

Gina said, "Bridgeport is *way* better than the North Side."

Tim buzzed us in. His apartment—though situated on a floor above an old lady who boiled chitterlings each morning, stinking up the hallways, and a floor below a bunch of Ukrainian tuck-pointers with an aversion to bathtubs—was spotless and mod. He got all his furniture from Restoration Hardware and was particularly fond of pieces that came attached to some famous figure from history, such as the Picasso chair or the Freud desk. Everything was done in shades of forest green and amber and beige. His old nonworking fireplace, framed with embossed ceramic tiles, was utilized as a stage in which he arranged his favorite library puppets. When not in use at his job, the puppets made themselves comfortable in Madame Alexander doll furniture in the fireplace; little Emperor Hirohito and Churchill nestled on a miniature settee with FDR's dog Fala, while Gene Tierney, William Powell, and Myrna Loy perched on satin-tufted footstools. Tim proudly instilled in his youthful library patrons a decent working knowledge of old Hollywood and New Deal democracy.

Tim welcomed us in, looking pleased, so I knew something was wrong. There, on the cream wool slipper sofa, sat Kabuki Tart. Two steaming mugs waited on the coffee table, but Tim's breath stank curiously of Johnnie Walker.

"I'm so happy to see you," he cried desperately and pushed us into our seats. Gina settled into the Picasso chair and gazed around the apartment, while I, thrown into the 1952 Metro recliner, pitched backward and hit my head on the windowsill.

"Little top-heavy," I mumbled, indicating the recliner, as I carefully placed myself back in the chair.

"*I'll* say," replied Kabuki Tart, indicating my bust with staring zombie eyes.

Tim introduced us all. Kabuki Tart asked what I thought of Governor Ryan.

"Big and doughy," I said.

He said, "Ever since he passed that moratorium on the Illinois death penalty, my father's killer has been living the high life in Joliet!"

Tim dragged me out of my seat into the kitchen, ostensibly to help him pour more tea. Tim's cat, Len, had found his way to the Psychic Friends Network and launched himself into Gina's lap. Tim dumped out a crystal ashtray from his kitchen counter, full and still smoldering, into the garbage. Nina Simone shrieked, "My . . . name . . . is . . . *Peaches*!" ominously from the stereo.

"Oh, God. Oh, God," muttered Tim as he threw back an impressive swig of Johnnie Walker Red.

"What's going on?" I whispered.

"That's what *I'd* like to know! First he's staring off into the distance, mooning about his lost youth, then he tells me that since we've started hanging out, he's never *felt* the way he feels right now, then he's pacing around and ranting about the governor, then he goes fetal on the couch, crying about the tart shop. Then, just as I'm preparing to comfort him, in you come, throwing yourself and your"—he glared at my chest—"flesh globules about, and he turns into a disgusting frat boy. Half the time he says he's 'open to new feelings,' and the other half he spends excruciating about how his girlfriend dumped him after his father was murdered."

"Ouch," I said. "Run, don't walk."

He sighed. "Aw, hell. I've already spent like a hundred and fifty dollars on this guy. Not to mention my expensive emotional investment."

Tim is one of those cynical boys who hates everything, yet deep inside longs for love. He poured two mugs of tea, even though I tried to make my preference known by nudging the Johnnie Walker toward him. He ran his hand through his hair abstractedly, too frazzled to stop and wonder why we had come over.

I said, "Why don't you just take a break from dating altogether for a while?"

He opened his eyes wide in shock and responded, "A break? Look, I'm thirty-three years old, and I don't have time to fool around. I want a steady boyfriend."

"Exactly," I said. "So forget this guy and move on to someone more, er, gay."

"Like who? I *hate* gay men." Then suddenly, eyes alight, he said, "Wait, there's Chip."

"He's not gay," I protested.

"Lisa, honey, sorry to be the one to break the news, but your brother is so gay, he makes me look like Mike Tyson."

I said, "My brother is an indie 'zine publisher, and while he is extremely lame and faggy, he is *not gay*."

My voice had risen passionately during the exchange, and I had shouted the last dozen words. Kabuki Tart's voice called out from the living room, "Who's not gay?"

I shouted, "My *brother*! My brother's not gay!"

Gina said, "Yeah, he is."

"I knew it!" shouted Tim, triumphant. I stomped into the living room, smart-ass Tim close on my heels. I shoved the mug roughly into Gina's outstretched hand, spilling scalding tea on Len's tail. The cat screamed and leapt at me, claws extended. Tim had a mini-coronary tugging the hissing, spitting animal off my flesh globules.

"Len doesn't like you," observed Gina.

"Well, thank God we have a pet psychic here to tell me that!" I snapped. My sweater was now hopelessly snagged by vile cat toenails. Len jumped out of Tim's hands, scampered across the coffee table, and hid on top of the bookcase. Kabuki Tart went fetal on the couch.

"You must have noticed that he never dates any women," she said.

"I thought that was because he was icky."

I retreated to the relative safety of my recliner. It came out that Chip had told Gina he was gay years ago, when he was twenty. I thought, *Why not me? Why not tell me?* I was the only person from Bridgeport who has ever had a gay friend, so it wasn't as if I would judge him harshly.

Gina said, "It's not that. It's just that I confide in Chip, so he feels comfortable talking to me. Who do you confide in?"

I stared out the window, brooding. I hated confiding in people.

Tim dabbed at his eyes mockingly. "This is so beautiful, it's just like an intervention."

I stood up and announced, "I have to go now."

Gina said, "You *always* run away when you should be confiding your feelings." I stared crossly at her until she got up. She advised

Tim to move Len's litter box back to the closet if he wanted to avoid further accidents.

He stared at her in amazement. "How did you know?"

I pulled her after me into the stinky hallway.

Kabuki Tart unfurled himself and sat up. "*Who's* a pet psychic?" he asked. I closed the door behind us.

By the time Gina dropped me off at my apartment, I wasn't feeling quite as pissed off. It's hard to stay mad at a grown woman who wears ponytails every day and thinks animals talk to her.

"Do Ma and Daddy know?" I asked.

She said, "Not really. But they must suspect inside."

"Why? I didn't."

She said, "Well, you're more absorbed in . . . other things."

According to Gina, Chip watched *Dynasty* reruns every Thursday night on cable and always managed to mention to our dad how sad it was that Blake Carrington had trouble accepting his gay son. All Daddy would say then was "John Forsythe . . . sixteenth most annoying man on earth."

"Don't be mad," said Gina. "I'm sure he'll tell you himself one day."

I scoffed. "I'm not mad. I just resent that his gayness now makes him seem like an interesting person instead of the social retard he actually is."

I opened the door of my apartment, dismayed to see my life as I had left it. What I needed was a means to hold and conceal everything I owned. More closets, more trunks, more dressers . . . yet the apartment must remain spare, empty, white. How can I do it? It should look like nothing on the outside. It should hide everything.

Chapter 13

I had an excellent morning at Fishman's. Wearing a really tight velvet peasant-girl bodice with white lace mantilla, I leaned out of the balcony built against the back wall and blew kisses to a group of paid fans and real admirers on the floor. *Tosca* boomed out over the audio system. Afterward Mrs. Lubbeth helped me down the ladder propped up in the stockroom. Since Thanksgiving was the next day, we had to start pushing expensive party clothes for the Christmas season (i.e., marking up garments with velvet trim 20 percent and moving them to the "Essential Holiday Wear" section). For the first showing of the day, I would have to change into a more glamorous costume. Mrs. Lubbeth unleashed me from the bodice (even with velvet, it would be hard to persuade shoppers that the serf look was in), and into a silk harlequin-patterned queeny dress and much tighter corset, with a huge taffeta ball-gown skirt. Mrs. Lubbeth tucked a large ribbon of lace into my décolletage and at my wrists, for a bit of flounce and holiday charm.

I said, "Holiday charm? You mean, you and Mrs. Consolo have a lot of lacy blouses and things you haven't been able to get rid of, and you think I'll inspire our customers to 'go lace' for Christmas."

"My, my, how quickly we learn," she said. She looked as proud as a mama goose watching her imprinted gosling follow her across a six-lane highway. She steered me in front of the mirror so that I could get a look.

"Ohhh," she swooned, "plum is *really* your color."

"Yes," I agreed, "very regal. Who am I supposed to be now?"

"Hon, think 1952, think electrifying, think brilliant coloratura soprano! Think *Lucia di Lammermoor*!"

"But I don't know that one too well, how should I act? What's it about?"

She pushed me out into Women's Wear. "The usual opera theatrics—passion, sexual intrigue, mayhem, and madness. But try not to overdo the madness. Your corset can't take hysterical flailing."

I was scheduled at eleven-thirty for a quick showing, then off to cookware to help Chef Dumas from Odysseus whip up Greek fare. Thankfully, I would not be required to do any real cooking, just to stand there oozing Mediterranean glamour.

My Lucia costume was a *huge* hit, and we drew a big audience. The eleven-thirty show was supposed to be a small one, but my "mad scene" incited a frenzy in the crowd, who stormed the little platform and tried to touch the hem of my dress. I think I gave a decent performance as Lucia descending into insanity when I staggered around the dais, wailing and clutching a butcher knife. (The disturbing effect was diminished by Cookware's humiliating request that I pause, hold the knife aloft, and say, "Wüsthof-Trident butcher knife, thirty-nine dollars after rebate, or part of the deluxe Chef Set for two hundred dollars, including meat cleaver, peeler, and a set of six handsome steak knives in woodblock stand.") Mrs. Lubbeth assured the ladies present that only gorgeous harlequin-patterned Dior gowns could inspire such passion. We sold out our stock of purple, plum, garnet, and cabernet couture, not to mention a crumpled box of odd lace scraps Mrs. Lubbeth declared "Lucia flounces." I made six hundred dollars in commission.

I hurried downstairs to Cookware. I hoped that a free meal would be part of the bargain, seeing as how I peddled their steak knives during the most poignant moment of my lunacy. Chef Dumas was already busy at the food processor, showing the crowd his secret recipe for baba ganoush. A reverent silence greeted me as I swept in toward the hot plate. Men bowed, women gasped, and Dumas gave me an oily smile.

"You are Maria Callas, yes?" he asked, kissing my hand.

I made vague, "as you were"–type gestures with my free hand and curtsied to the people.

Dumas said to the crowd, "Next, my recipe for vegetarian moussaka. The secret? Luscious, hot, plump sweet potatoes." He ogled my chest as he said these last words. A quick downward glance showed that only one translucent layer of gossamer separated my exposed nipples from the crowd of hungry shoppers. All eyes were glued to my globules as I struggled to stuff them back in their corset.

Dumas commanded the audience to handle the luscious plump potatoes *gently,* and not to mash the life out of them.

Once I had secured my breasts in their cage, I was able to relax and watch the demonstration. It was only after we had all sampled a few of the chef's special olives that I noticed someone waving frantically at the back of the crowd. It was Honey Dietrich, vying for my attention!

She called out softly, "Yoo-hoo, darling," and everyone turned, as if watching a slow tennis match. How jealous they all must have felt, seeing Chicago's celebrated socialite waving to Fishman's adored fake-Greek saleslady. To be part of our coterie of famous personalities, to be in with our exclusive crowd, these were the most desperate wishes of the throng of little people in our midst.

Chef Dumas waved back to Honey and said, "How *are* you, darling? You look lovely as always." She blew him a kiss in response. Nobody was waving to me after all. At least, one person was paying me some attention: Babbington Hawkes, who managed to both scribble and smirk in my direction. He was dressed in a flamboyant Aegean blue suit, baby-blue dress shirt, and gold silk tie. La Dietrich, in her usual honey-beige cloud of cashmere.

Suddenly I felt like an old drag queen at a quiet Armani trunk show.

Chef Dumas began to prepare a platter of saganaki as I rested my elbow on the counter, chin in hand. I sighed and watched him set it on fire while the crowd ignored me and applauded the burning *fromage*. Imagine, being upstaged by flaming cheese.

A moment later I was shocked out of my reverie, as the whole crowd turned to the strobe of camera flashes at the cookware entrance. The same people who freaked out during my mad scene were now paparazzi-ing Dumas's latest spectators: young Aristotle Onassis and dry-husk Jackie Kennedy! I stood up suddenly with a sharp intake of breath. This momentarily expanded my rib cage, causing a seam thread to break and snapping one end of the lace ribbon out of my cleavage like a rubber band on a slingshot. Jackie clung to Ari's arm and shot me a look of Napoleonic triumph. She wore a yellow two-piece swimsuit, showing off hipbones that belonged on a geometry compass. Ari, demure in a white terry towel wrapped casually around his waist and *nothing else,* waved happily to me.

"Watch out!" screamed a customer up front. Dumas spun around in time to beat out the cheese fire that had crept up my lace and was now engulfing my bodice. Bernie from Admin appeared out of nowhere, party fro wobbling furiously, and doused me with a fire extinguisher. Afterward, Dumas waved away the black fumes issuing from my smoldering, ruined Dior gown as the crowd gaped in stunned silence.

"Opaa!" shrieked Babbington Hawkes.

I dreaded the second show. How could I perform as the spirited diva when it hurt to move my arms and neck? Little bubbling sores were sprouting where the flaming cheese had splattered.

"I guess you can sit this one out," said Mrs. Lubbeth doubtfully, referring to the next show. "The only thing is, you'll have to pay out of your own pocket for the burnt Dior, so I think you could use some more commission. But it's up to you."

"It wasn't my fault!" I said. "Make that dumb-ass Dumas pay for it. He's the one who ignited me."

"I'm sorry, hon," she said, "but he signed a contract with Fishman's before his cooking performances, absolving him from any mishaps associated with saganaki. Apparently, there'd been some trouble at Odysseus in the past with waiters catching on fire and trying to sue the restaurant. But as I said, it's completely up to you, dear."

"I'll do it," I grumbled.

"That's my girl," said Mrs. Lubbeth. "You're one step closer to getting a brown name tag!"

The wrenching pain coursing through my hands and arms made it hard for me to enthuse properly about that prospect. Mrs. Lubbeth saw my discomfort and began buttering my burns.

She suggested I keep moving before the next show in order to keep my energy up, so I milled around the store in a scarlet silk robe embroidered with a peacock on the back. I put on dark glasses and refused to sign autographs.

"My hands," I said to the gawkers closing in for a better look at the fiery diva. "They are too buttery."

I found myself in the irregular department. Doris was arranging a table full of irregular turkey socks. The socks were printed with little brown turkeys (roasted, not living), but the toe region had been split into three segments.

I asked Doris, "Were they supposed to be socks with five toes, or just normal socks?"

"I don't know," she said, "but they fit *me* just fine."

I said, "Maybe they were supposed to look like turkey claws or whatever."

"Maybe," she said. Then: "I'm sorry you were burned by the cheese. It's really terrible."

"Yeah," I agreed, "and Fishman's is making me pay for the dress. And I'm getting butter all over everything."

Doris nodded sympathetically. Then she said, "I have an idea." She handed me a pair of turkey socks and suggested I put them on my hands until the showing, to keep the butter in place. I said I couldn't afford to buy anything else from the store until I made enough commission to pay off the Dior gown.

"Go ahead," she insisted, pressing the sad irregular turkeys upon me, "my treat."

"Well, thanks," I said, carefully inserting my fingers Vulcan-fashion into the socks.

If I'd had any self-esteem, I would have stayed away from Men's Wear, but I felt myself drawn in. It was hard not to imagine that somehow Hui had orchestrated the whole cheese debacle as a means of vicious interdepartmental retaliation. I went up to the fourth floor and stood behind a fake ficus, watching the action on the bridge of the *Christina*. Peeking through the dusty plastic leaves, I was reminded of the Crump hallway, and my imagined assignation with Kato behind the potted palm. If only Phranque were here to soothe my burns with expensive charcoal/mud compote instead of Lubbeth slathering me like a scone.

There they were, Ari and Jackie, still clad in their yacht wear. I noticed a young woman standing between them near the ship's wheel. Ah, booze-addled Christina Onassis, on a break from the junior-miss department. The paparazzi snapped dozens of photos while customers shoved against one another in a rush to buy fifty-dollar white bath towels. The three "actors" looked very cozy, all linking arms on the beautiful mahogany bridge, as I—the burn victim, the buttered freak—stood watching from the distance.

"Please remove yourself from my department."

I jumped at the sound of a voice and the touch of a hand upon my shoulder sores. Hui looked down at me with undisguised revulsion. He said, "Calamity seems to follow you wherever you go, and your presence is unsettling to Mrs. Kennedy. Hasn't she suffered enough loss in her life without the further peril of your grease fires?"

I said, "You know, she's not *really* Jackie Kennedy."

Hui snapped his fingers, and a security guard appeared instantly. I protested that I had a right to go anywhere I wanted in the store. I tried to cling to the ficus, but my three-toed sock-mittens impaired my grasp.

Suddenly Ari looked over in our direction, leapt off the bridge, and sped over. He dove through the crowds, pushing onlookers to the side, and arrived panting as Hui and the security guard were about to haul me off.

"Wait!" cried Ari. "Can't we all just get along?"

Hui stopped and stared at his young magnate. "You'd better hoist your Jolly Roger and get back on the bridge," he said, pointing to the floor at Ari's feet. There, at his square feet, lay the soft terry towel. Ari stood before us naked, unashamed, boxy.

The security guard pulled me away. Unable to help myself, I looked back over my buttery shoulder and said, "I like the cut of your jib, Aristotle Onassis." The crowd erupted in cheers.

I endured the second fashion show. The costume changes were agony, but Mrs. Lubbeth handed me two Vicodins, so by the show's end I was loose enough to wave bye-bye to the crowd and fall headfirst into the orchestra pit.

My male escorts—Who were they? I remember nothing—must have carried me around on the little stage. There was no way I could have walked on my own after the first change of clothes. At one point I remember looking out at the audience and weeping, "*Quel dommage. C'est fromage!*" Afterward, I was left on the cot in the back room. I screamed for more butter and Vicodin, but no one heard. Drifting in and out of sleep, I thought, *So this is truly fame, in all its sordid loneliness.*

I awoke to a long pointed beak in my face. "Turkey!" I gasped hoarsely. "Happy Thanksgiving."

"Hi," said the beak. "Great show! Everybody loved it. How are your burns?"

The beak, stretching on into infinity, gradually shortened its perspective, and sadly became Doris Mingle. Standing behind her were Mrs. Lubbeth, beaming proudly, the shoe people, Nan, Mrs. Consolo, even Gulag Anna. Everyone was smiling down at me. Everybody loved me.

Mrs. Lubbeth leaned in and said, "Lisa, we have a surprise. Doris here took up a collection to help you pay for the wrecked Dior. All the employees contributed something, so impressed were they with your willingness to go on with the show."

They handed me a bag of cash. I got to hold it and say thanks, then Lubbeth took it away to go settle up my debt.

"Thanks, Doris," I said. "That was awfully nice of you. I feel just like George Bailey."

She shrugged happily, skinny smiling pretzel-rod Doris Mingle.

Nan said, "I was gonna start a collection, too, but she beat me to it."

Mrs. Consolo patted Doris kindly on the shoulder and said, "That's the kind of spirit I like to see. It reminds me of the old days of storewide pageantry, when we all pulled together to help each other."

One of the shoe people said, "Right, it's just simple Christian charity. It's no coincidence that we are called 'Fishman's,' you know. Jesus said we should be fishers of men."

Everyone was all happy and friendly until she had to drag Christianity into it. Then we squirmed uncomfortably in the glare of organized religion.

Nan rolled her eyes and muttered, "*What*ever!"

Anna asked, "Jesus from Sporting Goods?"

Chapter 14

I awoke early on Thursday morning. My parents promised to drive me back home after Thanksgiving dinner. I wasn't holding much stock in this vow, as it was impossible to roll Daddy off the couch once he began his post-Thanksgiving tryptophan snore fest. But perhaps I could talk Chip into giving me a ride, if I threatened to out him. It was beginning to look like his gayness would pay off for one of us.

I dug through my closet. It was important to find conservative, dull clothes for family holidays. Nana DeRosa and Grandma Galisa would be there and anything more flamboyant than black bombazine sent them into convulsions. Grandma exchanged her Michaelmas daisy-patterned housedresses for black ones after Grandpa died a couple years ago, while Nana began to dress in mourning shortly after her honeymoon. Come to think of it, Poppie DeRosa dressed in black for most of their marriage, too, though he had asked to be buried in an electric-blue tuxedo with tap shoes and top hat.

I chose a white silk blouse and chocolate wool trousers, Max Mara, understated, elegant, Thanksgivingy. Nice brown chunky-heeled Donald J. Pliner slip-ons, though the angle of the heel to the arch was just a tad wide for this season. Everything fabulous was all about right angles now. This was probably the third and last time I could wear them; others would notice the outdated heel. Family wouldn't notice or care, as slippers and tennis shoes outranked couture in the house of Galisa.

It made me mad to see all my expensive clothes all over the floor, but I didn't have enough room in my closet, so it wasn't really my fault. I wanted to know what kind of people could stand living in apartments with closets this small. Nuns, I supposed, with their three identical habits or poly suits. I liked the pared-down wardrobe and the neutral colors, but I couldn't wear a habit unless it was all cotton. It was hard enough being celibate and poor without wearing polyester on top of it all.

Last night, while soaking in the tub (had to wash off all the butter), I decided it was time to do away with the trills and flourishes that bogged down my life. Whittle down to the bare essentials, you know, like how Thoreau lived. His essays on Cape Cod had inspired me to buy my Birkenstock Lord-boards, back when I thought it was possible to spend months walking up and down the beaches of Wellfleet and Nantucket Sound and not work. But it was too expensive to get out there, and forget about staying anywhere simple and decent, like an extremely cute seaside cottage with wild roses growing everywhere. Cape Cod was all inhabited and costly and not cool anymore. Asia is where it's at. I was sure I could find affordable chic spareness in certain parts of Japan, but I couldn't swing the airfare.

On the other hand, I probably could swing a small redecoration project in my apartment. I'd stay within a budget by keeping to my all-white palette, but move it into minimalist white and away from the white of the not-interesting North African wool textile. I could see it in my mind, the angles, the geometric symmetry. Yes, everything white and enamel, except for some stainless steel and chrome and gray terrazzo floors, to warm things up.

After my bath I called the automated–bank account thing (checkbook was sort of imbalanced right then), but I couldn't remember my secret code or account numbers. I figured I probably had enough available credit on my assortment of Visas to remodel the apartment. I realized the purchase of new furniture could turn out to be expensive, but it was an investment in my well-being.

I stuffed some recent *Architectural Digest* and *Metropolitan Home* magazines into my leather satchel and headed out. Daddy had remodeled Leisure Lady plenty of times and knew not only the cost of such labor, but the importance of altering your surroundings for psychological impact. Too bad he totally misread the impact of visceral-red shag carpeting.

When I walked into my parents' house, the smell of giblets and grease greeted me. There's nothing to match the cloying scent of gummy gravy at ten o'clock in the morning. Gina and Chip lay on the floor of the living room in their pajamas, watching the Thanksgiving Day parade. How could so much not change in twenty years? I've often wondered what might have become of me if I had not moved out. . . . Maybe I would still be smoking pot in my bedroom with a wet towel shoved under the door, listening to the Eagles while Gina regaled me with gory tales of Catholic martyrs. These days, I would not be caught *dead* listening to the Eagles; Don Henley used to have that wild, seventies rock star fro, but now he just looks like Jane Wyman. Plus his lips are nonexistent— I never noticed that when he had his beastman beard. I'm only attracted to men with full, sensuous lips (see Ebert). I guess there is something to be said for maturing tastes.

My dad sat in his Barcalounger, critiquing floats. He kept a small notebook in which he recorded his thoughts on the changes in TV over the years. He seemed not to notice, or at least mind, the shift in programming from hackneyed blandness to banal violence over the years, but instead preferred to chronicle the career progress of William Conrad, Linda Lavin, and Norman Fell (number four on the infamous list). He was particularly upset over the decline in popularity of *Cannon* (Who wasn't?), though predicted that the likes of Mr. Roper and Alice were not meant for long-term televised enjoyment.

Daddy is the Ken Burns of seventies television schlock.

I came up behind and hugged him, an armload of vinyl recliner and orange sweater vest and bursitis. His wig, for once glued in place, remained rooted. He gave me a quick kiss on the cheek and scribbled a few marks in his notebook. I peeked: "Snoopy float—minimal crowd reaction despite death of Charles Schulz. Why?"

Ma trussed up the turkey with a series of ornate seaman's knots. She tried to get the drumsticks to cross, but somehow one continued to sag into the roasting pan while the other shot up skyward, like a Rockette midkick. The turkey looked both mutant and—if such can be said for a headless carcass—embarrassed. It had probably not thought things would end so miserably. There was nothing shameful in being murdered for someone else's dinner, but to be served in a such a grotesque, humiliating manner, legs spread awkwardly, could hardly have been what it envisioned for itself when innocent and young, a gobbler with a future.

Ma had taken some trouble to "gussy" herself up, as she liked to say. Instead of the ubiquitous track suit, she wore beige slacks (elastic waistband fighting for its life) and a cotton turtleneck printed with fall leaves. Her dyed blond hair was attractively shaped into a middle-aged lady's helmet, and she had smeared on some coral lipstick from 1973.

"That's more like it," she said, indicating her approval of my outfit for once. Immediately, I doubted the fashion future of Max Mara.

I started to pour some coffee, but she insisted on making a fresh pot. "That's been sitting there for four hours," she objected, taking the pot out of my hands. "*Some* of us have been up since five-thirty, dusting the dining room and making sourdough rolls."

My ma was like a magician, and could make her insomnia and neurotic need for busywork suddenly seem like my crime.

Thanksgiving marks a melancholy time for us. In 1993 the holiday was spent eating White Castle at the sparkly boomerang kitchen table as Daddy lay on the sofa crying. Ma stayed in the living room with him. She sat at the end of the sofa rubbing his feet, quietly comforting him. At low volumes, the timbre of her voice can be nongrating and kindly.

"Nice job," Chip had said to me then, swallowing a fish nugget. Gina defended me. "It's not her fault, Chip. We all said we liked it."

"Hey, I was just going along with the rank and file." Then he looked at me and said, "You ruined Daddy's store!"

I got up then, grabbed my fringed motorcycle jacket, ignoring the living-room drama, and left. A lot of that holiday was spent waiting for the Ashland Avenue bus. It was a cold Thanksgiving in Bridgeport, and no one was out on the streets.

Daddy had brought home a bolt of fabric earlier that year and worked tirelessly on a notebook of sketches. He was attempting to introduce his very own line of clothing for the first time, instead of merely buying the cheaper garments that rolled in from the sweat-shops of Taiwan. He had spent months finalizing three designs and sewing prototypes in our basement after work. The first was an asymmetrical purple suit, huge shoulder pads, cinched waist, slim skirt longer on the right side, and flared coattail jacket (longer on the left). The second, a simple pair of jeans, low slung, with inordinately wide legs—the predecessor to the extremely successful "big pants" movement of the late nineties. Third, the one-legged pantsuit.

He asked one of the girls who worked part-time at the store to come by for fittings in the evenings. By April he had finished all three designs, but was undecided as to which he liked most or would be the quickest seller. He couldn't afford to have all three produced at once, so he thought he'd pick the best one to go first, and then its success would finance the production of the remaining designs.

"What do you guys like?" He questioned us over and over that spring. Ma said not to ask her; she liked everything and had no idea what would appeal to other women. Gina asked if the jeans could be made into straight-legged overalls.

Chip sputtered, "I'm a guy! Why would *I* care about women's clothes? I don't! I hate women's clothes! Are you trying to say something? Just say it, whatever it is." As usual, we ignored his out-burst—just one of hundreds that year—though in retrospect I now see that I had perhaps been blind about certain elements of Chip's personality.

"Lisa?" asked Daddy. His face, still youthful-looking beneath the Bon Jovi wig, glowed with childlike enthusiasm. He admitted to being too partial to his creations to choose objectively between them, and besides, he reasoned, at twenty-four I would know bet-ter what young women liked. I reminded him of the year I sug-gested introducing burnout wear into the matron line.

"Oh, that was great." He dismissed my failure and utter lack of fashion sense. "I think it was ahead of its time, Leese. You have really good taste, just like your old man."

We had good taste: I, with my fringed garments and fingerless gloves and dude cap; he, with his blond wig and truss.

I felt disappointed as the girl modeled his prototypes. I didn't really like any of them. Of course, if I had known that within one season Thierry Mugler and Claude Montana would release similar garments to worldwide acclaim, I would have chosen Daddy's asymmetrical purple suit. And who could have predicted the popu-larity of clown pants?

I examined the one-legged pantsuit. Styled as a sort of jump-suit that buttoned up the front, it clung to every inch of the body. Daddy favored double-knit polyester as the fabric of choice. It had a plunging V-neck with notched collars in contrasting colors (lime-green pantsuit, pink collar; royal-blue pantsuit, orange collar). The right leg of the suit was tight to the knee, then flared out into a giant bell. You could practically hear it gonging as the model paced up and down our living room.

"You've never seen anything like it, have you?" Daddy asked eagerly. "I think it's the most original thing I've ever done." His eyes shone with a curious light that I'd never seen before. He looked proud and thrilled, stood taller, and it wasn't just because he'd put hot rollers in his wig that day.

The left pant leg, such as it was, had an inseam of about a half-inch. It was really a half of hot pants. A hot-pant half? Well, it *was* hot, in a weirdly exciting way. On a woman more packed and stacked than our model, a nice round crescent of rear end would hang out of the hot-pant side.

"It's extremely original, Daddy," I said. "Do you think the Bridgeport woman is daring enough to wear it?"

He studied the garment for a few moments, then said, "I could reverse the legs on some patterns, if a lady is more comfortable exposing her right leg instead. I don't want to offend someone who prefers one leg to the other. No, sir, that's not what I'm all about."

It was impossible *not* to throw my support to the one-legged pantsuit, to the innovation obviously most adored by the sweet, conscientious, clueless retailer with almost no business sense at all.

"The one-legged pantsuit! The one-legged pantsuit!" cheered my family, grateful that someone had stepped forward to cast the first ballot.

My father had poured a lot of money into making dozens and dozens of the garments, so assured of their universal acceptance was he. He redecorated the store display window with five mannequins in one-legged pantsuits in varying hues, striding purposefully into the future. He'd hung huge banners both indoors and out that read: TWO LEGS BAD! ONE LEG GOOD! Unfortunately, he didn't cut back his buying budget for other collections, so not only was the store way overstuffed with clothes, but anything that was not a one-legged pantsuit was relegated to a messy rack against the wall, or to a dark corner in the back.

Then he waited.

He sent press releases to the local newspapers, *Women's Wear Daily,* and many fashion magazines. I told him to send the publicity to the avant-garde press, punk-rock 'zines, Malcolm McLaren, anybody.

But he said, "My Bridgeport ladies don't read that stuff. If it's good enough for the *Tribune* and the *Sun-Times,* it's good enough for them."

As it turned out, the one-legged pantsuit was not good enough for the *Tribune* or the *Sun-Times*.

PRACTICAL JOKE DRAGS STYLE EDITOR OUT TO BRIDGEPORT, whined the *Trib.*

SEWING-ROOM MISHAP RESULTS IN HIDEOUS PRANK, lamented the *Sun-Times*.

The national media did not bother to respond, as my father had included in the press kits snapshots of his creation. After work, he'd sit at our boomerang table and push his pork chops around.

"Prank?" he'd say. "Practical joke?"

Ma—I had to give her credit—wore the one-legged pantsuit day in, day out. At five foot nothing, she needed Daddy to custom-make one that would fit her. She chose for its colors fuchsia with the collar in sort of a cheddarish orange. She wore nylons under it (thank God) and black patent pumps. Her bubble butt resisted the hot-pant, and her left cheek usually burst out below. On any given day, you could usually see my mother running to the grocery store, gardening, or vacuuming in her one-legged pantsuit, a massive globe peeking out the hot-pant side, the control top of her nylons and even the beige grandma panties underneath clearly visible.

"Is this really what you had in mind?" I asked my dad one day as we watched, from behind, Ma weeding between the yews.

His eyes had become sadder those first few months, with pouches beneath and an upside-down V in between. He stared at Ma's backside and said, "The female form is a work of art. The one-legged pantsuit *proves* this. Why can no one understand?"

The truth is, one item cannot really break a successful business, but it can close the casket on a dying enterprise. Daddy had lost faith in himself by the time fall rolled around that year. He had done nothing to promote the other clothes in his store. He spent too much and made too little—well, it's the age-old story of retail. Worst of all, he had alienated his older customers by pushing a garment on them too extreme for their tastes. The women of Bridgeport had at least five other clothing stores to choose from in our neighborhood, not including the big national chains. Why would they patronize one that many believed had turned into some type of strange Halloween shop with limited costumes? I bet rock stars would have worn the one-legged pantsuit, but we didn't have that kind of clout.

If Daddy had been younger, or perhaps had been a man with stronger convictions in himself and his work, or perhaps had simply been rich—a lot of variables could have affected the outcome of thirty years in the apparel industry—he might have rode out the disaster and turned a profit by the following year.

"I can't do it," he said. He lay on the sofa every day, wigless, and stared at television. "I'm tired, and I don't know what women want to wear."

He let the broken forty-ouncers and taco-riddled vomit accumulate on the sidewalk outside Leisure Lady. Mikolajczak stood outside the butcher shop every day, watching for my father.

"Sal," said Ma, "everyone makes mistakes. This was your first design! You can't expect your first try to go off without a hitch."

"I'm fifty-eight," he had responded. "The time to try new things was about thirty years ago."

She said, "You can't give up."

He said, "I'm fifteen thousand dollars in the hole, and my sciatica's about to drive me out of my mind. I got a buyer for the store, and I'm getting out."

He switched channels on the TV—*Matlock,* I think. Funny how you remember the small things in troubled times, what was on TV, how small Daddy's head looked without his toupee, the dog that was not yet dead putting its nose on Daddy's elbow. Funny how in troubled times, if the television is on, you cannot help but turn to stare at it, even if it's Andy Griffith, even if a grown man is quietly sobbing on the sofa right next to you.

That was Thanksgiving 1993. Gina said grace over White Castle bags as my brother and I fought for the onion rings. After I'd gone back to the North Side, the dog waited patiently by the edge of our curb, then calmly threw itself in the path of a speeding tow truck.

By comparison, Thanksgiving in the new millennium was a day at the beach. Grandma Galisa and Nana DeRosa came accompanied by several extended-family members. Grandma sat in the living room and watched TV with my dad while Nana stood at the stove and criticized my mother's cooking.

"You know, you ruin the mashed potatoes when you put in all that cream cheese and sour cream," complained Nana.

"That's how we like them, Ma," said Ma.

Nana held up her hands in surrender. "What do *I* know? I've only been making mashed potatoes for five hundred years."

Ma muttered something under her breath about what else Nana had been doing for the past five hundred years.

Nana's English was excellent. She prided herself on having learned the Bridgeport tongue within six months of arriving here from Sicily in 1930. She pretended not to understand my dad's mother sometimes, even though Grandma had been born here.

Nana liked to say, "Hey, not everyone can learn to speak good English. It's a gift and I got it." Grandma Galisa liked to say that people who are born American citizens don't need special gifts.

I squeezed in between Daddy and Grandma on the sofa (she wouldn't budge over), and showed him the magazine pictures I'd marked as potential ideas for my apartment. He tried to talk me into shag rugs, but I wasn't having it.

"This is very stark and cold." He frowned, thumbing through the pictures. "All these square, modern lines don't look very comfortable to me."

"But that's what I want," I said. "Spareness is better than comfort. I want it to look like a terribly hip bank."

He shook his head. "I don't know, honey. I like a big squishy chair and sofa. I like warm colors, like gold and red."

"No, only white—and not warm winter white, but cold enamel white."

"Morgue white," offered Chip.

"Exactly. Porcelain tiles. Chrome. You know what I'm talking about."

Daddy said, "I have a white leather chair in the basement you could have. It's not real leather, but it's very close."

"No, that's all lumpy and stuffed. I just want lines. No curves."

"No curves?" asked Daddy, eyebrows shooting wigward.

"No curves?" asked Chip.

I repeated firmly, "No curves."

Grandma woke up out of her coma and whispered, "What curse?"

Ma screamed for us to come in and eat.

As we all sat around the big dining-room table, Daddy forced us to be grateful and announce one thing each of us was thankful for.

Gina said, "Animals, and our ability to communicate psychically with them."

Amidst the squawks of "Huh?" and "What the hell does that mean?" I took my turn and mumbled, "Cigarettes."

Chip said, "I'm thankful for the independent press!"

Grandma said, "All this interesting food."

Ma said, "My beautiful daughters and my son, my son."

The aunts and uncles listed various personal ailments that had been trounced by medical science. It's nice, while awaiting dinner, to join your fat disgusting uncle in thanking God for curing his ingrown toenails, or to praise heaven for yanking out Aunt Bertha's gall bladder so efficiently.

Daddy said he was thankful for his home, wife, and children.

Nana said, "*I'm* thankful my Stell has such a wonderful family. Money isn't everything."

As predicted, Daddy fell asleep on the couch almost immediately after pie. Gina offered to drive me home in the station wagon, and we decided to stop at the Wysockis' house on our way.

Fred welcomed us in, and the Dragon Lady made us sit in the family room with a bunch of uncomfortable-looking Polish and Korean people. Everyone drank cups of coffee and stared at the walls. Dinner must have been brutal. I guess I would rather pretend to listen to my uncle complain about his feet than sit in silent scrutiny.

Fred saved us by taking us down to the basement where some Wysocki kids played Nintendo. We sat in a rec room furnished in sixties Danish modern. This was pretty close to what I wanted for my apartment, but there were a lot of wooden things and cushions upholstered in Swedish blue. Close, but not quite right.

Fred said, "You know, my parents have been married for over forty years, but at every family gathering, everybody else acts like they've never sat down at the same table before."

I said, "Our family acts like they were forced to sit down together forty years ago and have never been allowed up."

"When my mom brings the turkey to the table, the Polish side of the family calls it Fido."

"That's horrible!" cried Gina.

"You win," I said.

I brought *Metropolitan Home* out of my satchel and asked Fred what he thought of my ideas for redecoration.

He said, "Will your landlord let you put in a terrazzo floor?" Gina peeked at the magazine and said that that was the same floor the old Goldblatt's department store had.

"Well, the landlord will probably condo the building soon, so I'll just buy my apartment, and it'll be okay."

"Wow!" Fred exclaimed. "That'll cost a fortune. My friend just bought a two-bedroom condo in a filthy warehouse in Wicker Park for three hundred large."

I shrieked, "What?! Three hundred thousand bucks for an *apartment*? He must be mad. It should be like only ninety thousand at most."

Fred laughed, "You're dreaming."

I sighed irritably. "Okay, fine, forget the terrazzo floor. Where do you think I could find quality modern furnishings for cheap? Don't say Fishman's; they're too expensive."

Gina said, "How about a restaurant-supply company? I bet you could find stainless-steel tables and stuff; you know, the things people would usually hide in the restaurant kitchen that you would put right out in the living room." Sometimes my sister is absolutely *brill.*

Fred suggested the Salvation Army, but I didn't want my home to look like a bohemian retreat. Anyway, white things from thrift stores were always unquestionably dingy (i.e., my bed sheets), dragging me back to the Marrakech textile marketplace I was trying to escape.

He said, "You realize, of course, that the whole modern look is extremely Easy. I'm into it. My mom won't lend me money to redecorate the tavern, though."

Fred's Easy Hour would be so much more successful if he could get rid of the wormy oak bar and the dartboard and the customers. He got up, went over to a closet, and brought back a cardboard box full of old *Playboy* magazines. As we looked for examples of the Easy lifestyle, Gina wandered over to the fish tank against the wall. She knelt down next to it, put her hand against the glass, and every so often nodded seriously. Fred raised his eyebrows at me.

"Don't ask," I said.

Fred said, "What do you think about Easy Cover Duels?"

"Easy Cover Duels?"

"Yeah, it's my new idea for the Easy Hour. I'll play a song on the stereo system, then follow it immediately by its Easy—ergo, better—cover version. So far, this is what I've put on my Cover Duels CD compilation: Bob Dylan versus the Living Voices, ('Like a Rolling Stone'), Julie Andrews versus the Aluminum Group ('Wouldn't It Be Loverly?' from *My Fair Lady*), and Creedence Clearwater Revival versus Leonard Nimoy ('Proud Mary')."

I smiled. "That is *fabulous*. You're going to make the Easy Hour an enormous success, Fred."

"Decor is still the problem, though. God, why is Mom so tight-fisted? Look what I want." He showed me a photo of a bachelor pad in a magazine from 1970. It was all green velvet and fluffy bear rugs and barware shaped like chemistry beakers.

"See how Easy things used to be, how Easy they still *could* be?" he said wistfully. "The lifestyle was about pleasure and love and fashion. Not working at a job. Not pretending your Polack relatives aren't racist."

I said, "Not scrimping for rent, not getting singed in an embarrassing burnt-cheese incident. Not having Aristotle Onassis prefer Jackie to Maria Callas." He looked at me questioningly but said nothing.

I said, "I guess Jackie O is pretty Easy, huh?"

He said, "Jackie *O* is Easy, but Jackie *Kennedy* was distinctly unEasy until 1964."

"Huh," I said thoughtfully.

Gina appeared at my side, done with fish talk. She asked Fred, "Does your mother do belly dancing in front of the aquarium?"

Before he could answer, I stood up and said we'd better go. I promised to come by for the Easy Hour on Sunday night. We tried to sneak by the Wysocki UN meeting in the family room, but the Dragon Lady saw us and blocked our way with pie.

"It's special," she said, shoving a plate at me. "Kim chee pie." Gina hid behind me.

"I'm full," I declined politely, but she put it in my hands anyway. It smelled like fermented cabbage and whipped cream. Fred shook his head.

I gave it back, pleading I was stuffed to capacity.

She nodded sympathetically. "Try to lose weight? Me too. I lose five pounds. Wanna know how?"

She ran downstairs into the basement as Fred sighed, "This is so *not* Easy."

The Dragon Lady came back with a videotape and showed it to me. "See? I exercise every morning in the basement with the TV." I imagined the Dragon Lady doing squat thrusts with the television strapped to her back.

Gina gasped and pointed to the videotape title. It was called *Belly Dancing for Beginners.*

Chapter 15

No inventory of retail misery would be complete without including the day after Thanksgiving. We had to arrive an hour early to prepare for the crowds, and I wasn't even allowed to be Maria Callas for more than one trivial fashion show. It felt like the old days, when I was just a struggling fake Maria, pretending to be fabulous on my lunch hour. Boy, I hated returning to those difficult times of being nobody, three weeks ago.

Though brief and lacking the extras I had become accustomed to, the fashion show was a hit. The theme was "Urban Christmas," and I got to wear a mink coat with severe Coach loafers and handbag. The idea was that Maria might have worn this same outfit while Christmas shopping in New York in 1959. After the show, I sashayed around the department while keeping an eye out for Ari. Hui had threatened to set his Men's Wear goons on me if I walked into his department again.

The Santa throne was out again, but this time Santa was sitting on it. I remembered the days before I was famous and had to sit on the throne myself, while kids mistook me for Santa's sexless man-woman helper. A little girl pointed me out to Santa and asked for a fur coat like mine for her dolly.

Santa said, "That coat is made of little murdered animals. Do you really want Santa to go out and kill animals for you?"

She looked at him with big moon eyes and whimpered. I got the hell out of there. Why didn't they just hire the Ukrainian Santa from last year, whose only English words were, "Okay, Pokémon"?

I decided it was safer to give the coat back to Mrs. Lubbeth, who gave me ten minutes for lunch in exchange. I dragged Nan downstairs to the commissary, where we shared my last pink Sobranie. They have a no-smoking rule that is abandoned during the Christmas season.

I relished one lungful after another. I had a little overdraft problem with my checking account and only had enough cash on me for the El ride home after work. I didn't think I had any cigs left at the apartment, but now that I would be cleaning and redecorating everything, I might find an old butt or two under the couch.

Nan said, "It's a bummer, having to switch next week from the Greek Islands theme to the Christmas theme. There is nothing glamorous about Christmas."

I stopped, midpuff. "We're not really going to stop, are we? I mean, it's been so successful."

She took the pink bone out of my fingers and said, "Well, yeah, but that's the plan. Didn't you see the memo this morning?" Ever since I had become the fashionista of Fishman's, I hadn't had time for memos and protocol.

Our ten-minute break was almost up. I followed Nan dejectedly out of the commissary when someone tapped me on the shoulder. It was Ari, topless and snug in a white terry towel, wearing flip-flops and wraparound sunglasses.

"Aren't you cold?" I asked.

He motioned for me to sit down at a nearby table, and Nan waved good-bye.

He said, "I've been looking for you everywhere. Why haven't you come up to Men's Wear?"

"Hui banished me," I said. "You know, there's something I've been wanting to say, Ari. You've been great to me during this whole Greek Islands theme. Even in front of Hui and Jackie. Even during the cheese-fire nightmare. And the ham sandwich . . . I won't forget the ham. So I just wanted to thank you."

"You're welcome, Lisa. I guess it looks like our day in the sun is coming to an end, though, isn't it?"

"It's true, then? They're not going to extend the Greek Islands through Christmas?"

He nodded. "And the teachers' union is still on strike. That means I have to go back to being just a junior janitor on Monday."

It wasn't fair. Finally I'd made something of myself, and Fishman's was going to yank it out from under me. Only young Ari understood.

"You miss teaching science, don't you?" I asked.

"Science, especially at the grade-school level, inspires passion in me. For example, the bumblebee. Though aerodynamically unsound, it flies. We must ask, *Why?* I cannot find this kind of thrill throwing sick sand around and mopping up the men's bathroom." He put his hand over mine and said, "By Monday, I will be back cleaning toilets, and you'll be back waiting on customers. But in my eyes, you will always be a star. You are the one thing that makes this strike bearable. What do you say to a night on the town? A date . . . anywhere you want to go."

"Why?" I asked. "I'm grumpy and pudgy and broke. I have no talents and no future. If you like me, then there's something wrong with you."

"Perhaps," he said. "Nevertheless, I find myself strangely attracted to you against all reason. It is Fate."

It wasn't much of a compliment, but I'd take it. Though boxy and custodial, Ari was the hottest science teacher on strike I'd ever met.

Was it fortune, or maybe misfortune, that things began to happen as they did after lunch? As far as Fate was concerned, I had a big target drawn on my backside.

My cell phone rang as I took my place behind the cash register. I held my index finger up to a shrunken old lady, indicating I would be with her in a moment.

"Lisa, guess what," shrieked Tim Gideon from behind the reference desk in Uptown.

"I don't have time to guess; I have to start waiting on customers again."

"Okay, I'll be quick. Babbington Hawkes wrote a full-length feature on Fishman's Greek Islands—"

"Oh, no!" I groaned. "I can't take any more."

The old lady said, "Excuse me" a bunch of times, but I just kept my forefinger in her face.

He began to read from the newspaper.

CHEESE FIRE IGNITES NEW STAR

By Babbington Hawkes

Dearest friends, I should be sailing the Aegean right now, but since I can't, I've found the next best thing: the Greek Islands Spectacular at Fishman's. It reminds me of my trip to Greece years ago to attend Yanni's concert at the Acropolis (the one where he made his mother cry)—it is *that* fabulous! The crown of achievement must assuredly go to the awkwardly named Lisa Galisa, who portrayed Maria Callas during the monthlong event. Although unconventionally average-looking, she brought a level of pathos and drama to the role, and even managed to sell scads of designer gowns while embarrassing herself time and time again. I found myself disliking everything about this parvenu of lumpish aspect, yet somehow wanting to see more. The customers seemed drawn to her, whether out of pity or morbid fascination, I do not know. I *do* know that everyone but *everyone* around town wondered how she had simultaneously captivated and horrified us. The proof is in the Honey, dearests: Our favorite socialite, Honey Dietrich, was overheard at the

Saganaki Explosion to say, "That girl has star quality, sugar." I admit, she must have *something,* to be
feted with feta and yet manage to drive that
Fishman's crowd wild. Hey, if it's good enough for
Honey, it's good enough for me.

"He said I'm average-looking?" I asked breathlessly. The old
lady banged her shrunken fist on the counter, but I was too excited
to pay her any attention. It was published praise, the likes of which
I would probably never witness again.

"Yeah! And there's even a photo of you, post–cheese holocaust,
looking all bewildered and sad, and in the background young Aristotle is gazing at you like a lovesick sheep while Jackie Kennedy
sulks behind him."

My God, I thought, *I* am *a success; I* am *Maria Callas.* I snapped
my phone shut as Mrs. Lubbeth stampeded toward the counter.
The little old lady set her lips together primly while Lubbeth
scolded me for taking personal calls instead of waiting on customers. She told me to straighten up the dressing rooms, and I
floated back there dreamily.

I had almost finished hanging up all the clothes when Doris
Mingle ran spastically into the changing area. She said Honey
Dietrich had just waltzed into Irregulars and demanded that Doris
find me.

"Me? What does she want me for?" I asked, following Doris.

"I hope it's to help her find some designer irregulars. I can't do
it again."

Leaning against the table that held piles of three-pronged
turkey socks and problematic underwear was Honey, draped in a
replica of the mink I had modeled earlier. She straightened up and
beamed that famous salt fortune–heiress smile.

"Darling!" she exclaimed, kissing me right on the lips. "You
were marvelous today. *Everyone's* been talking."

"Cool," I said.

Honey stared at Doris, changing her high-wattage socialite smile into a tiny line of ice. "Run along," she commanded. Doris gulped, and ran along, banished from her own department.

Honey linked her arm through mine, and we walked, weaving in and out between racks of irregular trousers. "Lisa, my sweet," she began, "you have been absolutely wonderful these weeks as Maria Callas. As you no doubt realize, even my friend Mr. Hawkes has come to appreciate your indefinable charm. What I'm trying to say, dear girl, is that I need you. I need someone with your verve, your unique style, your sort of don't-give-a-damn sensibilities. I need a personal assistant. You are it, and I won't take no for an answer."

Her personal assistant . . . *Honey Dietrich's* personal assistant. Obviously, this was where all my hard work had been leading. Suddenly it all became clear. I had thought perhaps Fishman's would appreciate everything I'd done during the weeks of Greek Islands, but apparently they'd rather celebrate the gluttony of Christmas with vegan-tyrant Santa. Where was my thanks from Mr. Fishman, my raise, my promotion? I alone was responsible for the popularity and record-setting sale of Fishman's binding under-garments, not to mention impractical ball gowns and fur tippets, and how was I indemnified? With no raise and no gratitude and burning cheese and Lubbeth back to her comfortable old barking routine. So I made some decent commissions, so what? Fishman's wanted me to be a loser again.

I wasn't having it.

"I would like nothing better than to be your personal assistant," I said. "It would be an honor." It would not be honorable to ask about the salary; undoubtedly the salt-fortune heiress could afford more than $208.25 per week.

"Oh, goody!" she exclaimed. "It'll be *such* fun. I'm a complete mess when it comes to running my life, darling. I really need some help." She handed me a calling card (a tiny engraved honeybee above her tiny engraved name, address, and phone number) and told me to be at her apartment at eight A.M. sharp, Monday morning.

I said, "But . . . but I have to give two weeks' notice, Honey."

She pouted, and replied, "Hmmm . . . no, I don't think that'll work out for me at all. I have a lot of Yuletide festivities that'll require your immediate attention. Do whatever you must, but if you want to work for me, I expect to see you at eight o'clock on the dot."

I swallowed uncomfortably and nodded.

She started to walk away, then turned back to me and said, "And if you don't mind, sweets, it's Ms. Dietrich from now on."

The rest of the afternoon ticked by slowly. I dreaded telling Mrs. Lubbeth my news. It wasn't her fault that Mr. Fishman didn't offer anybody in our department a raise, though on the other hand she didn't have to demand that I kowtow to every crotchety matron who pummeled her shriveled paw on our counter.

I found her standing by Santa's throne. She watched him through narrowed eyes and worked her lips around, forming a curse. Good, she was putting the old kibosh on him. Everybody hated Santa.

I was about to join her in evil-eyeing him, when she stuck her fingernail under her bridge and extracted a raspberry seed. Santa went on break.

She sang to herself, "All I want for Christmas is my full upper denture."

Before I lost my nerve, I said in one breath, "Mrs. Lubbeth, Honey Dietrich just offered me a job as her personal assistant and it's a great opportunity for me I can't pass it up but I have to start Monday so I can't give you notice and I'm sorry but this is the way it's gotta be."

She looked at me with wide eyes and round red mouth. "Oh *no*! You can't leave us at the beginning of Christmas! What will I do?"

I repeated, "It's a great opportunity for me. I can't pass it up—"

She sighed, and sat heavily on the platform beneath Santa's throne. "You're a good girl, Lisa. I don't want to stand in your way, and God knows Mr. Fishman is a bit tight with his money. But can't you give me two weeks?"

I shook my head. Poor Mrs. Lubbeth . . . kindly, demanding, hogger of commissions. She saw Maria Callas in me when others saw only poverty and celibacy. She paved the way for my life to become less dull, more prosperous. But doors were opening for me now, doors to money and fame and possibly Roger Ebert.

She said, "I'll miss you, hon," and girdled me with tenderloin arms into the soft folds of her Pucci caftan.

At five o'clock, my career at Fishman's ended. It was kind of a drag, no going-away party, no cake or presents from sad coworkers. Everybody in Women's Wear was busy beating back customers by the time I left, and I never got the chance to say so long to my friends. Oh, well, I was sure I'd be back sooner or later with Honey, when it was time to restock her wardrobe. I saw a senior maintenance guy slacking off by the front doors, so I wrote Ari a quick note and asked the guy to deliver it. How would Honey feel about her assistant going on a date with a junior janitor, or a science teacher for that matter? Would it put my new job in jeopardy? Appearances were very important to high society. On the other hand, Ari was so smooth and Easy, he could probably win over any socialite's prejudices.

My cell phone rang nonstop from the moment I exited the store. First Tim, ordering me to meet him for drinks, then Gina, begging for just half an hour so that she could pick my brain for career advice, then Chip, wanting to borrow money so that he could put out the first issue of his underground magazine.

"What's it called?" I asked him, stalling for time. Nobody in her right mind lends cash to jobless chess enthusiasts.

"It's gonna be called *Prole*."

"*Parole*? A jailbait Sal Mineo fanzine? Nice."

"No, no," he retorted, "*Prole*. Duh, like proletariat? You know, the working class."

How can someone who's never held a job write about the working class?

I told Chip I'd think about it. I needed to psych myself up for drinking with Gina and Tim Gideon, and I didn't have time for dullsville political theory.

I convinced both Gina and Tim to meet me downtown. On a cold Friday night in winter, there's nothing like settling down in a warm cozy bar for the evening.

I got a table for us at Rosebud. A little Lambrusco, a little veal parmigiana. A little chat with the pet psychic and the grouchy children's librarian. The waitron brought the wine to the table before Tim and Gina got there, uncorked it, and poured me a glass. I tried to sip it slowly, but being there alone with the prospect of the new job on Monday made me nervous. Some say it's bad form to drink a whole bottle of wine by yourself in public.

Tim arrived, threw his briefcase under the table, and announced he was learning Vietnamese. "I *know* those little kids in the library are talking about me," he said, "and I'm going to find out what they're saying. They're going to *pay*."

I said, "Have you considered taking anger-management classes?"

"Classes?" he mused. "Well, I *would* like to make more efficient use of my anger." Tim loved the harsh dissonance of Vietnamese, a language part Chinese, part French, with every word one brutal syllable. They talk out of the backs of their throats, just like South Siders do. He asked if I'd been out with the licorice whip again. I had. I'd forgotten.

"We met for a quick drink last week. It was okay," I admitted, "but I was fifteen minutes late, and he acted pretty miffed at first."

"So?"

"Nothing. It's just that Luke seems kind of anal-retentive."

"Well, as they say, opposites attract."

Was I anal-expulsive? That didn't bode well.

I poured him the last of the Lambrusco, and he wrinkled his nose as he lifted the glass.

"Not a big fan," he sniffed, then shot it like a frat boy with a beer bong.

Gina showed up moments later. For once she had had the sense to change out of her overalls into adult clothes, though I was aghast to see her in leggings. Nobody wore those anymore.

Tim was pleased to see my sister; he believed she had an "in" with Chip that I had not, and that maybe she could fix them up.

I said to her, "If you're so tight with Baby Chip, why don't *you* float him money to start his idiotic magazine?"

She answered, "Because I work at McDonald's." Then she said, "But maybe not for long. I want to become a full-time animal communicator, Lisa. How should I go about it?"

The three of us spent a good thirty minutes trying to figure out ways to break into the psychic business world. Venture capitalists don't seem interested in such things. We ordered more Lambrusco.

She said, "I don't want Ma and Daddy to know about it until I've made some headway. Promise me you won't say anything to them."

I said, "I promise. Now that I'll be working for Honey Dietrich, maybe I'll meet some moneyed investors looking for *pet* projects and can send them your way, ha-ha."

They stared at me speechless. I had not planned on revealing my new career with such a lame joke. Then all the questions came out at once.

"You've finally done something right!" shouted Tim. "How did it happen?"

"I thought you liked working at Fishman's. Why are you leaving?" asked Gina.

"I did, but this is so much better for me. I will meet the right kind of people, you know, like Ebert and others who can help me realize my full potential."

"For what?" she persisted.

"For . . . for being successful! For being more than a clerk, an errand girl with armloads of Chanel suits, saying, 'Yes, ma'am,' all the time."

Tim said, "I think it's fabulous, and now you'll have *much* more leverage with Luke." Gina sighed, and excused herself to the ladies' room.

Tim's comment kind of gave me a weird stabbing feeling in my stomach, either a twinge of conscience or too much Lambrusco. Part of me still wanted to date Luke, but my motivations were a bit murky: I was lonely. He was attractive and not despicable-acting. He knew Roger Ebert. These were all the reasons I could come up with. I thought, *Is that so wrong? No, not wrong! Freewheeling!* Yet there was that peculiar stabbing feeling in my stomach again. I began to wonder what sort of person I actually was. The Lambrusco was not sitting pretty in my stomach, and my drunk was just itching to get out. She whispered, *I'll tell you what kind of person you are: a lonesome, celibate lunatic destined for failure. Let's face it, the Shakers saw more action than you. You think it's so terrible to date more than one guy? Who cares? You've got a lot of time to make up for. Date the licorice whip, date Ebert, even date that janitor for all I care. Trust me, it's not like any of them are going to get too attached to you.*

I told Tim my drunk was inviting herself to our threesome. He took the wine away from me and said he couldn't handle both of us tonight.

I said, "My drunk is the kind of girl who thinks I can go out with Luke *and* Ebert and . . . whoever . . . all at once and it's okay."

"For once," he said, "she's making sense. Men are pigs, even fabulous ones. Ebert is a man and, like any man, would probably *enjoy* bedding a woman currently dating his personal assistant. This is your world, sordid sty that it is, and you better get into the game."

I said, "For a gay man, you know an awful lot about the dating habits of breeders."

He sighed impatiently. "What have I always said? I only date straight men. I know what I'm talking about here."

Gina returned to the table and said, "What'd I miss?"

"Nothing," I replied.

Tim rapped his knuckles on the table. "Let's talk about security-market predictions for today's pet psychic."

Chapter 16

*W*oke up at the crack of dawn on Sunday morning. Stupid ringing phone interrupted a fantastic dream about Ebert and tearaway dojo trousers. I had spent the previous night hauling my furniture down to the storage room in the basement, and I was still drag-ass tired. I kept the white tuxedo sofa and of course my bed, but exiled everything else. Damn it, there was still warmth in my apartment, due to the oak floors. I know everybody's crazy for oak floors, but I really needed something gray, mallish. Like comfy cement.

"*Who* is it?" I croaked. I hate, hate, *hate* early mornings.

"Ray," the voice repeated.

I said, "I've told you people a thousand times, I don't want a subscription to the *Tribune*."

A lengthy pause, then: "It's Ari, Lisa. You asked one of the maintenance guys to give me a note with your phone number on it?"

"Oh, Ari! Why didn't you say so? Don't play tricks on me so early."

He said, "It's almost noon, and it isn't a trick. My name is really Ray."

"Noon? How embarrassing, Ari."

"*Ray,*" he said.

"Sorry. I'm sort of used to calling you Ari. You seem more of an Ari than a Ray."

There was silence. Perhaps that wasn't very nice of me, perhaps he was sensitive about his janitor name.

I said, "Never mind. Ray, is it? Then Ray you shall be."

"Thanks."

I told him about my previous evening of furniture moving and plans for white spareness and no curves. White-on-white expressionist paintings, plenty textural and mod.

He said, "It sounds like a corporate lobby."

I said, "Excellent."

He wanted to know why I left Fishman's, especially why I had quit and why I hadn't bothered to say good-bye to him in person. Even though I had only left Fishman's two days ago, it now seemed like I'd always been in Honey's world, where there were no good-bye parties, no cakes. Nobody worked, so nobody ever had a job to leave.

He asked to see me that night, but I said, "The old Lisa would never have accepted a date less than four days in advance. The new Lisa extends it to six."

"Oh, come on," he said. "I want to know what's going on with you, how you are. We were planning to rewrite Greek history, and then you just took off."

New Lisa was freewheeling, in demand by varied gentlemen. "All right," I relented. What the hell, the old Lisa never had any dates anyway.

By seven o'clock I realized that I was really looking forward to seeing Ray. This could only portend disaster. It did not fit into my plan of freewheeling, of rotating multiple boyfriends. Something exciting lurked beneath his gray janitorial coveralls. . . . Was it his inner Ari, the smooth, Easy man of the world? Was it his weird obsessive fascination with science at the grade-school level? Like Ebert, there appeared to be more to Ray than met the eye, except I actually *knew* Ray, I was actually going on a date with him, and this filled me with an awful foreboding. It's so much easier to go out with someone you don't really like.

By the time he picked me up, I was operating on equal parts dread, anticipation, fear, and unreasonable hope. He unlocked the passenger-side door, opened it, and I slid in. Not slid so much as fell. It's hard to maneuver wearing a brown leather skirt over rubbery Fishman's body-slimming undergarments. When he reached his side of the car, he just stood there at the door. Finally he knocked on the driver-side window, and gestured expansively toward the lock.

I shouted, "Don't you have the keys?"

A dark cloud crossed his face as he unlocked his door and got in.

He said, "You just failed the test from *A Bronx Tale.* You were supposed to reach over and unlock the door before I got to it."

I said, "Aristotle Onassis would not have expected Maria Callas, a world-class superstar, to be an opener of doors."

Thus our date began.

I suggested a trip to Wysocki's Tavern, home of Fred's Sunday-night Easy Hour. I liked the way Ray asked, "What is this 'Easy' that you speak of?"

"It was monsoon season," I began. "My flight out of Bhopal was delayed, and I was going to be rerouted through Addis Adaba. I sat in the airport bar sipping a gimlet when a man in Tyrolean gear sat down beside me, introducing himself as Mr. Yow. We argued about IMF social-policy issues for a while. After he left, I noticed a microfilm capsule sitting next to his empty martini glass. When I finally arrived in Brasília, I went straight to the embassy and read it. It was a biography of Percy Faith. At the end was a Norwegian address and invitation to an après-ski party next month. Music and laughter drifted up to the embassy windows—Carnival. I went down to the street and disappeared into the crowd.

"That, my friend, is Easy."

The look of stunned astonishment on his face told me he was *having it.*

When we got to the bar, Ray's eyes lit up. He said he had not expected me to suggest such a dive. I could see he was one of those types who likes dives. He said *this* was the real Chicago, not Rush Street or the House of Blues or Gibson's. He said this was where the backbone of Chicago lived and worked, the South Side.

I Bridgeported, "Go Sox! Hooray, Mare Daley! Love dat Sout' Side sahh-sidge, dere."

He looked at me curiously, and I admitted that *that* was my real voice, my real Bridgeport-native, nasal, chokin'-on-a-Polish, slobberin' Old Style voice. His eyes sparkled, and he arched an eyebrow and smiled warmly at me.

I said, "You're not supposed to like me *because* I'm from the South Side; you're supposed to like me *in spite* of it."

He grinned, and said, "I'm not sure I like you at all."

Fred had really done up the tavern beautifully. Colored Christmas lights were strung up everywhere now; he had taken down the St. Pauli Girl mirror and the poster of the whorish Killian's Red babe and replaced them with posters of Easy icons like Astrud Gilberto ("Girl from Ipanema"), Caetano Veloso (bossa-nova giant), Claudine Longet, Telly Savalas, Virginia Rodrigues (enchanting Afro-Brazilian contralto), George Lazenby (the one-film and Easiest-by-far James Bond), and New Easy darlings, the Elevators.

Fred wore a smashing blue poly shirt with a pattern of 1920s flapper faces all over it and snug tangerine-colored trousers. The regulars, oblivious to the decor changes, stared either straight ahead at nothing, or up at the mute TV (*Diagnosis Murder*).

"Terrific outfit, Fred. How do the regulars like it?"

He looked down proudly at the poly. He said, "Aw, if they give me any shit, I just say they're Bears colors. That shuts 'em up." I introduced the guys and marveled that way at the end of the bar sat two slackers, digging the scene.

Fred said he saw one of the slackers the day before at the doughnut shop across the street, so he gave the guy a little flier advertising the Easy Hour.

Ray said, "I hope that doesn't drive away your regular customers. They don't look too Easy."

"No," said Fred, "they're difficult. Plus they tip lousy and make a lot of Korean jokes. Anyway, I'm trying to capitalize on the southward hipster migration. No one can afford to live in Wicker Park or even Pilsen anymore."

I said, "*I* can't afford Wicker Park anymore, either, but you don't see *me* running to the South Side."

Fred said, "Bridgeport is the community of the future."

"How can this be? My parents still live here, and nowhere they live can be hip or desirable. Their assignment is to live in the past and die peacefully without any inkling of what is going on in the world."

I lit up a nasty Kool (found a stub under my bathtub, yay!) and asked Fred about the redecoration scheme for Wysocki's. He said he had only just begun, and now that he had joined his mother's Geh Club, he'd soon be able to make massive changes. Geh Club was an unconventional savings and loan program for the Korean side of Fred's family. Members had to put in a certain amount of money each month, and then they took turns withdrawing the lump sum for individual use.

Fred had made fun of Geh Club for years, calling it the Korean Mafia. He always talked about friends and family in the club who missed payments, then suffered sudden "accidents," black eyes and broken bones attributed to walking into walls or falling down several flights of stairs. I asked him why he would join now.

Fred looked uncomfortable. "Because I don't trust the white man's bank?" Ray and I exchanged glances.

Fred sighed. "Okay, I just wanted to do something to make this place my own, even if I have to suffer the humiliation of Mom's Geh Club. I'll never be able to start my own business, but if I have to keep running this bar the way it is now, I'll throw myself under a truck."

I was reminded of our suicidal dog. It had chosen death over life in the Galisa home. Maybe it saw Daddy's melancholia as a sign that things would never improve, just as Fred saw Wysocki's Tavern doomed without a tremendous amount of cash and skillful interior design.

A customer buying packaged goods at the front counter looked around for someone to ring him up. He spotted Fred and shouted, "Hey, gook!"

"What a jag-off!" exclaimed Ray in disgust.

Fred straightened up, turned toward the front, and said to Ray, "Forget it, man. These guys are on their way out. Easy is on its way in." He marched to the cash register, ran his hand through his bowl cut, and muttered, "It *has* to be."

After a couple drinks, Ray confided that if the teachers' strike didn't end soon, he was going to lose his mind. He said, "I miss science." It was a very cute and nonmagnate type of thing to say.

I leaned over and said, "I like science," and planted a kiss on his cheek. He smelled of Aramis, a dad-ish cologne, yet somehow it suited him.

He looked curious. "Really? What interests you?"

"I don't know. The planets? They're kind of cool."

I kissed him again. He smiled roguishly and said, "Astronomy inspires a lot of passion in you, Lisa. That was *all right*." I said there was more of where that came from.

Then: "Oh my God!" I blurted out. "It's my mother!" Not really the words men like to hear after they have basically been promised sex. But there she was, waddling in, waving to Fred, decked out in turquoise velour. Daddy trailed behind, talking with Chip. My sister was not there; apparently it was "clean-the-deep-fryer" night at McDonald's.

"They think they're invited guests of the Easy Hour," I complained.

Fred said, "They are."

I was forced to make introductions when I realized I didn't know Ray's last name. Nobody cared, my family was so busy falling all over him. Comments such as, "Lisa has a date?!" and "I've never met any of her boyfriends before, have you, Stell?" were made. Ma called Ray "hunky."

She said right in front of him, "Now that's what I call a good-lookin' guy. I always liked big men."

"Ma! He's right here!" I jabbed my thumb at him for emphasis. He smiled and waved.

She swatted my words away, like smoke. Thankfully he went to the men's room, so I could berate my mother in peace. Chip sat next to me and asked again if I would lend him money for the first issue of *Prole*.

He said, "Ma and Daddy are giving us a hundred dollars, and Bruce's parents are forking over two hundred. We've already set up Bruce's Mac Classic in our basement, we just need money for printing and buying a used scanner."

Ma said, "My son, my son the newspaperman!"

"Ma," grumbled Chip, "it's a *'zine*."

"God, here," I said, opening my wallet, "twenty bucks, Mike Royko. Take it and get lost."

Daddy and Fred chatted about the new changes at the tavern. Daddy said he sure admired Fred's entrepreneurial spirit and wished that he were young again himself. They made a nice picture, the two of them dressed in blue shirts and orange trousers. Brasil '66 blared from the stereo. Christmas lights twinkled all around.

Ma said, "You boys have practically the same outfit on."

They answered in unison, "Bears."

Diagnosis Murder was just ending, and Daddy, unable to resist the call of any nearby television, watched the silent action. I asked if Dick Van Dyke was on "the list."

"Certainly not!" he replied, piqued. See, though my dad is strangely obsessed with TV and rooted firmly in 1976, he is not completely predictable. Who would have guessed that Rob Petrie was *not* one of the most annoying men on earth?

Ray came back from the bathroom. I whispered, "I am so ready to go," but he demurred, preferring to watch the spectacle of my parents and idiot brother.

Resigned, I ordered more Old Style. My drunk, that freeloader, ordered an ouzo chaser. "Hey, Ray," I said, "I just realized I don't know your last name."

He took a card out of his wallet and handed it to me. It had his name along with JANITOR/SCIENTIST underneath. There were also two tiny pictures, one of a mop and bucket, the other of that bunch of ovals symbolizing some type of atomic activity. I read aloud, "Ray Fuchet," pronouncing it to rhyme with *Nantucket*.

"It's French!" he protested. "Fu-*shay*."

I gasped in disbelief, "Your name is Ray Fu-*shay*?"

Ma shrieked, "I *told* you a rhyming name was goddamn-knockout gorgeous!"

At midnight, Ray drove me and my drunk home. She made the most inane conversation while I thought of ways to destroy her. I had vowed to stop letting her muscle in on my life, but when I get nervous, like when I'm around a man, she slips in and takes over. I rolled down the window and gulped fresh, cold air.

When we pulled up in front of my building, Ray said, "I had a really good talk with Fred about Easy, and I think I understand its allure. From what I gather, the easy-listening culture of the 1950s and '60s originated as an unconscious strategy to tame the uncertainties of living with the bomb. The possibility of global annihilation forced society to place undue relevance on the present, on pleasure-seeking for its own sake. The future became foggy, frightening, unpredictable, and ultimately irrelevant."

My drunk tried to answer—something brilliant, no doubt—but she had lost her advantage while I was sucking up fresh air. I said, "Ray, I am so impressed! You have given Easy as much thought as I have. I knew it was right to share the concept with you. And while I agree that Easy revels in the past and savors the present, I have to say I think that that is so only because it desires something greater for the future. Easy is hopeful and life-affirming; if the future was irrelevant, Easy would die. Easy is all about taking chances and moving forward."

"My God," he said quietly, eyes wide, "you're an optimist."

That was kind of a dreadful thing to say to someone. He might as well have accused me of being sensitive or religious.

He walked me to my door and kissed my cheek.

"Coming up?" asked my drunk. Oh, God, how did she get out? I'll kill her.

He smiled. "Going home."

"Right," I said. "Just checking." Blotches of flame appeared on my cheeks. That rat-bastard drunk . . . three shots of ouzo, and she's reading signals like a dyslexic engineer.

I said, "I was just being polite. I have to get up early for my new job tomorrow." *Please stop talking,* I begged myself, *please shut up and go inside. Don't ruin everything by speaking candidly and being yourself.*

The science teacher grinned at me maddeningly, then turned and walked slowly back to his car, whistling "The Girl from Ipanema."

Damn you, Ray Fuchet.

Chapter 17

*W*oke up with hideous hangover. Ugh, all ouzo and no sex make Lisa a dull girl. That was it—I was determined to fire my drunk. I was so used to starting my days before Fishman's with a beautiful Sobranie and a giant latte, but now that I was going to be among high society, I was scrambling around with a Kool and some hair of the dog. Oh, well, I had no time to ponder. It was extremely important to show up for my first day at Honey's wearing the Right Thing, but I had no idea what it was. Too glam, and she might feel I wasn't serious or dependable. Too schoolmarmy, and she'd think I was just a dud clerk incapable of mixing with her crowd. I opted for a gray pantsuit (two-legged) with frock coat, pearls (false, of course), and really decent high-heeled loafers, very Suzanne Pleshette. I parted my hair on the side, combed it down to just above my ears, then pulled it back in a loose bun with soft little wispies. I looked at my reflection in the mirror and thought, *Tosca*. Lubbeth and Consolo at that moment probably were cracking the whip over the juniors.

I arrived at Honey's high-rise with a minute to spare. She lived near the Loop in that curvy black glass building right on the lake, the one that has a reputation as a big lothario hangout. Everyone says that Oprah used to live there, but couldn't handle the swinging.

The doorman asked for my name. I told him and he didn't even giggle. He had one of those elegant stern faces like Captain Von Trapp, and he spoke into the intercom phone in low, measured tones. I felt intimidated, as even the doorman obviously had more class than I. I shut Bridgeport, its flat vowels and harsh *R*s, from my mind.

The elevator operator asked for the floor, and I told him, "Penthouse." That was twice in a month's time that I'd taken an elevator to a penthouse, though Crump's building looked like a soup kitchen compared to Honey's high-rise. I remember when all *penthouse* meant to me was naked girls in frilly socks climbing library ladders.

Things can change.

The night before, when I had told Ma and Daddy that I quit my job at Fishman's and was starting work as Honey Dietrich's personal assistant, Daddy smiled with relief and said, "So long, retail hell!" Ma said she always *told* me to go to secretarial school.

"I'm not going to be a secretary," I retorted. "A personal assistant is so much more, and there probably will be no typing or filing."

Daddy said the retail world could grab hold of a man's soul and suck it dry. The thing is, he never complained once about retail until the one-legged-you-know-what disaster. There is a thin line between love and hate, and it's called failure.

I exited the elevator and walked through Honey's private vestibule, a marble-tiled foyer with gilt mirrors and rotund French furniture and tasteful flower arrangements. I rang the buzzer outside the double mahogany doors, and a maid answered immediately. When I removed my coat and tried to hand it to her, she just pointed wordlessly to a closet around the corner. I smiled in an all-servants-together type of camaraderie, but she just said Ms. Dietrich awaited me in her bedroom.

The apartment was set up with the living room at the hub, with all other rooms and hallways radiating from it. Enormous walls of glass unveiled vistas of Lake Michigan and some of the northern lake shore. It had the feel of a Paris apartment, with lots of valuable antiques and everything in shades of raspberry and ice blue.

Silk lampshades with gold tassels sat atop every lamp and a sparkling crystal chandelier hung from a gold leaf–plastered frieze on the ceiling. The maid directed me down a dark hallway decorated with lithographs of seventeenth-century animal drawings and French watercolors, at the end of which was Honey's bedroom. She sat propped up in bed, wearing a peach silk peignoir set and half-glasses, reading the newspaper. The bedroom was the size of an average Bridgeport bungalow.

"Lisa!" she exclaimed. "Darling, I need *so* much help. I'm *so* glad you're here. First off, I need a refill." She waggled an empty china cup on the tip of her index finger. Lenox, nice. "Kitchen is that way." She made a sweeping, meaningless gesture toward the vacuity from where I came. I found myself back in the Parisian hub, as I'd come to think of it, uncertain which spoke would lead me to the kitchen. After a few errors, I found it. It was one of those rooms rich people have that serves no real purpose. It looked as though no one had ever cooked anything on the massive Aga stove nor had any veggies ever been chopped on the gleaming center-island butcher block. A chrome refrigerator of the kind found in large upscale restaurants stood imposingly next to the sink, which was a marble basin with copper taps newly polished. I peeked inside the fridge—ah, just as I thought: a giant bottle of Evian, a little tin of caviar, fancy horseradish, and nothing else. The set-up was so clichéd, it had the fingerprints of a prop stylist all over it, but apparently this was how Honey really lived.

"Ahem." The maid cleared her throat. She ran a feather duster over a large wall rack of spices in stainless steel jars with hand-printed labels. "May I help you?"

"Oh! Just getting coffee for Ms. Dietrich."

The maid's eyes widened slightly. "Madam does not usually keep the coffeepot in the refrigerator. You'll find it plugged in on the counter." She went about her dusting business, posture rigid as a corpse and frowny face full of disdain.

If there was a hierarchy of servants, shouldn't I, as personal assistant, rank above the charwoman? The thought made me stop in my tracks and wonder just what kind of salary Honey was going to pay me.

Back in the bedroom, I handed Honey her cup and decided to broach that subject the wealthy find so distasteful: money. I tried to cringe and sound contrite.

"Well," she said, taking a sip, "I confess I hadn't really thought of it. What do personal assistants make nowadays?"

I suppose I was expected to consult some type of salary hand-book the way high society consulted *Who's Who* or *Burke's Peerage*. I made a bold statement (or lie), tripling my former pay: "I believe Roger Ebert's personal assistant makes six hundred dollars a week."

She smiled lazily. "I adore Ebes, don't you? *So* smart and has such wonderful Fourth-of-July parties. That's good enough for me. Six hundred it is. And dearie, I never bother with taxes and all that crazy rigmarole. My accountant used to make me fill out so many papers and W forms, whatever they're called, it gave me a royal headache. So it'll have to be cash once a week."

On impulse, I curtsied. I had no problem with obsequiousness if it would get me money and prestige. I hoped in actuality Licorice Luke made well over six hundred a week at his job. It made me sad to think that Ebert might be a cheapskate. And even if he was, nothing could have made me refer to him as "Ebes." It sounded like Jeeves, that smart-ass valet. Roger Ebert was an intellectual and knew a lot about movies and politics and had divine Modiglianis and gave wonderful Fourth-of-July parties; why couldn't people give him some respect? *When we're married,* I daydreamed, *I will drum out of town anyone who dares call me Mrs. Ebes.*

I sat on Honey's tufted footstool while she embarked on a ram-bling monologue, thinking how easy this personal-assistant racket was: all I had to do was run around and get coffee and act like I was listening, then she'd hand me six hundred dollars. I guessed ol' Licorice Luke and I were now contemporaries in the service of society. *Maybe,* I imagined, *when Ebert has his Fourth-of-July party, Luke can wrangle an invitation for me, too.* Ray's square face suddenly flashed into my mind, but I banished it. After all, I was a freewheeling personal assistant on the cusp of an elite adventure, and I could date whomever I wanted. It wasn't like Ray and I had anything special, just one date. What's more, a date that ended in me practically groveling for sex and him whistling as he drove off. So why was I freaking out about him? Oh, hell, I knew why. It was because I *liked* him, and—if experience has taught me anything—the only result could be catastrophe.

"Dar-*ling,*" pleaded Honey, "are you paying attention?"

"Of course. Christmas . . . party . . . tree," I repeated the words that had made it through the haze.

"Yes," replied Honey, "Esmé has my address book somewhere. Ask her for it, invite the gold stars, then set about getting the apartment decorated for Christmas. I usually use Crest of Fine Flowers, ask for . . . oh, what's her name? Redhead. Maybe a blonde. Always gives me a deal. Should have done it a month ago. Oh, well, beg them to fit me in. Need holiday garb, too. Let's spend a day at Kate Spade and Prada and Armani, then we'll go visit your little friends at Fishman's and find replicas in the, um, 'affordable' department."

"Right," I murmured, rummaging through my satchel for a notebook in which to inscribe her ramblings. "Irregulars . . . call Doris."

Honey removed her half-glasses and gave me one of her infamous frosty smiles. "That's a painful word: 'irregular.' Don't you think? Perhaps if you lived through the war as I had, sugar, you wouldn't so carelessly toss around painful words. Why, I consider myself just plain lucky to be able to buy clothing at all." She sighed here, apparently reminiscing about the old hardtack days when she and Washington led the troops across the icy Delaware to attack the Hessians quartered on the Trenton side.

She put on her glasses again and resumed reading Mary Cameron Frey's society column in the *Sun-Times*. She mentioned, as though an afterthought, that she was disappointed Mrs. Lubbeth had not fired that horrible scarecrow, Doris, and that maybe I ought to mention to my former senior that if she wanted to keep Honey's business, she should consider hiring a non-Mingle. I gulped and scribbled down her instructions, page after page. Honey Dietrich expected me to earn every penny of those six hundred dollars.

Esmé gave me the evil eye whenever our paths crossed. Please, what kind of maid is named Esmé? It was obviously made up. And since when were they imperious? Didn't she know I once pretended to be Maria Callas? Fame counted for nothing.

The maid was writing out a grocery list at the William Randolph Hearst table. Throughout the morning, as I ran around getting tea and sandwiches for Honey's "elevenses" with her art dealer, making the bed, and writing notes to myself every five seconds, Esmé would materialize out of thin air and pronounce my movements as perilous to Honey's furniture and tchotchkes.

"Be careful!" she admonished, when I brushed too closely by a piecrust table laden with figurines. "Those are Lladró. Very expensive, in case you don't know."

"Watch out!" she gasped as I almost touched the twenty-seven-foot mahogany dining table. "I just polished the wood. That's a reproduction of the seventeenth-century English refectory table from the Hearst Castle."

Other times, when I was not actually moving or touching anything, she'd walk by and simply state, "This window was designed by Frank Lloyd Wright" or "These silk curtains came from the Hollywood mansion of David O. Selznick."

"Excuse me, Esmé?"

She looked up from her list with the grim expression of one who has just smelled something awful. "What is it?"

"Ms. Dietrich wants me to get the apartment decorated for Christmas and to start planning her holiday party, so I need her address book," I said.

The look she threw me could have frozen me into a punch-bowl ice sculpture, had my heart not already been chilled by years of Fishman Christmas shoppers. She said, "That's your job? Planning parties? Holiday decoration? *I* always used to do that for madam."

I said nothing. I wasn't here to win over the maid.

She went over to the little escritoire and withdrew a small book covered in faded rose silk, embroidered with the letters *HBD* in white on the front. She returned to me slowly, her small frame tensing visibly with each step. Her black hair was parted severely down the center and drawn back into a tight knot, emphasizing her gaunt, hidebound features. Her crisp gray-and-white-striped dress made from old-fashioned Marseilles clung to her bones. She tried to hand me the book, but when it came time to release her hold, she seemed unable to relax her fingers.

"Please take care of this," she said. "When you're not using it, it should go back in the escritoire.

"Uh-huh," I replied, yanking the book from her hands. I thumbed through it. There were, indeed, gold stars placed next to a good portion of the names. Look, there was even the home phone of hizzoner Mare Daley. There was Dennis Farina's number (no gold star—why?) and the Cusack family and several Steppenwolf company members and three pages devoted to various subentries under *Kennedy*. Rival socialite Sugar Rautbord had a listing, and I could see there had once been a gold star next to her name, but it had been torn off. "Cool," I said.

Esmé turned a violent pink. "I don't like you," she said in a pinched voice.

Who does? I reasoned. *I'm making six hundred bucks a week to get Roger Ebert's home phone number, so I'm not sweating it.*

I called the florist and asked for the redhead or blonde. All I had to do was say I was calling on behalf of Honey Dietrich, and I was put right through.

"We'll have to hurry," said the florist, Jean. "Ms. Dietrich usually orders her Christmas decorations before Thanksgiving. What theme is she going for this year?"

"Theme?"

"Yes, last year she did 'Parisian Christmas.' The year before, it was 'Nutcracker.'"

I placed my hand over the receiver and prepared to shout for Honey's input, but she was lying on the velvet chaise with a lavender sachet over her eyes. Esmé hushed me and said madam was stricken with a migraine after the tête-à-tête with her art dealer over the Calder.

"I need to know today," prompted Jean. "We're coming downtown to decorate for Oprah's holiday show, so I could swing by and we could start planning."

"Great," I replied. By that time, I should have been able to elicit some ideas from Honey.

In the meantime, I had to go outside and run two blocks over to Fnok's (Honey's latest restaurant darling; it was more sick-making than Nub) and pick up a bowl of pumpkin bisque for her. When I suggested she have it delivered, she balked at the dollar-fifty delivery charge.

"Why should madam pay for delivery when she has a *person* who can pick it up?" mused Esmé to the wall. Honey agreed it was idiotic. Nobody mentioned the idiocy of paying sixteen dollars for a bowl of soup. On the way back, I had to walk carefully so as not to spill the carton in the white paper bag. December bit through my light cloth coat and tore my sleek hair out of its bun. It began to snarl and frizz in the wind. Even with most of the perm cut off, it still had an undeniable Rhea Perlman quality.

Back in the apartment, chattering and shivering, I poured the soup into a Lenox bowl and brought it to Honey on a butler's tray of bamboo.

She took a slurp. "Tepid," she commented. "Warmsy?" Obediently, I took the soup back into the kitchen, used one of the thousand copper pots hanging from the ceiling (all were dusty), and reheated the soup. I remembered that once Luke told me part of his job was to fact-check some of the columns for the *Sun-Times,* take notes during interviews, and run interference during squabbles at the newspaper's annual Christmas party. I suppose his duties were more important than mine, but there's a quiet dignity to warming up soup for a glamorous old war veteran.

After luncheon (not "lunch," I was informed), I handed the dirty saucepan to Esmé. She considered it for a moment, then handed it back to me.

"Let me make something perfectly clear," she said. "As the housekeeper, I am in charge of all the other help: the driver, irresponsible lout that he is; the chef, who runs madam's dinner parties with the assistance of hired caterers and the cooking sherry; the weekly cleaning person, who pretends not to understand plain English; and you, the modern equivalent of a 'lady's maid.' Therefore *you* will tidy up after madam when you are here. Understood?"

I lifted my eyebrows slightly and turned away. That is the genteel version of throwing your palm in someone's face and shouting, "Whatever!"

I scrubbed the copper pot with an SOS pad, which turned out to be rather a mistake, but seeing as how the pots didn't seem to be used very often, it would be a long time before anyone noticed the deep scratches all along the bottom.

On my thirty-minute lunch break (not "luncheon," the gentry's privilege), I sat in the building's lobby and smoked a Kool. Checked my messages: Tim, Luke, Ray. Called Tim with a run-down on my first day—brutal, he said, but worth it—and Luke, who wanted to see a movie on Wednesday. I said yes before I could talk myself out of it. Also called Ray on his janitor's cell.

"I'm making more money, but I'm kind of a servant," I said when he asked how it was going.

"Everyone misses you at the store," he said. "You'd like the new Christmas theme."

"What theme? I thought they were just doing the usual Christmas."

"Nope. They decided to go with 'Christmas in Washington.' All the departments are decorating for the different administrations. Women's Wear fought really hard to get the Reagan years. Mrs. Consolo said they needed it to unload all those red John Galliano dresses."

"Do you get to dress up as anybody?" I asked. It sounded really fun. Not like being a pot scrubber and soup fetcher.

"No. I've been busy running around with sick sand every day, but Mr. Fishman says I might get to be Santa. There've been a lot of complaints about Vegan Santa, telling kids not to eat turkey and so on. During his break, he puts up a sign that reads 'Santa Is Feeding His Reindeer Non-GMO Corn and Soybeans.' It's ruining the shoppers' Christmas spirit."

"What's Men's Wear doing?"

"Clinton. Philomena in Crystal snatched up the Kennedy administration, and it's Camelot as far as the eye can see. You-know-who is really happy she can still dress up as Jackie."

Jealousy surged within me, but I showed massive restraint and said nothing. Doris Mingle got saddled with ol' "Waste not, want not" Herbert Hoover. If irregulars aren't the epitome of wasted commerce, I don't know what is.

"Hey," I said, "there's one more thing. I just wanted to say I was sorry."

"Sorry for what?"

For the chaos and annoyance I knew I would sweep into his life. "Oh, for, you know, getting a bit smashed last night and making a complete fool of myself, et cetera."

He said, "I thought you were charming."

"I didn't mean to be. I was nervous. Oh . . . you mean . . . huh." He didn't *seem* to be teasing me. "Thanks."

"You're welcome."

"But you didn't have to call me an optimist."

He paused for a minute. "I apologize," he said seriously.

We made plans to go out over the weekend. This meant I now had two dates in one week—a first for me. Excellent. Freewheeling. Yet also intimidating, frightening. In all likelihood, problematic. A precursor to certain trouble. I snapped my phone shut and resumed my old morose personality.

I took a monstrous drag on my Kool, when the doorman tapped me on the shoulder. He wrinkled his nose and coughed.

"Oh, Jesus, don't tell me I can't smoke in the lobby," I complained, extinguishing it. "There's an ashtray on the table, for God's sake."

"You can smoke," he replied. "Just not those"—he peered at the crumpled soft pack in my hand—"*Kools.*" He pointed at a discreet sign on the wall behind me: NO MENTHOL.

He held out a slim gold box of cigs, compliments of the management. I looked at him in amazement, and he said he had a brother in Austria's duty-free. I took a couple bones. Ahhhh, Sobranie!

Jean the florist and I stood in the Parisian hub, talking holiday decor. Honey was in her own private exercise studio with her personal trainer, doing Pilates. I tried to get some decoration feedback out of her before her workout session, but she got mad at me, stamped her foot, and said, "I hired you so that I wouldn't have to be *bothered* with little details. Just make a *decision.*"

Jean stood there patiently with a clipboard, awaiting direction. "Budget?" she asked.

"What was last year's?" I hedged.

She consulted Honey's file. "Twenty thousand. But with less than four weeks until Christmas, it may be more difficult to obtain desired items at that price."

Twenty thousand dollars. Twenty thousand! What could cost that much money? Jean kindly enlightened me: six Christmas trees, complete with ornaments, lights, velvet-and-silk tree skirts; wreaths; hundreds and hundreds of feet of fresh balsam garland twined with taffeta ribbon, and studded with pinecones rolled in real gold leaf, replaced weekly; centerpieces and floral arrangements for each room, replaced *twice* weekly. On top of that, there were the "stylist" items, such as the regiment of life-size wooden nutcrackers used one year, and the replica of the Eiffel Tower last year. There were mirrors to be purchased, candles, furniture, new fireplace screens and fire tools to reflect the current theme. New rugs in the proper color scheme; tapestries flown in from France with appropriate scenes painstakingly hand-stitched by cloistered nuns; new crystal and silver tableware engraved with Honey's initials and the current year; handmade Christmas stockings for all the rooms, plus more for Honey's closest friends (last year's total was ninety-two); hundreds of amaryllis bulbs potted in Chinese urns to be given as gifts; a crèche made every year with porcelain figures dressed in thematic garb—last year's baby Jesus wore a jaunty mohair beret while Mary kneeled by the manger wearing a miniature Gaultier robe and Joseph stroked his goatee made of human hair; the Wise Men brought the infant king gold, braided Tiffany bracelets, Chanel No. 5, and an autographed first edition of Sartre's *Being and Nothingness.*

I paced around the hub, my mind a blank wall. It was hard spending someone else's money, especially someone who could ruin me if I made an error. I'd learned that when people trusted my opinions, I wrecked their lives. At this moment, Gina was awaiting my direction on her pet-psychic future, fully aware I had brought about the cataclysm of Leisure Lady with my business advice.

Christmas decorations had always been a big deal at home—pipe-cleaner snowflakes, felt Santas stuffed with cotton balls, and various aluminum Christmas trees in silvery blue, white, and pink—but I could draw on none of these for Honey's theme. All I could see before me was a vast, yawning chasm.

I said, "How about 'Spare Christmas'?"

Jean looked up from her notes. "Spare? What do you mean?"

I explained my theory of white and gray and right angles and comfy cement. The openness that reveals nothing, the flat surfaces that appear to offer no secret places, but in reality offer a permanent mask for the resident. Who would *not* want that? Who wanted everything *out* there, ick, where everyone could see?

Christmas 1994. A year after the collapse of Daddy's store, yet he still spent a big chunk of daylight on the couch, ranking forgotten celebrities. Ma drove the station wagon up to the North Side to pick me up on Christmas Eve and also to shop for loads of seafood on Randolph Street. After Midnight Mass, Galisas stayed up for hours scarfing shrimp and mussels and reminiscing.

"Your brother and sister want to start a new tradition tonight," Ma had said as we picked through the bins of DiNardo Bros. "It's some kind of bonfire."

It's been going on for years now, everyone on Morgan Street knows about our family bonfire. The idea is to burn symbols of one's personal failure in hope of making a change in life. It would make more sense to hold the event on December 31, but my siblings wisely predicted that we would never want to spend New Year's Eve with Stell and Sal. Chip had originally suggested December 21, the winter solstice, but Ma objected on the grounds that it was "pagan," and therefore suspect. Though she saw nothing pagan about whooping it up around a bonfire, burning effigies to appease the failure gods.

We were antsy all through that Midnight Mass at St. Barbara's. Even I, who usually had no time for family traditions and the trouble and ulcers they wrought, was excited about burning stuff in the backyard. Like three little kids, Gina, Chip, and I fidgeted and whispered throughout the gospel. Santa had never been able to bring us much over the years, but at that moment we anticipated the coming hours as though great bags of money were about to be dropped down the chimney. If you can't afford to get stuff, the next best thing is torching stuff you don't want.

When Father Piraino stood at the pulpit and read the words from Psalm 23, "The Lord is my shepherd, I shall not want. He maketh me to lie down in green pastures: He leadeth me beside the still waters. He restoreth my soul," Daddy wept.

He put his arms around all of us and whispered, "My cup runneth over."

Ma whispered, "Since when does Piraino read from the King James version?"

I watched Daddy stifle a quiet laugh as he squeezed her, wiping the tears with the back of his hand. Ma complains, yet, somehow, restoreths.

Afterward, Ma began assembling the seafood extravaganza with Nana while the rest of us ran around looking for things to burn. Gina chose the year's collection of schedules she'd tacked to her bulletin board each week.

She said, "Next year, I'm going to have more important things to organize than cleaning the grease trap and buying tube socks."

Chip was not sure what symbol he wanted to burn. We poked around in his room, looking for indications of failure. I found many for him, starting with *Catcher in the Rye,* the little maroon book that inspired decades of white adolescent angst. He protested and put it back on his shelf. He also refused to burn his Olivia Newton-John records and the Morrissey collection, as well as a self-help book I found under his bed called *Admitting Truth: Homosexuality, Families, and Honesty.*

He grabbed it from me and said, "I can't burn that. It's—it's not mine."

In retrospect, it's not that I believed him or disbelieved him. I just didn't think about him at all.

"How about this?" he asked, reaching into a coffee can at the very top of his closet shelves. He brought out a dime-bag of really decent weed.

"Are you out of your mind?" I gasped.

Chip bounced the baggie in his palm, considering it. "I don't know. Maybe it's making me lazy. I get stoned almost every day, and I still haven't registered for classes at DeVry yet."

"Listen, let's fire up a joint right now before the seafood buffet, okay? I'll help you find something else to burn. Besides, if you toss this on the bonfire, the Bridgeport pigs will be out here in five minutes to throw you in the clink on Christmas Eve. You can't do that to Ma and Daddy."

I convinced him, but now that I think of my twenty-five-year-old brother still living at home and running a 'zine out of my parents' basement, I wonder if I did the right thing.

He ended up choosing the roster of the '93 Bears.

"But you don't even like sports," I objected.

Chip looked down rather miserably at the sheet of paper, saying only that it would make our dad happy.

As for myself, I selected one of the various dude caps I had stashed in my old closet in Gina's room. My sister said that was a ridiculous idea.

"On the contrary," I responded. "It represents my formerly poor fashion sense."

She said, "I still don't think that symbolizes a failure. Everybody hates the way they used to look. Why are you really burning it?"

"Do you see this cap? I wore it for years. I felt it really expressed something about me, perhaps a love of AC/DC, perhaps embarrassment of perms gone wrong. At any rate, it's hideous, and I want to trash everything that reminds me of . . . of the days of my disgusting wardrobe." I'd almost mistakenly said, *that reminds me of myself.*

I lay back on her bed and gazed up at Ursa Minor on the ceiling. Gina looked down at me and said she sensed sorrow. I said nothing.

"It was just a feeling I had," she had said, "that deep underneath your jag-off attitude, there's a sea of sadness."

Even in the dim lamp light, the constellation ceiling stickers glowed. That Ursa Minor was one bright little bear.

I was so baked at that midnight feast, I could only sit hunched next to Chip and struggle to operate the fork. I supported my body by resting my left arm on the table and wrapping it around my plate as my right hand shoveled in red snapper with white wine and garlic.

Grandma Galisa pursed her lips and asked my mother, "Who raised those pigs?"

At the word *pigs,* Chip and I erupted in giggles. My brother made *whoo-whoo* siren sounds as I mopped up sauce with a mortadella sandwich. Daddy wandered into the living room with lobster salad and switched on the TV. He found reruns of old game shows and settled into his chair, awaiting the bonfire.

Ma screamed, "Sal, it's Christmas Eve! Do you have to turn the television on right now?"

He said, "Just tell me when the bonfire's ready. I'll come out."

Gina sat on the arm of his chair. "Daddy, it's one-thirty in the morning. Come back and eat in the kitchen."

He tried to cast his eyes from the box, but failed. He said, "Wink Martindale goes well with any salad."

Chip, Gina, and I started that first bonfire in Daddy's outdoor fire pit, a sort of spaceship wok. I remember it was a really cold night and Chip kept dropping kindling on the patio and swearing. The light went on in our neighbors' house, the Krespis, a taciturn family who always watched us through their kitchen window. We'd been known to throw a few parties in our youth that naturally carried over to the Krespis' yard and house, even though they were never invited.

Mr. Krespi came out in a blue plaid flannel robe and retired-man slippers. "Everything all right?" he called out timidly.

"Yes, Mr. Krespi," said Chip, abnormally chatty from the pot, "we're just having a Christmas bonfire. Why don't you join us? We have plenty of food, and you can burn anything you like. Our family is burning symbols of failure."

Unable to resist such a gregarious fellow as Chip, though he tried and tried, giving up only when Chip walked over and towed him back to our house by his bathrobe sash, Mr. Krespi called good-bye to his wife, then disappeared into our kitchen to eat shrimp cocktail. When we finally got a decent little blaze going, my father was dragged away from the television, and everyone came out to the patio, bundled up in winter coats and gloves.

Nana said, "Oh, this is just crazy. I think you're all mentally ill," as Chip danced around gleefully with his Bears roster.

"All right!" he shouted. "Who'll go first? I guess it'll be me. I submit to the fire gods last year's roster of the worst Bears team in history!"

Daddy looked confused. "It wasn't so bad. They had seven wins."

Chip looked stricken. Why did he even bother pretending to care about sports? Certain kinds of boys liked football, and he wasn't one of them.

Everyone looked at Chip, who was determined to ride it out. "But there was no Sweetness!" The men nodded seriously. The mere mention of Walter Payton brought misty nostalgia to all present, recalling the glorious 1985 Super Bowl victory. My brother smiled with satisfaction and threw the paper on the fire. He scored cool points with Daddy.

Gina gently placed her schedule in the blaze, and I tossed my dude cap in. It gave off a weird chemical odor and burned blue, but it was too late to do anything about it. Mr. Krespi declined to burn anything, but stood there stiffly, bringing a joyless Cotton Mather piquancy to our Christmas Eve torch fest.

Daddy went back inside while Ma hemmed and hawed about what she should burn.

Chip said, "How about your lottery tickets? You know it's just a stupidity tax." He handed her last week's loser, which had been taped to the fridge.

Ma argued. "What's so stupid? I'm helping pay for roads!"

Chip sang his version of the popular lottery jingle: "Somebody's gonna Lotto, but it's not gonna be you."

Angry, yet hopelessly smitten with the cleverness of her son, her son, Ma grudgingly let the losing ticket ignite. Just then, Daddy emerged from the house with Ma's one-legged pantsuit draped over his arms.

Amidst cries of objection, he approached the bonfire. Ma begged him not to throw it in, saying she loved it. Gina said the poly was dangerous to burn. Nana and Grandma both looked scared.

"Dad, you can't," said Chip, trying to block the path to the fire.

"But it's the symbol of my failure," argued Daddy.

"Excuse me," said Mr. Krespi, "but I just saw a very moving drama on television tonight, and the message was, 'No man is a failure who has friends.'" He spread his arms wide, indicating the motley assortment of loved ones present who nullified Daddy's failure.

Ma cried, "Of course, Jimmy Stewart! Hear that, Sal?"

Defeated by our chorus of protest during that first bonfire in 1994, Daddy slumped wearily in a rusty, webbed deck chair. He held the pantsuit in his lap and the flared leg fluttered in the winter wind. "*It's a Wonderful Life* was on channel two," he sighed unhappily. "I missed it."

The florist checked her watch again. Honey's workout session was almost over, and I had not committed myself completely to "Spare Christmas."

She said, "If you really want gray aluminum Christmas trees and barbed-wire wreaths, I'll have to get started today. It's your choice. Are you sure about the Kabuki figures in the crèche and the manger filled with dried seaweed?"

"I'm not sure about anything," I replied in despair. "This is only my first day, and Ms. Dietrich doesn't want to be bothered with questions."

Jean smiled sympathetically. "Well, I've done Ms. Dietrich's holiday trimmings for five years now, and I've learned that she does seem to like a—well, a *festive* atmosphere. Bright colors and luxury items and such. Not that 'Spare Christmas' is without merit, but perhaps it's not quite right for this home."

Bright colors. Lux. Then I got it. We spent the rest of the hour making a bare-bones outline, and when Jean left, I went in search of Honey. I wandered into the workout room, the bedroom, the conservatory (really decent terrazzo floor, but dying aspidistras around a zen fountain), and the various other rooms filled with silk upholstered furniture—the cushions of which appeared never to have supported the heft of a human figure—but could not find her anywhere.

Esmé startled me as she jumped out from behind a marble statue of a giant bee. "Poking around? Can I help you find anything?"

"I'm looking for Ms. Dietrich," I said. "I'm making holiday arrangements."

"Madam went to Crump's for an emergency facial and aroma-therapy. Perhaps the stress of having hired an incompetent has afflicted her." She led me to the wall of windows looking out over Lake Michigan. Look how calming the icy waters were, she said, see how they beckoned one out of the black glass building where one didn't belong in the first place.

I'm not much for exchanging heated words with people, but I had a good forty pounds on Esmé and the inherited toughness of a long line of welterweight boxers on Ma's side of the family, so I was not afraid of the scrubwoman. I advanced on her, and she withdrew against the marble bee.

"Listen, Hazel. You think you can intimidate me, frighten me into quitting? Just try it. We can step outside on the balcony right now, and I can show you what it's like."

She smiled thinly but retreated, walking backward out of the room into the Parisian hub. She said, "No need for barbarism. I trust you'll make a disaster of things on your own."

Lisa: 1; scrubwoman: 0. Time to plan frigging Christmas.

I closed myself up in a little-used office off the hub for privacy and phoned Fred at the bar. After I told him about my job, I said I needed his help for a special project.

"Guess what I'm planning for the social set? It's going to be *the* holiday event of the season: 'Easy Christmas.'"

"Ah!" he replied. "Excellent idea."

We made plans to get together so that I could get his opinion about appropriate decor.

"By the way," he said, "what's with those fliers your sister put up all over Bridgeport?"

Oh, no. I felt a situation coming on.

He said, "She left a stack here. Let's see, it reads, 'Trouble communicating with your pet? Need answers to behavioral problems? Want to know what's going on in Fluffy's mind? Call Gina Galisa, animal communicator.' Then there's a phone number and a photo of Gina with her eyes closed and her ear pressed against a dog's head. Hey, it's your old dog!"

"I know that picture," I replied. I closed my eyes, too. Fred recited the number on the flier (it wasn't my parents'), so I hung up and dialed it.

"Gina Galisa," answered my sister.

"If you're so psychic, how come you didn't know it was me calling?" I said.

She said, "I'm not interested in reading people. So I guess you found my flier, huh? I got a cell phone! But I can't stay on long, somebody might be trying to call."

"Gina," I pleaded, "what are you doing? Why aren't you at work?"

"Day off. Even fry cooks get days off now and then. I already got two calls from people in the last two days. One was kind of a crank, but the other was real. A lady wanted to know—"

I interrupted. "I don't want to know what she wanted to know. You've gotta stop this. You can't be a pet psychic!"

"Why?"

"Because it's weird and there's no future in it."

"But I'm charging thirty dollars a call. They send me a check afterward."

"Sure they will. Listen, can we just talk about this in person? I have to come down there anyway on Friday to meet with Fred." She agreed to meet me, but I was worried. I heard in her voice something I'd never heard before: enthusiasm, pride. *Oh, God,* I thought, *I have to stop it. Nobody wants a personal assistant with a pet psychic in the family.*

Chapter 18

On Thursday night, Luke drove us over to the Music Box Theater to watch some French film. It was one of those movies where everyone is very pale and miserable. I made a real effort to be early, to be waiting downstairs when he drove up. Although he seemed happy to see me, he made no mention of my punctuality.

Finally I said, "I was right on time, wasn't I?"

"Yes, you were."

"*Right* on time. Early, even. It's just . . . well, I thought you might not have noticed."

He glanced over at me. "Do you have to be congratulated for simply doing what you were supposed to?"

"Yes, I do." What is the point of doing anything if no one congratulates you? I remembered when Ray congratulated me for not stabbing anyone during my infamous mad scene.

Luke bought Sno-Caps at the concession stand. I don't think I need to say any more about *that*.

At one point in the movie, where the little French girl's tattered shawl blows away in the winter wind and she watches it drift out of sight, tears in her eyes, I yawned and looked over at Luke. He also had tears in his eyes. I found this simultaneously touching and hilarious. He was so sad that he must not have realized his hand slipped down from my shoulder and kind of fell inside my shirt, under my bra. It was peculiar being groped while the little French girl froze to death in the gutters of Paris.

Afterward, he dropped me off at my apartment with a nice peck on the cheek. Although he had mauled me in the flickering blue light of foreign cinema, he apparently did not feel right about kissing me properly in the cold hard light of reality.

In the pit of my stomach I felt a sudden urge, a longing for a huge ham on rye, a glass of blackberry schnapps, and a square-headed man.

"Thanks," I said, exiting the car. "Those Sno-Caps really hit the spot."

Esmé generally kept out of my way, except to make comments in Honey's earshot, like "Something smells rancid. What could it be?" or "Hmm, where did these crumbs come from? Someone must have been wandering around with a handful of ham *again*." But Honey, floating about in an orderly world handled by an efficient personal assistant, appeared not to notice. The only real trouble I had with Honey came three days after the consultation with Jean. The florist people had come by with fabric samples for me to sift through as well as heaps of magazines.

I said, "We're definitely going with stockings and tree skirts in double-knit polyester, fuchsia, and cheddar orange, others in lime and sky-blue. Think marvelous, think Pucci, think bold stripes of color, think Frank Stella."

Honey, doing her nails at the Hearst table while Esmé stood sentry with the polish remover and a rag, looked over and said, "Orange? Darling, did you say you're doing some of my decorations in *orange*? I absolutely *detest* orange, and I'm not crazy about lime green, either, sugar."

The room was quiet as all awaited my response. Esmé licked her mummified lips expectantly. The decorators held their magazines still.

I said, "Easy is on the cusp right now, Ms. Dietrich, but this is completely up to you. The hippest bar in Chicago has seized upon it, and every Sunday visiting celebrities converge upon it—you know, of course, that Sunday is the new Monday, which was the old Saturday. It's all about the lux decadence of the fifties, sixties, and seventies. It's the new scene, and everybody's digging it. Roger Ebert, Nancy Sinatra, Jr., Princess Stephanie of Monaco, Athena Onassis, Stephen Hawking, Richard Chamberlain, Eve Plumb, Lou Ferrigno—they're all Easy." I meant to say Salvatore Ferragamo, not Lou Ferrigno, but I was nervous and it came out wrong.

Gaining steam, I continued. "Jean was just telling me how Sugar Rautbord wanted her to help throw an Easy New Year's Eve party, but she told Sugar she was already committed to you. Of course, if you want to do something else, Ms. Dietrich, something less daring, something more beige, just say the word and I'll send it all away. Shall we stay safe—or shall we get Easy?"

Jean looked like she had just swallowed a handful of roofing nails. Naturally, a professional like Jean would never divulge client secrets, but self-obsessed socialites such as Honey would never think of that. You could read it plainly across her face: *I must have what Sugar wants.*

"Lisa, where is this Easy bar you speak of? Can we go?" she asked, straddling the fence between suspicion and desire to be au courant.

"Only in the most happening neighborhood in Chicago: Bridgeport."

Everybody gasped. They couldn't seem to handle Bridgeport until Jean came to my rescue.

"Right," she said. "It's the new Pilsen."

Honey furrowed her brow. "I don't know about this; I'm a downtown gal. I thought Pilsen was the new Wicker Park."

"Aha," I said slyly, "you've caught on."

Suddenly, Honey was having it.

She made me promise to take her on Sunday to the secret, hip Bridgeport bar that everyone was talking about. *Oh, Baby Jesus,* I prayed silently, *I'm doing all this to help celebrate your birthday, please don't let the longshoremen be at Wysocki's this week.*

On my lunch break, I went down to the lobby to smoke and call Tim Gideon. The doorman, anticipating my ritual, left the box of Sobranies on the glass coffee table.

"Reference!" screamed Tim.

I cut to the chase. "How am I going to get Ebert to Wysocki's this Sunday?"

He whistled. "Whew, that's a tall order." I quickly told him about the developments with Honey's Easy Christmas and my need for celebrities at Wysocki's. He asked how things were going with Luke.

"Eh," I replied, the universal term for middling. "We went to a foreign film last night. He bought Sno-Caps and then he cried."

"Ugh, Sno-Caps are the worst."

"Yeah. Then he rounded second base when the little French girl bit it. Luke's a nice guy, but he was kinda getting on my nerves."

"Well, you just forget about your nerves, Miss Selfish. It was too early before, but now that he's groping you in the public arena, I think you can use sex as a leverage tool with him. You get him up to your apartment tonight, and you let him do whatever the hell he wants! That's how you get him to bring Ebert on Sunday." Then he shouted, "Does anyone here know the alphabet? Anyone? You, little boy, help this man find the letter *B* on the side of the stacks. Come on! It's like a snowman leaning against a wall, I've told you a thousand times. *Hen gap lie.*"

"Huh?"

"It's Vietnamese for 'thank you.' Listen, I gotta go, it's mayhem here. Just make it worth Luke's while, you know—a favor from one personal assistant to another. Who's next?! Step up, please!"

Sleep with Luke? I had spent the whole duration of the movie thinking about Ray Fuchet. But this was the business of business. Personal assistants using other personal assistants to claw to the top. *I can do it,* I told myself, *it's easy.* I emptied the box of Sobranies into my handbag.

After lunch, Honey and I were scheduled for an appointment with Mrs. Lubbeth. When I had called her to set it up, she'd sounded so excited to see me.

"Hi, hon!" she cried. "Gee, I know it's only been a week, but I miss you so much. How's your job?"

"Fantastic. Um, look Mrs. Lubbeth, when we come to see the clothes, can you just bring out a lot of polyester retro stuff? You know, sparkly swing dresses and bell-bottom pantsuits. That's what we're into right now. Like your Pucci caftan would be fab."

Actually, Honey was against caftans, but I had to convince her of the popularity of op-art Easy patterns and fabrics.

Lubbeth agreed to highlight their retro couture, then I took a deep breath. "Also, is Doris Mingle going to be there?"

"Yes, and she's dying to see you. She talks about you nonstop and how you were responsible for helping her sell out of the three-pronged turkey socks."

Here goes. "Well, Honey finds Doris irritating and I kind of told her that you fired Doris to please her—to please Honey, that is— so could you possibly fire her before we get there? I wouldn't want Doris to be embarrassed if Honey saw her and started to rant."

Mrs. Lubbeth didn't say anything for a minute. I thought we had been disconnected, and I vowed to get a tinier, flatter, newer cell phone.

But she finally said, "Well, thank you for being so concerned about embarrassing Doris; I can see that was really troubling you. I don't think I will be *firing* anyone today, but I'll give Doris the afternoon off, if that will suit you."

"Oh. Okay," I said. Then we hung up. Hey, I was just the messenger. I brooded. *Doris Mingle, why must you be a thorn in my side? She should be grateful to get the afternoon off. She could spend some time doing Mingley things, like knitting teapot cozies and playing with her cat. She could get home early and relax, eat canned soup in front of the TV. That would probably be a day of luxury for her. Oh, there it is . . . that stabbing, churn-*

ing sensation in my stomach. Christ, don't tell me I've gone soft on Doris Mingle now. For months she irritated me, trying to be nice and friendly. And even though I ignored her, she took up the Cheese-Inferno collection for my burnt Dior. I couldn't understand why someone like that would be kind to me. It made no sense. Yet she was able to weave her black art of niceness upon me, and I found myself reluctantly regarding her as a human being. Thinking about what her dull, lonely life must be like. How she probably went to sleep in an extra-long twin bed at night, wondering why she was so unpopular and pathetic even though she never hurt anybody and actually went out of her way to be a decent person. Maybe she cried before she fell asleep, holding her kitty cat in a tight embrace. Maybe she was an insomniac, lying under the covers for hours, trying to think of who could be her friend and finally coming up with no one.

Honey's driver dropped us off at the store around two o'clock. Fishman's, Mingle notwithstanding, has a certain appeal from the customer's perspective. It's not quite as chi-chi as Marshall Field's, but it does have a homey quality that works in its favor around Christmastime. We were always woefully understaffed, but the customers got to recognize us, since we were there all the time. And even though the pay was lousy, the benefits were decent, plus Mr. Fishman threw one hell of a Christmas party each year.

I wanted to run down to Janitor Land and look for Ray, but we were in a hurry. Walking toward Women's Wear, we passed Hui, who had been negotiating with Santa Claus on the throne. Children whined as the grown man in the gorgeous Armani suit and claret silk tie leisurely took up their gift-demand time with Santa.

"Silence, little fool," snarled Hui at a small boy who had ventured too close. He stepped down from the throne, and Santa was overrun with young vermin.

Hui strode by us, though he paused to incline his head deferentially to Honey. As for me, I received only a sour smile, which was more than I expected, I guess.

Entering Women's Wear, I was struck with a sense of nervous familiarity, like walking into the ballroom of a wedding reception where hundreds of your relatives are standing around. I wanted my old coworkers to feel like I was still one of them, even though I'd *kill* myself if I were. Mrs. Consolo rushed out of her couture corner to hug me. She made a divine Nancy Reagan in her red faille dress and had even frosted her short brown hair to match the former first lady's. Only the bronzed skin gave any clue that she spent her winters in neither D.C. nor some dude ranch out west, but in a cozy tanning bed in the Fishman's salon.

"You look wonderful, Lisa," she said, as though I had been gone for a decade. "Mrs. Lubbeth has really missed you. Well, we all have."

"You're certainly Miss Popularity," said Honey, flashing me the salt fortune–heiress smile, though this time she showed a bit of fang.

Mrs. Consolo said Lubbeth was waiting for us in the private showing room. I pointed out the balcony that had been specially constructed for my airborne Callas kisses, which had now been draped with garlands of boxwood and holly and glittering red berries.

"How nice," said Honey Dietrich in a bored voice. "I must tell Babbington."

Mrs. Lubbeth stood by the rack in the private room, hands clasped in front of her, beaming. She hesitated, then barreled toward me, drowning me in yards of chiffon and satin.

"Well, what am *I*? Pâté de foie gras?" quipped Honey. Her shrill giggle came dangerously close to sounding high-strung and uncontrolled.

"Oh, Ms. Dietrich, how lovely to see you," said Mrs. Lubbeth, disentangling herself from me to shake Honey's gloved hand.

"What do you think of the Women's Wear Reagan era? I have here some of the most thrilling outfits. I had to yank them out of the hands of less-deserving ladies. I know they will look devastating on you."

Placated, Honey sank down into the velvet couch and ordered me to start taking notes. She needed an outfit for her party, of course, but also one for Christmas Eve with Cardinal Francis George; a Christmas Day outfit of "festive conservatism" for her family's dinner; a gown of staggering beauty and originality for New Year's Eve; and a quietly elegant suit appropriate for her well-known New Year's Day unannounced society visits.

"That horrible girl isn't here, is she?" asked Honey, looking around. "I shall never be able to concentrate if that bumbling idiot rushes in here, knocking things over and trying to sell me Filene's Basement rejects."

A strained expression tugged at the corners of Mrs. Lubbeth's mouth and eyes, but she assured Honey that only she, Mrs. Lubbeth, was here. I saw now that there is a sort of loyalty amongst Fishman's employees, in that they can mock one another, but outsiders cannot.

I had to hand it to Lubbeth. She really did find the Easiest suits and dresses. They were the kind of garments that, had they been mixed in with regular clothes, you might pull out and scream, "My grandma has this same thing, and they want ninety dollars for it!" But assembled as they were in one uniform Easy army, they drew you in with their shocking colors and shiny fabrics and eyesore patterns.

We had no trouble finding the Christmas Day outfit (red Capri pants with velvet ballet flats and a Pucci high-necked side-wrap blouse in black, white, red, and green, very Suzy Parker circa 1953). An evening with the Cardinal proved a little more challenging, but we found a gold brocade jacket and matching long skirt. (Honey said, "I want to stand out at five o'clock Mass, yet I don't want the ushers to linger around me with the collection plate, if you know what I mean.") Her idea of "quiet elegance" for New Year's Day consisted of a thrifty plan to pair the gold brocade jacket with black-and-gold silk wide-legged trousers. New Year's Eve glamour came in the form of a one-sleeved orange Donatella Versace gown (torn lining, 60 percent off) studded with rhinestones. It made me think of Daddy: One sleeve, he'd say, why not one pant leg?

Honey said, "You know, Mrs. Lubbeth, I've come to adore orange. It's the new black."

That left the Easy Christmas party outfit. Mrs. Lubbeth kept insisting on a red Dior, but Honey said it wasn't fabulous enough. Usually you can talk Honey into anything, but she had developed a firm opinion on what was Easy, and wasn't budging.

She stood up. "Not a total bust," she said, as the seamstresses gathered up the outfits, making last-minute measurements and tearing hems. "But Lisa, you had better find me the perfect party outfit soon, or I will be too, too peeved."

We tallied up the cost for the day's haul—five thousand dollars.

"That's what the Versace gown alone would have cost if the lining had been intact," noted Honey. She liked to be congratulated on getting good bargains, especially if that meant other customers could not get the same treatment.

Mrs. Lubbeth smiled, and said, "What you saved today, Ms. Dietrich, I will more than make up for on the marked-up velvet ensembles in Women's Wear."

"I loved the Reagan era," sighed Honey wistfully. "See? Trickle-down economics *does* work."

As we left Women's Wear, I readied my Sobranie. I needed a smoke really bad. When we passed the throne, Santa waved at me and called out, "Ho, ho, ho, little girl! Why don't you come sit on Santa's lap?" A long line of angry young mothers gave me the evil eye. God, Santa's a *pig*.

"Oh, you must!" whispered Honey, shoving me in front of the children. "Let her through, children! It's Mrs. Claus."

Hardly. Would Mrs. Claus wear a white wool Jil Sander coatdress? I don't think so. Staring down at Santa, at his disheveled saliva-drenched fake beard, his Cryptkeeper wig, his puffy grasping mittens, I thought I detected something familiar about the dancing brown eyes.

"Hi, Santa," I said, throwing myself heavily onto his lap.

"Oof," said Santa.

"Have you been a good girl?" he asked.

"Pretty good."

"Please share your cigarette with Santa. Santa left his Chesterfields on the El," he said. I handed him the cig, and he dragged deeply. Mothers gasped. Santa usually smokes a pipe, so I don't see what the big deal is. He continued. "Ahhh, yes. Have you been nice to all the janitors you know?"

"Very nice," I said, bouncing up and down.

"Be careful, little girl," he groaned. "Santa has a full bladder."

I whispered, "I know what *you'd* like for Christmas, Santa. I made up a little limerick:

> *A young man with a mop and a bucket,*
> *saw a girl with a cig, so he took it.*
> *All he wanted for Christmas*
> *was to get down to business*
> *with the girl fond of kissing Ray Fuchet."*

Santa laughed and gave me an unwholesome squeeze as the mothers prepared to storm the throne.

"It's Fu-*shay,*" he corrected, standing and putting up the SANTA'S FEEDING THE REINDEER sign, to the outraged cries of toddlers.

"My, my," said Honey, linking an arm through Ray's, "you're quite a sexy Santa." She took off her fur coat and handed it to me, saying it was too hot and would I mind carrying it. I trailed behind them as Ray looked sheepishly over his shoulder at me. Honey removed Santa's hair and beard and tossed them on top of the coat, while children gasped and pointed at Santa unmasked.

"Darling Santa, I have to buy my cousin a tie," she purred. "Would you mind coming to Men's Wear with me so we can try some?" We all got on the escalator, even though Honey told me I could go wait in the car.

Men's Wear was rather empty. Where Reagan prompted people to buy, buy, buy, Clinton made shoppers want to browse without making any decisions. Although Hui's cigar stand was enjoying some brisk sales.

While Hui would have liked to ignore Ray and me, he had no choice but to fawn over Honey Dietrich. He showed her the most expensive collection, and she lovingly tied each one around Santa's fun-fur collar.

"Now, none of that Regis matchy-matchy stuff," she said, banishing the solid colored ties in rich hues. "I want Easy!"

"Easy, yes," murmured Hui, faking it. I whispered to him what Easy meant, and he gave me a slightly grateful look. After all, it *was* the season for kindness.

Finally Honey selected one. She told the men she hoped they would both come to her holiday party, then she turned to me and barked orders about invitations.

Hui gave an eel's smile and said, "Perhaps Santa will come in something less motheaten."

Ray said, "Maybe you can show me a suit, Hui. You don't look too busy up here."

Hui lost his composure. "It's this Clinton theme! Nobody is inspired by Bubba's hillbilly track suits. They should have given Clinton to somebody else. At least Jesus in Sporting Goods could have used the theme to sell hideous gray sweatpants."

Trying to be helpful, I said, "Why don't you dress up as someone hip from his administration? In Nancy garb, Mrs. Consolo is doing wonders for Galliano."

Hui looked around at the empty department and said, "Nobody would see me, it's dead up here! Anyway, who am I supposed to dress up as?"

"Vince Foster?" cracked Ray Fuchet.

Chapter 19

*L*eft Honey's at five o'clock and called Luke on my cell. Per Tim's advice, I invited him over for a home-cooked meal and cocktails that night.

"Tonight is the night, Lisa," Tim had said. "Say good-bye to horny and desperate saleslady, and hello to bed-friend of Ebert's personal assistant."

"It doesn't sound very romantic put like that," I objected. "I . . . I *like* him, too. I think it's just foreign films that I don't like."

"Yeah, sure, whatever," replied Tim. "Just make sure you strip those nursing-home cast-offs from your bed, all right?"

On the way home, I returned to Fishman's to pick up new sheets for my bed, and it about killed me to pay non-January white-sale prices. Got a set of spare, white Ralph Lauren sheets in 100 percent cotton. Other sheets were cheaper, but did not display that *RL* logo prominently on the top sheet, which was so key.

Looking around for a clerk to ring me up for the sheets, I had spied in the corner, surrounded by piles of irregular bedding, Doris Mingle. She was folding blankets by herself. I thought Lubbeth gave her the afternoon off. When the clerk finally showed up at the register, I pointed at Doris and asked what she was doing up here on the fifth floor.

The clerk scrutinized me for a second, then said, "Oh yeah, you work in Women's Wear, right?" I quickly corrected her; I *used* to work in Women's Wear.

She said, "It's just for today. I heard some customer didn't want Doris to help her, so Mrs. Lubbeth tried to give her the day off. But

Doris said she didn't have anything else to do and could she please stay at work. Can you even believe that? So Mrs. Lubbeth sent her to us, but of course nobody here wanted to work with her, either, so we messed up a load of folded blankets and pashmina throws and made her refold them. Isn't that *so sad*?" The clerk relayed this with a certain amount of relish.

"It *is* sad," I agreed. I picked up my shopping bag and turned to the elevators. A few moments after I pressed the Down button, a bell chimed and the elevator doors slid open. Doris picked up her head and started to wave to me. I ducked inside the elevator, pretending I didn't see her, but at the last second I changed my mind and waved back. It was too late, though; the doors had already closed.

At home, in spite of my having purchased no new furniture, my apartment had begun to acquire the not-lived-in look. Without all the framed photographs and other junk crowding the living room, it actually resembled a corporate lobby. I was glad I had not redone everything in chocolate, as I had originally wanted. The brown palette would have provided an inviting warmth I wanted to avoid. I removed the extra pillows from the tuxedo sofa and cleared everything off the old stainless-steel coffee table, except for an empty black vase. It was such a brilliant idea to throw out the houseplants I'd tried to keep alive on my windowsill and just keep the pots, after spraying them with white paint. They were clustered in a regimented little row at the end, voided of life.

The room that really needed to look good was, of course, the bedroom. With crisp new white sheets, the bed looked so tempting. The top of the large black lacquered box I kept by the bedside was cleared off, too, ready to hold Luke's watch and wallet while we frolicked under the Ralph Lauren logo.

I had promised him a home-cooked meal, but the only meals I knew how to prepare well were heavy, messy Italian dishes. Nobody wants to get down while reeking of garlic and onions and sausage. I ordered in some sushi, and the guy from Pacific Café acted like he had never heard of someone requesting only black and white sushi. Was I the only person who color-coordinated dinner with home furnishings?

After a quick shower, I dressed in silvery lingerie (way uncomfortable, but not as uncomfortable as body-slimming underwear), a silver pajama set that was very stark, very work camp with opulent overtones, and high-heeled black-and-silver mules. The makeup bit was difficult because on the one hand, I didn't want to get it on the new pillowcases and end up looking all used and passed around like Marilyn after a Kennedy romp, nor was I a healthy outdoorsy type who could go around barefaced. I decided on lots of waterproof black mascara and pinky-silvery lips sealed with a kind of nonsmearable glaze. The hair, as usual, was a problem. Without a perm my hair still had some natural curls, but they were mad and unbridled, not cute and feminine. I tried to straighten them with a crimping iron, but they stood out from my scalp in dry stiff peaks, like overbeaten meringue.

Luke arrived just minutes after the sushi. At least I had time to arrange it on several square plates on the coffee table as though I had prepared the meal myself. He plopped down on the sofa and cried out. Evidently, he'd been expecting cushions.

"Before I forget," I said, "I wanted to invite you to the Easy Hour." I explained about Wysocki's Tavern and told him they were having a "hush-hush celebrity benefit" there on Sunday.

"That sounds fun," he agreed. "Count me in."

"Think you could pass the word around to your boss and the rest of the *Sun-Times* office?" I asked. My voice sounded sickeningly cloying even to me. But he said he'd do it. His eyes traveled to the sashimi and nigiri that I was passing off as handcrafted creations.

"Mmm, homemade sushi and martinis," I said, digging in.

"Homemade?" asked Luke. "Then who was that Asian guy I saw coming out of the building just now complaining about lousy tips?"

I swallowed a hunk of mahi mahi and asked Luke if he'd ever seen a silver lamé g-string up close. He swallowed the martini olive, toothpick and all, and shook his head.

"Maybe you will," I said, pouring us more drinks.

The silver shaker of martinis looked so nice on my bedside lacquered box, in between the glasses. Luke had not bothered to remove his watch, possibly to time himself against past performances. As for myself, I couldn't wait to throw off the silver thong. I'll never get used to wearing it; having inherited Ma's bubble butt, I've spent a lifetime trying to get my underwear *out* of there.

Lying quietly in the brand-new sheets, waiting for Luke to amass the Trojan army, I looked around my room. My walls had clean rectangles where I'd taken down the black-and-white photos of the Art Institute, the Medinah Temple, the Lincoln Park Zoo in springtime, the lakefront in Boystown, the Fishman's Christmas window display. The pharmacist's cabinet in my bedroom had a fine coat of dust on top, where I used to keep favorite birthday cards from Gina and Chip and Mrs. Lubbeth. Stuffed animals, made by Daddy from fabric scraps each year of my childhood, used to sit on an old wooden rocking chair in the corner. Now they were banished, along with the chair, to the storage room in the basement. Nothing was there. Nothing of *me* was there anymore. Everything was perfect and lean and secreted in my home. I turned off the light and ran my fingers along the raised *RL* embroidery. Luke rolled over and there we were, personal assistant to personal assistant. The Trojans advanced and prepared to sack Greece. *It's war out there,* I thought, *and I'm about to bite the bullet.*

He reached for me and my hand flew, of its own volition, up to his shoulder and pushed him back. What was my hand doing? I had ordered no such movement.

"What's wrong?" he asked.

"I have no idea," I answered. I willed my hand to relax, but it held on. They say men are ruled by the desires of their loins. Women are guided by their hearts. Smart people of either sex are guided by their heads. As a South Sider, the descendant of welter-weight boxers, meatpackers, butchers, tailors, carpenters, it is only fitting that I am ruled by my hands.

"Are you sure you want me here?" he asked. He had kind eyes up close, which disconcerted me. *He* wanted to be here, and I have to admit I was seduced by that. I wanted the freedom of a wild adventure, to stop feeling like a big loser, to have a night of feeling not-lonely, not-unlovable in my cold, empty apartment. I wanted someone cute who would snuggle under the Ralph Lauren sheets and introduce me to Roger Ebert. I wanted to free myself from celibacy without shackling myself to heavy emotions, the kind that wreak havoc in people's lives. These had been my goals for a long time. They would make me happy. A vision of Ray's maddening boxlike head rose before me, accompanied by a sickening churning in my stomach, signaling to me that this Ray person might indeed wreak havoc in my life, and furthermore, could be damaged by me. I was sick of havoc; wreaking it, having it wrought upon me. I just wanted some lovely physical warmth without the prospect of destruction.

My hands stopped pushing him away and made up my mind for me.

"I do, Luke, I do want you here," I finally answered. And I did.

Afterward, while he slept, I lay under the covers thinking. At least I'd gotten one medicine ball, celibacy, out of the way, and now things would be better. *I* would feel better. I would feel happy. I lit a pale blue Sobranie and watched the ember glow in the dark. Decent.

Chapter 20

I managed to meet the decorators at Honey's building on time. Several Christmas trees were waiting, bound up in netting, by the elevators, and half a dozen people loaded box after box of garlands, ornaments, fake trees, and other decoration into the lobby.

I asked Jean, who was directing everyone efficiently, if I could just slip upstairs and finish my barrel of coffee before we undertook the daunting project. She smiled and said all was under control. I sighed happily and entered the elevator. It dawned on me that this must be what it was like having your own personal assistant: somebody handles things while you stand by idly with a beatific, ignorant smile.

When I walked into the Parisian hub, Honey and Esmé were seated together on the pale blue Empire love seat. Each rested her elbow on one of the massive arms ornamented with bronze lion heads. They turned their faces to me as a single unit, then Esmé dropped her hands into her lap, clasping them primly, while Honey rose to greet me.

"Lisa, I am very disappointed in you," she said.

"What did I do?" I asked, irrationally fastening onto the idea that she somehow knew I shagged Luke.

She held up her palm and closed her eyes, as if in pain. "Please. Don't pretend. I have the evidence." She held out the stub of a mint-green cig. She placed it in my hand, and I looked at it silently, uncomprehending.

"Darling, Esmé found it under the Hearst table. It had burnt a small hole in my antique Anatolian kilim." She took me over to the rug under the table and pointed out the tiny hole.

I sputtered, "But—but it wasn't me! I would never smoke in here. Ask the doorman, I always smoke in the lobby."

Honey said, "We *have* asked him, and he said you often take a cigarette or five from the complimentary box. Always these little pastel ones." Esmé smiled with contempt and triumph. It was no use protesting. The scrubwoman had set me up. I put the butt in the pocket of my coat, my cheeks burning in anger.

Honey cooed, "Now, darling, everyone is entitled to one mistake. Just don't do it again." Esmé pretended to dust various objets d'art, clucking her tongue loudly all the while. Honey went into her bedroom to dress for the holiday luncheon and bazaar at the Creosote Club, and when she was out of sight I stomped over to Esmé and lunged at her.

She drew back and said, "Careful. Madam abhors violence."

I growled, "I'm going to *get* you."

She smirked, and said, "*Are* you?"

I didn't have time to carry out my threat, since Jean and company entered the apartment then and Yuletide chaos ensued for the remainder of the day. I decided to make pots of hot chocolate to keep the workers' spirits up. We all need to remember the true purpose of the holiday and its meaningful diversions, like drinking cocoa, ordering workers around, and spending Honey's money.

The Parisian hub was strewn with drop cloths, trees, boxes, and many florist's helpers. It was just like Santa's workshop, except the elves were student temps from the School of the Art Institute. Honey wanted a tree in the hub, her bedroom, her office, the conservatory, the master bath, and the entertainment room, each decorated with a different theme. She requested the real trees be sprayed with pine scent, as they did not smell real enough.

Midmorning, I found a florist's helper napping under the conservatory tree, a trail of vinegary drool forming a puddle on the terrazzo floor. I nudged him awake. He pled forgiveness and said he had been up late studying for a test he was scheduled to take this afternoon.

"Hey, I know somebody who went to the 'Tute. My brother's friend. His name is Bruce, and he lives in his parents' rec room," I said.

He said, "Art school is hard." He got up, yawned and stretched, and as he did so, a flask dropped out of his pocket.

"I'll hold this for you," I offered, swiping it. Grateful that he wasn't tattled on, he went back to work, and I sampled the flask. Yuck, it was Rumpleminze, the most disgusting spirit ever to have seen the inside of a distillery. But it was not too bad when doused with hot cocoa.

The Parisian hub looked excellent. Pink-and-orange Christmas lights on the fur-trimmed beige Christmas tree, pink-and-orange satin-poly stockings (two dozen embroidered with *Honey* in gold thread and hung from the picture rail), pink-and-orange ribbon candy in Waterford dishes, pink-and-orange roses in a massive gold bowl atop the Hearst table. It looked good with the regular hub furnishings in raspberry and light blue. It did. Really. Though I thought perhaps I ought to take the bulbs out of the floor lamps, just to keep the lighting on the subtle side, and of course close the curtains every day.

The master-bath tree glistened in blue aluminum, trimmed with antique-glass mermaid ornaments, seashells, and blue lights. The conservatory tree was live, though it looked out of place among the dead aspidistras. The office tree was red aluminum and decorated with miniature books on beekeeping. The entertainment room boasted another live tree.

Honey had said, "I want one of the trees to look traditional. Can you find heirloom-type ornaments?"

Jean had asked, "You mean the kind of ornaments people keep throughout a lifetime and always put on their trees?"

Honey asked, "People keep their ornaments from year to year?"

The bedroom tree was a visual feast, a ten-foot Fraser fir decorated in the theme of jet-set travel. Little airplanes, trains, steamships, and sports cars formed the garland, while postcards from Monte Carlo and Saint Moritz and Portofino hung from every branch. Cute bottles of Valium dangled here and there, to cope with jet lag.

Each tree was topped with a queen bee wearing a twenty-four-karat gold crown.

At lunch break, I went down to the lobby to poke through the complimentary cigarette box, but the doorman informed me he had been told by the management to stop giving away cigarettes.

"Stop giving away cigarettes!" I cried. "What is this, China?"

"I'm just following orders."

Fascists! I thought, then remembering his connection, said, "What about the duty-free Austrian?"

He said, "I think Sobranie has stopped producing cigarettes, anyway. Although they have a Balkan pipe-tobacco blend that is really quite good."

No more Sobranies. No more free cigs. I pawed through my handbag and found five dollars. I took it to the White Hen, bought a turkey sandwich from the cooler, and browsed the cigarette rack behind the cashier.

"I guess I'll take a pack of Parliament," I said. The box is an okay shade of blue.

Back in the lobby, I sat down with my lunch and prepared to eat, but the doorman said they had a no-eating policy. Off the lobby there was a public rest room. I ate there, thinking, *This really brings a person close to Christmas.*

Honey came back from the Creosote Club in a highly charged state of excitement. She had seen Sugar Rautbord at the holiday lunch and bazaar and bragged all about her Easy Christmas. Honey knew she struck a chord—a chord of envy, the best kind—when Sugar responded, "How . . . *interesting.*"

"If she was *not* consumed with envy, she would have gushed all sorts of false praise," said Honey. "The fact that she replied so boringly *proves* she is being eaten up with rage!"

I have not completely grasped the complicated rules high society has for social interaction. In Bridgeport, if something sounds stupid, we say, "What a dumb idea, jag-off." Thank God black is white and up is down north of Madison Street.

Honey cringed a bit when she saw the color combo in the hub. She said in all her life, she'd never seen blue and pink and red and orange all together in one room.

I said, "Yes, Ms. Dietrich, and I hope your party guests realize how brilliant you are to have used the same color scheme found in . . . in . . ."

The napping 'Tute elf rescued me. "In Matisse's *Apples,* which hangs, as you know, in the Art Institute of Chicago."

Honey beamed at the decor with new appreciation. I beamed at the 'Tute elf and slipped him his flask.

I finally took off at five o'clock and stood for eons at the Red Line El stop. I hated taking the train to the South Side. It was always full of guys playing three-card monte. On the platform, there was a skinny black Santa collecting for the Salvation Army. His bell was muffled with towels. I asked him why, and he said people had been complaining about the loud clanging.

I rifled through my handbag and found fifteen cents left over from paying the train fare. I felt embarrassed dropping in such chump change, but Santa said it was okay.

"Want a cigarette?" I offered the blue pack of Parliaments.

He shook his head. He said he didn't want to give the kiddies the wrong idea about Santa and smoking. With a pang, I thought of Ray Fuchet.

The train ride turned out not so bad. I won at three-card monte! The marble was under the middle cup, anybody could see.

At my exit, the Thirty-fifth Street and Sox Park station, a

Salvation Army Santa stood ringing and chiming and pealing at full volume. They don't *dare* tell the South Side Santas how to ring their bells.

I said to him, "I won five bucks in a shell game on the train," and I dropped it into his red kettle. I really won ten bucks, but Santa doesn't have to know *everything*.

Ma and Daddy were putting up the fake Christmas tree. The ornaments we kids had made in school were preserved with a thick, lacquered coat of space-age polymer, threatening to outlast each Galisa. Peggy Lee Christmas songs (Easy) played on the radio.

It was "Hors D'oeuvre Night." The Friday evening each year spent decorating the tree was always Hors D'oeuvre Night: little pigs in blankets, water chestnuts wrapped in bacon and brown sugar, rye toasts with olive cheese spread, fondue (three varieties: cheese, creamy spinach, chocolate), tiny reubens. I helped myself and hung tinsel, half-assed.

Ma said, "Maybe *you* can get your sister out of her room. She's been yakking on the phone all day."

"All day?" I asked. "What about work?"

"Don't even talk to me about that. She saved up vacation time and is taking the next two weeks off to work on her new career, except she won't tell me what it is. Is it phone sales? It's not phone *sex*, is it? I'll kill her."

I said, "She's a pet psychic, and she conducts telepathic readings over the phone."

I loved the look on their faces at that moment, round red mouths and eyebrows shot heavenward.

Gina's door was closed, but I barged in anyway. She sat at her painted desk from childhood, the one with Winnie-the-Pooh stickers all over it, cell phone in one hand. She turned to me and held a finger against her lips.

She said, "Yes, I sense that Millie is a very difficult cat. She bites everyone, doesn't she? Yes, she wants you all to herself. When you picked her out at the shelter, it was really *she* who picked *you* out. But she likes your new apartment with the windows all around."

This went on for some time, though eventually Millie had had enough, and the customer hung up.

I said, "I'm sure you'll be getting your check shortly."

Gina said, "Yeah, the way I'm doing it, starting next week, is they have to send me a check or money order in advance of the call, then they'll wait a few days before calling and if I've received the check, I'll do the reading."

"Oh," I said.

She said, "Don't worry. It's all spelled out on my website."

Her phone rang, so I went into the basement. Chip and Bruce were in the midst of a grueling chess match on their computers, which were situated across from one another on a partners desk. They played their game like it was Battleship.

I watched them for a moment, then said, "The scanner's on fire."

They both looked at the scanner, which had little flames licking out from beneath its cover.

"You get it, Chip," said Bruce.

Chip retorted, "It's *your* turn to put it out."

Evidently, the scanner was not top quality and ignited regularly, causing arguments about its maintenance at the *Prole* office.

I asked Chip if it was true they had designed and set up a website for Gina. Chip said it was really Bruce's work.

"Check," said Bruce.

"Ah! The queen's sacrifice," said Chip. "I fell for it again." I grabbed my brother by his rounded shoulders and shook him, berating him with my favorite insult until he turned from the game.

Chip smoothed his sweatshirt and said with dignity, "Please do not call me 'chess fag.' I'll pull up the site, just calm yourself."

Well, he showed me the website. It was not bad. Just an intro-
duction to Gina, plus a satisfaction guarantee and the phone and
payment information. Again, she used the picture of her leaning
against our old dog. Chip said in addition to the fliers she put up in
Bridgeport, she distributed fliers at about twenty pet stores in
Chicago and bought print advertisements in *Dog Fancy* and other
pet trade journals.

I said, "There's no future in this."

He scoffed. "There was no future at McDonald's for her."

"She could have become assistant manager! She could have
gone to Hamburger University."

"Jesus, you sound like Ma."

Stunned, I whined, "That's a *horrible* thing to say to somebody."

I went back upstairs, prepared to fortify myself with fondue.
Ma had the three pots bubbling on warming plates on the dining-
room buffet. Thirty fondue forks were spread out on the dining-
room table (vinyl tablecloth replaced with white crocheted cloth).
Some had handles shaped like reindeer; others had handles topped
with the heads of famous sports legends; yet others had simple
Bakelite handles in red and green. What would happen if you
dipped a tiny reuben in the cheese fondue? I grabbed Lou Gehrig
and speared a sandwich.

Ma wobbled on a ladder in front of the Christmas tree and
asked me to steady her as she placed the star on top. "How's that
Ray fella?" she asked.

"I don't know; fine, I guess," I replied.

"What do you mean you don't know?"

"I mean I don't know! God, Ma, leave it alone."

"Well, what's the matter with you? He's a real catch."

More churning, stabbing awfulness in my stomach. I was still
waiting for a wave of happiness to wash away the growing unease I
felt about what happened the previous night with Luke. All day I
tried to keep that Ebert goal in mind, but it was crowded by feelings for Ray that had actually seemed to grow rather than diminish.

I didn't want to like Ray this much—so much in fact that he would disrupt all the goals I'd set for myself. It made me resent him, rather, like how I resented Doris for being nice to me when all I wanted was to be left alone.

"Maybe I don't like him that much. Maybe I like someone else."

"Who? Who do you like?"

"Maybe I like"—I was going to say Luke Sheehy, but somehow it came out—"Roger Ebert."

"Roger Ebert?" screeched Ma. Dishes rattled in the china cabinet.

"Roger Ebert?" wondered Daddy.

"Oh, please, Daddy, don't tell me he's on your list. For Christ's sake, he's not a TV star."

Ma climbed down from the ladder and slapped the back of my head. "Nice mouth at Christmastime. Now about Ray—"

I groaned. "Forget it, *please,* would you? I don't want to talk about it."

She said firmly, "I like Ray. I don't even *know* this Ebert."

"Well, Ma, maybe I don't want to be stuck with a junior *janitor,* okay? Maybe I want something more: an exciting film critic who throws wonderful Fourth-of-July parties and is a divine dancer and all that."

Daddy scowled. "I don't think that was very nice, what you said." It was the closest he'd ever come to yelling.

"I'm sorry, I don't know what I'm saying," I replied, rubbing my temples. "I don't know anything. Can we please just drop it?"

Ma rolled her eyes, turning away from me. She shrieked for everyone to come in and view the Christmas tree while she turned off the living-room lights. Chip and Bruce came up from the basement, reeking of pot, and a moment later Gina came out of the bedroom, her cell phone tucked neatly into the chest pocket of her overalls. From the radio, Frank Sinatra crooned a "hep" version of "Jingle Bells."

"Isn't it great?" sighed Daddy.

The boys headed for the hors d'oeuvres while Gina held our parents' hands and gazed at the tree. I sat by myself on the floral sofa. I thought, *I should get up and hold their hands, too.* Instead, I picked wool pills off the elbows of my sweater.

Ma looked at my sister and asked, "What's a pet psychic?"

Gina turned to me with a strange expression. Extreme interest, which transformed itself into comprehension, then a hardness that had never visited her features before. She said she had planned to tell them after she had made a little progress, at least that was what she hoped would have happened. I stuck the wool pills between the cushions of the couch.

"I didn't like being a fry cook," she said simply. "I like animals."

Daddy said, "I guess now's the time, Gina, being in your twenties, to try new things. Can it be a career?"

My sister explained her plans, showed them her fliers and the website on Chip's computer. I looked through the liquor cabinet with Chip. There wasn't much, and what was there, was old. He poured us each a glass of Harveys Bristol Cream.

"That was kind of rotten," he observed.

"Oh, shut up," I said. He didn't know the half of how rotten I could really be.

"You promised her you wouldn't tell them."

Bruce came in then and poured himself a little Harveys. I raised my glass and said, "To the happy couple."

Bruce looked around dumbly while Chip regarded me with suspicion.

"Come on, Chipster," I said, elbowing him all-lads-together-style, "I *know.* We can talk about it, we're all pals here."

Chip asked his friend to go check on the scanner. When Bruce went downstairs, Chip said to me, "What the hell is wrong with you today? *What* do you know?"

I had a bit more Harveys—it wasn't bad at all. "That, uh . . . you sit on the other side of the stadium. That Bruce is your longtime companion."

"Huh," he said. "You've never taken an interest in my life before, or anyone else's for that matter. Suddenly, you're blabbing about Gina's pet-psychic network and threatening to out me to Ma and Daddy."

I said, "I *am* interested in people's lives! And I don't care that you're gay. My best friend is gay."

"Ha! Your best friend. I've never seen such an antagonistic, flimsy, one-dimensional excuse for friendship in my life. Tim's *exactly* the type of person *you* would have for a best friend, someone as catty and shallow as yourself."

I stared at the boomerangs on the kitchen table and said nothing.

He continued. "And Bruce is my lifelong pal, but not my lover. I guess I have to tell you that, before you out the wrong guy."

Still I said nothing. I had become so awful that I had begun to frighten myself. It was like I had been rotting inside since last night and now it was oozing out of me.

Chip said, "Oh, is the clam closing again? Nothing new there."

Bruce came in and remarked, "Did someone say clams?" He went into the dining room and rummaged around the table, looking for seafood.

I got my coat out of the closet. The rest of the Galisas came upstairs. Gina watched me with an unhappy expression, her arms folded across her overalls bib.

Ma said, "Psychic communication might be possible, Sal. Gina says we only use one-tenth of our brains."

"That's rubbish," said Daddy, switching on the television.

I walked toward Thirty-first Street. Snow fell. I made an inventory of all that had taken place during the previous twenty-four hours: I'd had sex with a man for reasons I couldn't seem to fathom at present, lied to my employer, threatened a scrubwoman, upset my sister, infuriated my brother, smoked a pack of lousy cigarettes, and clogged my arteries with enough cheese and grease to fell a man twice my size. In the distance, Christmas lights blinked around the tavern windows. A neon pink OPEN sign was the most welcome I would find anywhere tonight.

"Hi, Lisa!" called Fred. I pushed my way through a crowd of hipsters. Fred had advertised Wysocki's in the *Chicago Reader;* the first time anyone in his family had advertised the bar. The Dragon Lady stood with her son, grinning happily at the new customers, the growing revenues. The plumbers and stevedores sat in a sour little heap at the end of the bar, surveying the modern scene and its younger set. It wasn't even Sunday, Fred's Easy Hour, and the bar was still packed with people.

Fred asked what I wanted to drink. I said Harveys Bristol Cream. He smiled approvingly: Harveys was *very* Easy.

"Guess what?" he said. "In two weeks it's my mom's turn to withdraw the Geh Club funds, so I suggested she take the money and finally go on that trip to Korea she's been moaning about for the last decade. She said, 'Hah! You think about vacations all the time! I'd rather stay here and come to your Easy Hour.' My *mom*! The *Dragon Lady* loves Fred's Easy Hour. Lisa, I think this might be a success."

"You haven't seen anything yet—Roger Ebert and Honey Dietrich are coming to the Easy Hour on Sunday," I said. "And maybe I can get Babbington Hawkes from *Chicago Society* to come and cover it for his paper."

Fred Wysocki looked so happy, I smiled in spite of myself. It was assuring to see a good friend enjoy success and achieve set goals. Perhaps, in some small way, I'd even helped Fred. It made my heart glad within its shell of crackling yellow fat.

"Is everything okay?" he asked. "You seem a little down."

"Fred, I think I've made a big mistake," I said in a small voice. It was an alien, miserable sound. Concerned, he reached over the bar and took my hand.

My cell phone rang. I took it out and looked at the display, saw Ray's number appear. My throat began to ache, and I put the phone back in my purse. Instead of feeling free and adventurous after sleeping with Luke, I felt wretched and guilty and lonely.

"What mistake?" asked Fred.

But I couldn't say anything more, even to Fred, my oldest friend. The shame I felt for showering him with vomit didn't even *compare* to what I was feeling right then. What had I done? Everyone hated me. I ordered more Harveys. A nearby plumber said, "That sounds good," and ordered one for himself. He didn't chat me up, thank God, just stared at his reflection in the mirror behind the bar. I did the same until eleven-thirty. Bridgeport was getting Easy, but underneath it was still a strange, cold town.

Chapter 21

I met Tim Gideon at the Bongo Room for breakfast. He was seated up front at a table, already nibbling on fruit and drinking a smoothie. We were surrounded by really good-looking gay men and half-slacks: people with neo-nerd glasses and disarranged hair and ironic T-shirts who work in offices during the week.

"Late," Tim tsk-tsked, "but decent Burberry trousers. Are your saddlebags smaller?"

I pinched them. "No, I don't think so. Do they look smaller?"

He shrugged. I usually shied away from prints, as my saddlebags stretched conservative plaid into wavy Peter Max murals, but Burberry fit well and everyone recognized it.

"Eggs Florentine," I ordered.

"Ugh," said Tim, "do you know how much cholesterol is in that?"

I looked at the waitron. "Can I have some extra hollandaise in a cup?"

Tim said, "Don't look now, but behind you is Elmar, the 'zine mogul."

I said, "There are 'zine moguls?" The guy behind me was dressed in typical Easy garb and shouted into two cell phones. Several yellow legal pads were spread out on his table in front of a few dull half-slacks and stripper-looking girls.

"How's Chip's 'zine coming along?" asked Tim. "Maybe he could get some pointers from the mogul."

I felt a sudden pain in my stomach at the mention of my brother. *Oh Chip, why did I berate you in front of your loser 'zine buddy and call you a chess fag?*

But I said, "It's good, I guess. They're doing an article on the Rainbow Man; you know, that guy who always showed up at sporting events in the seventies with a rainbow wig and a John 3:16 sign? They're also exposing corruption in Chicago government at the alderman level."

"No shortage of material there." Tim reached into his ever-present briefcase and pulled out the new *Chicago Society*. "For you, sweetums."

EASY CHRISTMAS
—SWEET AS HONEY

By Babbington Hawkes

Friends, you know how much I adore Christmas . . . the gifts, the figgy pudding, the excitable elves. I thought a Victorian Christmas, with its filigree ornaments and candlelit trees, couldn't possibly be improved upon. I was *wrong*. I have just returned from a midnight supper with gal-about-town and everybody's idol, Honey Dietrich. Her normally tony apartment has been transformed into a 1960s den of swinging luxury and jet-set decadence. At first, dear ones, I must admit I thought, *What is with all this maddening double-knit?*

Then Honey explained, "It's Easy, darling. You probably never saw the interior of the *Christina*, Aristotle Onassis's yacht, but it was all Easy, and now Easy has made its way from Skorpios to Milan to Sweden—which is the Easiest country by far— to Tunisia to Chicago. Picture yourself romping with Princess Stephanie on the Concorde; having drinks with Bunny Mellon in Palm Beach; taking in a Herb Alpert show at the Mirage and then flying into Augusta to watch the final round of the Masters. Imagine life as you knew it should be: plenty of Dom flowing and Bar Harbor and

Mary Quant and Wimbledon and après-ski parties at Vail."

Then I got it. "Easy" is just what dreary old Chicago needs, and I, Babbington Hawkes, am *having it*.

When asked who first inspired her to Easy Christmas, Honey simply batted her famous eyelashes and uncorked a magnum of Taitinger. *Very* nice. See you at the Easy Hour. (Don't you know where it is? Uncle Babbington will help you out— just this *once:* Wysocki's Tavern in Bridgeport on Sunday night.) *Everyone* will be there.

"Tunisia? Algiers is much more Easy," I grumbled.

"Algiers?" scoffed Tim. "Big deal. France with Arabs."

"Anyway, *I'm* the inspiration for her Easy Christmas," I said. "I want to see *my* name in *Chicago Society*. Would it have killed her just to credit me?"

Tim said, "Leese, you can't very well cite a *personal assistant* as inspiration. It'll destroy the imagery. Would *you* want to follow a trend started by a servant?"

I argued, "Hey, old sock, Mrs. Lubbeth always gave me credit."

He patted my hand. "But you were all just a bunch of . . . *shop* clerks. You're in high society now, old trout."

Some eggy substance got caught in my throat. The waitron brought me a doggy bag for the hollandaise.

We left together; Tim on his way to Vietnamese lessons, I to shop for paper for the party invitations (Honey wanted homemade personal invitations, but she was inviting over a hundred people).

We walked toward the Blue Line station at Damen. I asked how Kabuki Tart was.

"All right. But he's getting on my nerves, talking about his father all the time."

I said, "But the man was murdered by a tart-shop employee. Of course Kabuki is going to dwell on it."

He sighed irritably. "Aren't *you* all bleeding-heart these days."

We paid our fares and waited up top in the freezing cold. My cell rang—it was Ray again.

"Aren't you going to answer?" asked Tim.

"Too cold," I said. Coward.

"So whatever happened with Licorice Whip? Did you get down?"

I nodded and tried to smile. It felt crooked and sour.

"Excellent!" he exclaimed. "Was it fabulous?"

"It was something," I said. "I guess now I can count on meeting Ebert at the Easy Hour Sunday." But there was no thrill in my words.

"Ebert," said Tim. "Man, you could have the whole city at your disposal if you snagged Ebes."

The train came and we boarded. Someone had left a *Sun-Times* on the seat across from me. I picked it up and read the front page headline: Teachers' Strike Resolved—Back to School Monday.

I looked sideways at Tim. "I miss Ray."

He stared at me, then at the paper headline. "Oh, the janitor/scientist! Young Ari. Well, I think you've got a good prospect in Luke. I wouldn't mess it up, if I were you." He rose at the downtown Chicago Avenue subway stop to transfer to the northbound Red Line. "Janitor or grade-school science teacher?" he mused. "Which is more awful?"

I watched him walk down the aisle, away from me. He wore one of those dark gray wool car coats that men look so good in, blue jeans, and a light gray J. Crew sweater. The eggs Florentine did not sit well in my stomach, but my hangover at least had vanished, apart from a vague paranoia that had insinuated itself in me. The clear head, combined perhaps with cold air and clarified butter, had raised great disturbing clouds of doubt around me. Worse was the feeling that I had wound a broad chain of errors in my past that could not be untangled. Tim exited the train and walked down the platform, grinning as he passed my window.

Chapter 22

Honey wanted me to make invitations in the color scheme of her Christmas decorations. She wanted something fibrous and all-cotton from Crane's Fine Papers, but all that I could find in her colors were the pink and orange samples from the "Neon Bright" collection at Kinko's. I called her from the Water Tower and convinced her to go with honey-toned Crane's cards, which could be printed with pink or orange ink.

"Printed?" she asked. "I wanted them handwritten, you know, with a little winter scene drawn on the front."

I made a face that approximated the agony of a person just stabbed in the neck with a pencil. "Ms. Dietrich, Easy embraces artifice and technology. Easy would never handwrite something when an expensive printing press is at hand. Easy avoids amateurish, hokey—"

"Yes, you're right," she interrupted. "Printing is much better. Now, Lisa, Saturday is my day of meditation, spa work, and magazine reading. Please don't bother me anymore." And she hung up.

She had given me $125 to get the invitations, but Crane's said they would need at least ten days to engrave them. Damn, I had to get them in the mail tonight, or Monday morning at the latest. Who had a printer? Oh, *crap*.

I paused with the phone in my hand, took a breath, and dialed the number. "Hi, Chip, it's me. I need your help." I explained the situation.

My brother promptly forgot our fight yesterday and said I could come over and he'd help me use his computer and printer.

How confusing it all was: without alcohol or hangover, Bridgeport brought out familial warmth. Yet the only way one could tolerate it was while blotto. Could blood be thicker than Harveys Bristol Cream?

He said, "I warn you, it's a little crazy in the basement just now. *Prole* is in production, and we're entering the chess-club finals as we speak."

Ma, Daddy, and Gina stood outside, preparing to decorate for Christmas and erect the rooftop Santa. I'd passed the Wysockis' house and saw the Dragon Lady and her husband clinging to the gutters, stringing lights. They called for assistance, but I hurried by, anxious to finish my invitation project. They had just a short drop to the ground, with plenty of soft arborvitae to cushion the fall.

At our house, Santa had one leg in the chimney while Daddy manhandled him at Ma's direction.

"Shove him in further!" she screamed. "No, back out a little now; he looks like he has a peg-leg." Gina watched me walk up the driveway. She had been untangling about five hundred feet of colored bulbs while wearing fuzzy brown mittens.

I kneeled down and helped her straighten out the cords. I told her that Tim said once he moved his cat's litter box like she suggested, it stopped peeing on his clothes.

"Cool," she said.

I did not like asking for help or prostrating myself in apology, but I needed to do something to expel the gremlin who was kicking all the people in my life to the curb. I said, "Sorry I told the nut jobs about your pet-psychic business, Gina. Wish I hadn't."

She said, "It turned out okay. Anyway, I understand that you're unhappy and you need to lash out at everyone around you. Many people sabotage their own happiness because subconsciously they feel they deserve misery."

I said, "I hate when you watch Oprah."

We moved over to the crèche, a relic from the fifties with a Scandinavian-looking holy family. Daddy always liked to set up a line of chasing colored lights around the stable. He said we mustn't forget the true meaning of Christmas. We keep Baby Jesus in the junk drawer until Christmas Eve, then right before the bonfire, Daddy carries it out to the crèche and places it in the manger. One Christmas many years ago, our dog took Baby Jesus out of the stable and worried him like an old rag doll. Baby Jesus has a big dent in his forehead now, like a lobotomy scar.

I went inside and followed the wailing complaint of Tears for Fears down to the basement. Chip waved to me, holding the phone to his ear. He had recruited a few more people to work on *Prole* and also to round out the chess championship. In fact, there, in the midst of the chess competition, sat Fred Wysocki.

"Hey!" I exclaimed.

He smiled sheepishly and said he was always up for a game. The boys looked at me with annoyance for having interrupted the tournament.

"Care to make it interesting?" asked Bruce, holding out an old Chicago-cop riot-gear helmet full of cash.

"Sure," I replied, stuffing in five bucks. "My money's on the Asian."

Fred issued his disclaimer: "Hey, you know I'm only half Asian."

I considered Fred's opponent, a pointy and bespectacled boy resembling the Mel Cooley–looking elf on *Rudolph the Red-Nosed Reindeer,* but kept my bet on Fred.

"Guess what!" shouted Chip excitedly, hanging up the phone. "I've just been notified that we've been given official Illinois Chess Association club status!"

A massive cheer went up around the basement. Chess fags attempted to high-five one another, but missed.

. . .

The invitations looked fabulous. We used hot-pink ink on the cards, and Chip found excellent clip-art drawings of people getting smashed around a Christmas tree.

"I'm sorry I was mean last night," I said. "I am unhappy and need to lash out at those around me."

"'Sokay," he said. "Just keep your big fat mouth shut."

"Aren't you gonna tell Ma and Daddy?" I wondered.

He looked down at the cards and put sharp creases in the quarter-folds. Then he said he had to go downstairs and get back to work.

"We go to the printer on Monday," he said, "and I still have to pick up ad money. Plus that society mag wants to do a short piece on *Prole,* and I have to be back in time when the guy calls. Babbington Something."

Midlick, I sliced my tongue on the razor-sharp edge of an envelope. "How did he hear of *you?*"

Chip replied, "Oh, I sent out press releases for a benefit we're hosting at Wysocki's next month, and the guy called me right away, all excited for an interview. He said anything connected to Wysocki's Tavern was 'extremely now.'"

A sort of mad burning sensation took hold of my stomach.

Ma walked in then, looked at me, and said, "You've been into the sausage and peppers again, haven't you?"

I spent the rest of the afternoon addressing the one hundred invitations. It was a drag to find out that Honey had supplied me with only the *Sun-Times* address for Ebert. But I wrote his name very slowly, lovingly, on the envelope, sealing it with a kiss. When I finished, I sat in the living room with Daddy and snacked on salami and cheese and Chianti.

He said, "I wish you still lived here. It's hard on a family when everyone moves out."

I said, "I'm the only one who's moved out."

He looked down into his wineglass. "But it seems so empty here these days."

I came over and put my arms around him. His toupee slipped a little, but he didn't notice. My cell phone rang and he let go of me.

"That's okay," I said, making no move toward the phone.

"Answer it," said Daddy.

I said, "I can't."

We watched *Jeopardy!* for a while, both of us getting a lot of the answers right. It was the children's championship.

"What is an earwig?" I shouted. Alex Trebek shook his smug face sorrowfully.

Daddy growled at the TV, "You've just moved up to number ten, buster," and made adjustments in his small notebook beside the Barcalounger.

By the time I got back home, it was almost ten o'clock, and I'd had three messages on my cell and one on my home phone from Ray. I picked up the phone, then put it down again. I couldn't do it. The shame would come pouring out of me and engulf him.

Ray understood Easy. I had to admit he was right when he suggested that those of us in the Easy scene really viewed the future as irrelevant. Although I argued, claiming to be a forward-moving risk-taker, the truth was all along I *had* treated the future as irrelevant: living for the moment, ignoring the consequences of my actions, and fearing what lay ahead. I sucked, I was a sucky pessimist stuck in the present. I wanted to ride that Easy rocket to the future, but I had messed up whatever future I had with Ray.

I undressed and lay on my bed, staring up at nothing. With the lamp off and the shades drawn, not a speck of light made its way into my room. I could have been anywhere . . . maybe a suite of rooms at the Ritz with Maria Callas, maybe a lonely beach house on Nantucket, maybe in my lux stateroom aboard the *Christina*. I lifted back the shade on my window and looked up at the stars. I recognized Ursa Minor and the Big Dipper. They say that Aristotle Onassis refused to fit the *Christina*'s porthole windows with shades so that his guests would have no choice but to gaze up at the stars from their beds.

My phone rang. The familiar heaviness of resignation settled upon my chest, and I finally decided to answer.

"Lisa!" exclaimed Ray Fuchet. "I've been trying to get a hold of you forever."

"Sorry," I said, explaining about work and such.

"I wanted to tell you that I was going back to teaching on Monday. The strike is over. No more sick sand for me."

"That's great, Ray, I'm so happy for you. You deserve the best. I wish I . . ."

Silence descended as my voice trailed off in guilt. I ran my fingertips over the *RL* embroidery on the top sheet.

Then Ray said, "Lisa, tell me what's wrong. *Something* is. You don't sound like yourself at all." *Oho, that's the worst part,* I thought. *This selfish dullard is the real me.*

I said, "You know what? My stomach hurts. It's like a giant medicine ball has been thrust upon me and I've just been dying to get it out."

In the same breath, I told the truth and a lie, a feat that had gotten easier over time.

Chapter 23

oney's driver waited in the Mercedes. I had to help Honey put her evening outfit together, and we were going to be late. Earlier she had decided she wanted a white mink stole "on loan" from the Fishman furrier, but I'd had no luck. Even Mr. Fishman had his limits.

"White mink is kind of old-fashioned, don't you think?" I said. "So Doris Day. Of course, if that's what you want, Ms. Dietrich, I shall be only too happy to go back to Fishman's, but this feather boa just screams Easy." The feather boa also had its home under my bed for the last two years and was eager to get out in the world again. Brilliantly, I'd spray-painted it with yellow-and-black stripes, knowing Honey would adore the attention the striking bee motif would bring her.

Honey regarded herself doubtfully in the mirror. "Yes, I suppose. I certainly don't want to look stuffy and old-fashioned at Wysocki's tonight. What do you think, Esmé?"

Esmé, caught between wanting to fawn over madam and hating to approve of anything I had suggested, pursed her lemon lips and simply nodded. The doorman buzzed up then, saying Mr. Hawkes awaited us down in the lobby.

"Babbington Hawkes is coming with us?" I asked. As the personal assistant, there was a scandalous amount of information to which I was not privy. I had been rather hoping that Babbington would just glimpse my style from afar and write about it in *Chicago Society*. I faced certain doom if forced to come in close contact with him.

Honey ordered Esmé and me into our coats. Why was the scrubwoman coming with us? And what kind of socialite drags her servant out to cocktail hour? I whispered to Honey that maybe Esmé would feel more comfortable at home with her own kind.

Honey said, "Look, darling. I am taking a chance with this new Easy culture; the other ladies in my social set have not caught on to it yet, and I need an entourage to support me *out there*." She made a sweeping gesture with her arm, indicating the frightening world out there of unsanctioned, untried new trends.

Babbington wore a winter suit in cream wool with a navy shirt and a gold ascot. It gave him a jaunty, nautical air. His silvery hair was slicked back and, in the time since I had last seen him, he had grown and maintained one of those horrible little Clifton Webb mustaches. He kissed Honey on both cheeks and gave me a slippery snake's smile. We strode toward the car while Honey breezily reminded Babbington who I was.

"You remember my little personal assistant, Lisa, don't you?" she said.

Babbington said, "How could I forget? Opaa!"

At least there was no mention made of the scrubwoman. I guessed it was better to be acknowledged and mocked than to be completely ignored. Plus they made Esmé sit in the front with the driver, a sure sign of her lower status on the servant scale.

Honey and Babbington chattered about whether to spend Easter in Palm Beach or at Oprah's multimillion-dollar rustic cabin. I looked out the window at the cars speeding by us on the Kennedy, praying that the usual Wysocki laborer crowd would be invisible to Honey. I wanted a cig pretty bad, but dared not light a Parliament.

Babbington, it appeared, had acquired a new affectation. He withdrew from his overcoat pocket a Meerschaum pipe in burled mahogany, and packed it full of queer-smelling vanilla tobacco.

"Ugh," groaned Honey, "how can you smoke that wretched thing?"

"On the contrary, it's the heighth of nowness in Monte as well as Washington. You should see Madeleine Albright's pipe—pure ebony with gold inlay! I can only hope Colin Powell smokes a pipe, or this country is in for a rough ride."

"It's awfully stinky-poo," observed Honey.

"*You* don't mind, do you?" he asked, blowing a tremendous cloud of exhaust in my face.

"Of course not," I coughed, "though I prefer the Sobranie Balkan pipe-tobacco blend favored in London."

He stared at me curiously for a moment, then looked at Honey and asked where she dug up a rare gem like me. Honey laughed coquettishly. I longed to announce that the doorman had plenty of interesting info on the tobacco trade, but decided against it.

The only other time they spoke to me in the car was when we turned down Thirty-first Street. Babbington had set a mirror on his lap and cut a couple tiny lines of cocaine.

"Lisa?" he offered. I declined.

He said, "It might help decrease these," and pinched my nearest saddlebag, but again I demurred.

"Isn't she cute?" laughed Honey, snorting a week's salary.

"She's something, all right," replied Babbington, squeezing my saddlebag in a more forceful, prolonged fashion.

I opened the door as the driver came to a halt in the Wysocki parking lot and exited ungracefully. I wore a calf-length white leather skirt that was so tight, I had to plant both feet on the ground, then hoist my rear end up like a mainsail in order to rise.

"Full moon tonight," commented Babbington Hawkes.

A line of people stood outside the tavern. I reflected back on a childhood and adolescence spent in this neighborhood, and could not recollect a time when anyone waited in line to get inside Wysocki's. I spied faces from other restaurant and nightclub openings, scenesters, hipsters, artists, society mavens, local celebrities, the bored moneyed elite. Bridgeport had never seen such a spectacle, and likely never would again.

Mr. Wysocki, looking less depressed than usual, acted as doorman, checking IDs as well as the fire-code manual. He waved to me and asked us to come up front. The crowd watched us walk ahead of them.

Mr. Wysocki said, "Hi, Lisa, welcome to the Easy Hour. What a crowd! My boy did all this. My Fred." It was taking him a long time to usher people in because he never had to check IDs before. That's a plus, I guess, when none of your customer base is under sixty. He made a big production of asking Honey for her driver's license, thinking she would be flattered.

She hissed at me, "Doesn't he know who I am?"

However, this eventually convinced Honey how very exclusive Wysocki's was.

As at any party, the customers had divided themselves into little enclaves: Galisas at one end, media people at the other, club kids in the corner, longshoremen by the jukebox trying in vain to resurrect George Jones over the strains of Caetano Veloso and the 101 Strings. Honey, Babbington, and Esmé abandoned me to hobnob with society folk. Honey told me to make notes on who was there and to listen to what was being said about her behind her back. It sucks being stuck with myself.

It appeared that Fred had hired some of his younger cousins to man the bar while he cruised around making sure everything was going all right and that people were having a good time. His Easy Cover Duels were the highlight of every Easy Hour. Thus far tonight, we'd heard: Simon and Garfunkel versus Guy Lombardo ("Mrs. Robinson"), the Doors versus José Feliciano ("Light My Fire"), and Stevie Wonder versus Jim Nabors ("You Are the Sunshine of My Life"). Fred came over to greet me, looking smashing in a yellow velour V-neck with appliquéd silver apples and shiny green flared trousers.

"Congratulate me," he said. "I won the chess tournament." He handed me my take, ten bucks.

"Congratulations. I knew it was right to bet on the Asian."

"Half Asian," he corrected. "Or, as the chess club likes to call me now, the Krasian."

"As in crazy Asian?"

"As in the Asian Kramnik. You know: Vladmir Kramnik, the Russian chess champion."

"Oh, sure, Vladmir Kramnik."

He raised his palm for a high five. I slapped it, though it's hard to dredge up the grinding enthusiasm required for chess-club victories.

It was then that the landslide began, summit to trough.

I saw all my old Fishman friends enter across the room: Mrs. Lubbeth, Nan, Doris Mingle, Mrs. Consolo, and old Gulag Anna; Bernie from Admin; Hui; and the custodial staff, in the midst of which was Ray. He looked like young Ari more than ever, surrounded by adoring women, wearing the thick glasses of an intellectual industrialist and a long-sleeved red terry-cloth shirt that hinted at poolside days on the Riviera. I felt a deep pang in my stomach. Mrs. Lubbeth reached me first. Her wild blond hair was pulled back by a velvet headband topped with a fake poinsettia, and her usual caftan had been replaced with a black velvet tunic. The ladies gathered round me, asking about my new job, saying they missed me sneaking off to smoke in the handicapped dressing room.

"Me too," I said.

Said Mrs. Lubbeth, "Lisa has got a really important job now; she doesn't have time to miss a bunch of old salesladies!"

"Old? Speak for yourself," grumbled Nan, and everyone laughed.

Doris shook my hand warmly. I think she wanted a hug, but I couldn't bring myself to do it, not there in front of Honey's watchful eyes and Babbington's acid pen and Chicago's glitterati. She said she missed me and wished I was there to go to the Cheesecake Factory with her and Nan every Friday for lunch.

I stared at Nan, who replied she was not about to sit in the staff cafeteria anymore after the E. coli bagel–dog incident. I looked back at Doris, skinny-scarecrow, bag-of-bones Doris, in her grim nun frock and out-of-style shoes and jackdaw nose. Her weird wide mouth was stretched into a grin. It gave her face a kind of human look. Nan said Doris always treats the women's wear department to cheesecake each Friday, and everyone made silly idiot faces and patted Doris's gangly stick arms.

Talons gripped my shoulders. I turned to face the flared nostrils of Honey Dietrich, who smiled at the Fishman crowd and pulled me backward.

She whispered into my ear, "It doesn't look good for me to have you fraternizing too much with the shop clerks. A handsome young man over there in the *Sun-Times* contingent has been eyeballing you all evening. Why don't you go and talk to him?" She pushed me in the direction of Luke before I could say hello to Ray or good-bye to Mrs. Lubbeth.

I couldn't believe it. Standing by the bar was Roger Ebert, looking very dashing in gray flannel. Hawkes was monopolizing him. I felt sorry for Roger, who craned his neck in desperation, doubtlessly averting his eyes from the screaming queen in the Thurston Howell getup. Why did I ever think Babbington's ascot was where it's at? Gray flannel was where it's at.

Luke intercepted me as I drew closer to the goal of my lifetime. He put his arms around me and planted extremely moist, limp tongue kisses all over my face. People turned away. Even Roger Ebert was revolted.

I tried to wriggle out of his grasp and distract him. "What do you think of the music?"

He paused to relube his tongue. "Weird. Is this . . . is this, 'Welcome to the Jungle'?"

Guns n' Roses versus the Greene String Quartet. Hardly weird. I tried to give him my dissertation on Easy, but he had other things on his mind.

"You feel good," he murmured, hugging me. "I've been thinking nonstop about that night we spent together."

I said, "Roger Ebert isn't wearing his maroon sweater."

"Hell, no. He hasn't worn that for ages."

I couldn't believe it. No maroon sweater anymore. You think you *know* someone . . . Suddenly, I felt like I had just seen through a hokey magician's trick. That I had allowed myself to be fooled by silk scarves and flash paper, missing the real substance underneath, the cards up the sleeve, the trap doors, the truth. My eyes passed over Ebert, and I thought, *I don't know you.*

Luke massaged my saddlebags. Between him and Babbington, they will be extremely bruised and tender tomorrow. He confided, "You know, I've never been with such a big girl before."

"Me either," I said, trying to slip out of his arms again. I failed. Luke continued to lap at my face, and when I cleared the drool from my eyes, I saw Ray Fuchet staring at me from the end of the bar.

I pleaded with Luke to get me a blackberry schnapps. As he turned away toward the bartender, I tried to escape and get over to Ray. Of course, Honey materialized at that moment and asked me to get her a vodka on the rocks.

"OK, just a minute," I said.

She gave me one of those looks that brought to mind the frosty charm of Bea Arthur. "I really want one *now*. I'm too parched."

Flaccid and meek, I turned to the bar and ordered the drink. Luke placed the schnapps in front of me and commenced the tongue bath.

"What kind of vodka?" asked Fred's cousin.

I stole a sly look at Honey. "Absolut Peppar. With plenty of peppar."

"Darling, I have just met the *most* fascinating creature," said Honey. "You *must* meet her. In fact, I want you to schedule a rendezvous with her because she is a pet psychic, and your new job is to find me a dog."

In such circumstances, I ordinarily would have pretended not to know who Gina was, but the whole strange evening and sad display in front of Ray had broken down my defenses, and I confessed that the pet psychic was in fact my sister. As these things go, I could not have predicted that Honey would be so pleased at this news. She insisted I set up an afternoon for a reading next week, and in the meantime I had to locate some kind of appropriate pet.

"But what kind of dog do you want? I mean, there are hundreds of breeds."

"I don't care," she said cheerfully. "Something very needy, I absolutely insist upon a dog who needs a good home, so I don't care what breed it is, as long as it is very tiny, very chic, and very clean. None of this shedding or licking itself or odors. But I open my home to a poor little animal who needs one." She spread her arms out, showing how much love she had to give, and bonked Dennis Franz in the head.

"Okay," I said uncertainly. "One odorless, small, chic dog."

"And get me a good deal. I won't pay retail." She kissed Dennis's boo-boo, and I sneaked off to find Ray. I didn't *want* to confront him, to humiliate myself, but I felt it was time to seek him out and explain, to tell him the truth. I usually tried to avoid any situation where I had to say, "I'm sorry" or "It's my fault" or "Forgive me." But it seemed that in the last few days, that's all I'd been doing. Thirty-two years of error-filled living had prepared me well for my new role as public apologist.

I found Ray slumped in a booth with Fred and Chip. They were feeding him beer nuts and Old Style. They rose to leave me with Ray, and Chip clapped me on the back and said, "Nice going."

I sat across from him. His eyeglasses were on the table and big licks of dark hair fell across his brow, obscuring his eyes. He held up his can of Old Style, lifted it in the direction of the socialites and club kids and said, "It's our great beer, and they can't have it."

"Ray, I'm sorry you saw that, but let me explain."

"Okay," he said.

I gulped and, once I had determined to explain my behavior, found myself speechless.

He said, "You should have told me you had a boyfriend. Even Ari told Maria about Jackie."

"But I don't! He's not my boyfriend."

Ray said, "Well, that makes it pretty disgusting then, doesn't it?"

"I . . . I made a gigantic mistake." My throat was closing up, drying out.

But all he said was, "I better go now; I have to get up early for school. Good luck with Honey the Queen Bee." He got up. "Hmm. That reminds me of something. . . ."

I interrupted, grabbing hold of his sleeve, grabbing hold of any chance to explain in even the feeblest of terms how asinine I had been. "Ray? Ray, have you noticed that Ebert doesn't wear the maroon sweater anymore?"

He looked over at Roger, who was attempting to pry his arm loose from Babbington's claws, and shrugged.

I said miserably, "I never noticed until now. I mean, there is a lot I haven't noticed, haven't seen or understood, until right now."

He said, "Then Lisa, you better keep your eyes open around the Queen Bee. I have, no doubt, shared with you my opinions on the bumblebee. It's much too big to remain airborne, yet it flies around wherever it wants. It makes me *so mad.*" He slammed the Old Style down on the table and walked out of Wysocki's Tavern.

• • •

Eventually, my parents tracked me down in the corner of the bar and asked where Ray was. They had pinned all their hopes on him for delivering me from spinsterhood.

"He's gone," I said.

"We hardly got a chance to talk to him," said Daddy. "I had begun to explain my William Shatner theories to him but never got a chance to finish. He seemed very interested."

"Oh, Dad, come on," argued Chip. "You can't include William Shatner on your list just because you didn't like those Priceline commercials."

"Hey, TV is TV," reasoned Gina.

"I can't believe I saw Sipowicz!" said Daddy.

Ma said, "Oh, he's hunky."

It's not just being a spinster that worries me; it's also the idea that I may end up with these people as my caregivers. I know I'm going to return to Bridgeport as an elderly lady to live with my sixty-year-old brother, still publishing an indie 'zine out of the basement, and my sister and her thousand cats. My dad, mummified and stuffed, will be seated forever in the Barcalounger with the remote control entombed in his death grip, and Ma will be strapped down to her bed, screaming out obscenities in senile dementia.

At the end of the Easy Hour, I finally dragged Honey and company out to the Mercedes. I have to say for the scrubwoman, at least she was able to exit under her own power. The other two laughed and stumbled and fell to the ground repeatedly. So these were *their* drunks! God, was that what *my* drunk looked like to other people? Honey tripped on the sidewalk, and I yanked her up by the boa. She hacked and coughed, but thankfully no one noticed. Babbington continued to grab my saddlebags and leer. He'd seemed so classy and admirable back in October when he hated me. I'd had a lot of respect for him. But since he'd begun lunging at me and groping my sore, bruised fat, I found him repellent.

"Madam seems unusually befuddled," commented the driver as he helped her into the car.

"Madam has been under the influence of sinister forces," replied Esmé, looking at me.

Babbington crawled into the car and pulled me onto his lap. "I'm going to land you," he said. Between this disturbing fishing allusion, his Captain Stubing costume, and my constricting white leather skirt, it was impossible not to feel like maritime foe Moby Dick. His face loomed in close and he held me tightly, forcing me to regard his upsetting mustache. Then he conked out, whereby a severe case of sleep apnea took hold, exacerbated by his extremely tight ascot, which I declined to loosen.

When we reached the black glass building, Honey shook Hawkes awake, then the two of them and vile Esmé disembarked without a backward glance at me. The driver asked how I was getting home.

"Cab, I guess."

He said, "I'll drive you. I'm sure madam won't mind."

By the time we reached my apartment in Wicker Park, I was so exhausted, I could have slept for ten hours in the backseat.

"Wake up, miss," said the driver.

"I wasn't sleeping," I said. "Stress and constant stomach pains are keeping me awake."

I never used to have such stomach pains before I went to work for Honey Dietrich. Now I have so many, they could name a wing at Rush-Presbyterian after me.

Chapter 24

I found Honey lying in bed the next morning surrounded by nine humidifiers. She had a hot compress on her forehead and lavender sachets on her sinuses. Esmé was coaxing her to drink a little lemon tea as she made sad whimpering noises.

"If Babbington calls, you tell him I'm out jogging!" croaked Honey.

"Is she ill?" I asked Esmé. And if so, where was my salary? She forgot to pay me on Friday. It might have looked callous to utter these last important concerns aloud.

"Not ill," replied Esmé. "Just a tad too much alcohol last evening. You know, at the fraternity beer bath you dragged us to."

Honey said, "It was worth it! Sugar Rautbord was not there and *I* was. Kate Spade was there. She gave me a wallet. Roger Ebert was there. We're going to the Sotheby's movie memorabilia auction next month. Sugar gets nothing, while I get everything. All is right with the world, Esmé."

Then Honey told the scrubwoman to give me the envelope on the nightstand.

"Oh, my salary!" I sighed with relief. "I was wondering—"

"Oh, that," replied Honey grumpily. "Can't I just give it to you tomorrow? I'm very, very sick right now." Sick-making is more like it. I looked at the envelope uncomprehendingly.

Esmé shoved me out of the room. "You will find seven hundred dollars there. Madam would like a nice pet, appropriate for psychic readings. Come back when you've purchased one."

. . .

It was snowing outside, looking all peaceful and Christmasy. I detested the idea of having to trudge through it, looking for a pet. I called Gina from Honey's lobby. The complimentary cigarette box had been replaced with a box of mint Tums, which are sort of mentholated if you can suck the essence into your lungs.

"What's up, Lisa?" she asked. "I have a full day of calls to take. People want to find out what their pets would like for Christmas."

"I'm in a situation right now," I said. I explained my day's errand to her and my ignorance of the dog trade. I asked if I could just go to a pet shop.

"No! They buy from puppy mills, and their animals are unhealthy. Hang on, let me check my schedule." I rather missed the days when her schedule afforded her massive amounts of free time in between cleaning the grease trap at McDonald's and counting socks.

We arranged to meet at Lou Mitchell's Restaurant. I grabbed a handful of Tums and headed for the westbound Jackson Avenue bus. I got there early and ordered scrambled eggs and coffee. "Double-yolked," the menu promised. How did they know? Did they have a pet psychic in the hen house?

Gina came in and ordered orange juice. She checked her Palm Pilot and voice mail, then tucked them back neatly in her overalls bib. I slid the envelope of cash over.

"I need seven hundred dollars' worth of clean, purebred pooch." Nearby customers peeked over their booths.

"I think this is a bad idea," she said. "You don't buy a pet because you'd love a psychic reading. You get a psychic reading because you love your pet." Customers turned away.

I insisted that she track down a wholesale breeder of odorless small dogs, but she suggested that we go to the pound and select a truly needy animal.

"Gina, I think we all know who is truly needy here: it's me, and I need papers that prove the animal is valuable."

She considered this thoughtfully. "Hmm. Well, all weekend Chip and Bruce have been creating false press credentials on the computer. I don't see why they couldn't make fake papers for a dog. Then you'd only spend a fraction for the shots and stuff at the shelter."

You know, I take it all back. This *Prole* thing has turned Chip into a mighty useful citizen.

We went to the Anti-Cruelty on LaSalle Street. Everyone at the shelter knew Gina, as she had been volunteering there lately.

I said, "For an unemployed adult living with your parents, you sure get around."

She said, "*Self*-employed."

As we walked through the room with all the cages, it was impossible not to feel depressed. *None* of the pets looked pure-bred.

Gina carried on telepathic conversations with the dogs we passed. She said some of them had been through very rough times.

"Yeah, rough. Any look like good candidates?"

"I don't know. They all seem to be in need of, you know, real love and care."

I began to despair. "What about a cat? They don't need anything."

We toured the cat cages and found some mellow ones. Who knew what a purebred cat looked like? As long as they had all their legs and no chunks missing from their bodies, you could pass any one of them off as purebred. I stepped into the lobby and made a call.

"Esmé, it's Lisa. Could I speak to madam, please? Well, could you hold the phone next to her ear? It's very important. I'm sure you won't drop it in the tub. . . . Hi, Ms. Dietrich. I have wonderful news. I've found a breeder who turned down Sugar Rautbord for his prizewinning cats. *Cats.* Yes, he said she was too . . . too insensitive to own one. But when I told him I was representing *you*—yes! He was very excited. Oh, yes, very exclusive. What kind? It's . . . it's a . . . Parisian Hub Cat. My God, yes, Martha Stewart has one, so did that Italian contessa who disappeared from her villa, and, um, that English prime minister. No! Not the Labour one, the other guy. Well, there's only one cat left, but if you have your heart set on some kind of dog, I'd be more than happy—really? Excellent. No, no, I'll spare no expense."

I strolled back into the abandoned-cat room. Gina was crouched by one of the cages, communing. I said we had the green light on getting a cat. She gestured toward the cage, at the little gray feline inside. He was neither mangled nor diseased.

Gina said, "He said he lived with an elderly lady who died. He'd like to live with a nice lady again."

"Well, he's going to live with Honey. We're in business, baby."

The cat was not a bad sort. He sat still in his cardboard carrying box on the El to Bridgeport. Gina said the cat would like to have a pillow by the window in his new home.

"Who wouldn't?" I retorted. "*I'd* like to have a new stainless-steel couch and a bagful of cash, but you don't hear *me* complaining."

"Don't I?" she sighed.

Chip sat brooding at the computer. Bruce snoozed in the corner on our old rattan patio furniture.

"Hey, how did production go?" I asked, setting the cat transporter down on the desk. Chip stared at the monitor.

"The 'zine, *Prole*? Is it at the printer?"

He shook himself slightly out of catatonia and nodded. When I asked him what was wrong, he said, "What if it's a success? My whole life will change. I'll have to give interviews to *Chicago Society* all the time, schmooze with media types. It'll get too big to run out of Ma and Daddy's basement."

"I wouldn't worry about it," I said helpfully. "Now, this cat here—"

He interrupted. "What, don't you think I can make a success out of anything?"

I looked at my brother in his wrinkled button-down shirt with the pit stains. His wavy hair was matted on the top, and something brown and curled fell out of his ear. His desk was littered with mock-ups of the Rainbow Man article and old doughnuts and a transcription of an interview with a guy who drilled a hole in his own skull. Bruce rolled over on the rattan love seat and snored.

I said, "I think you already have. Made a success out of things, I mean. It's hard to create your own projects and work for yourself. That's why I'll always work for bossy ladies, 'cause I'm too dull and lazy to start anything on my own."

Gina came over and stood between us. She squeezed Chip's hand and reached for mine. I let her.

Chip somehow dug up a copy of a cat pedigree from a website. He mimicked its design as closely as possible, listing the breed as Parisian Hub, color gray, age two.

"His name is Don," said Gina suddenly.

"How do you know?" I asked. She gave me an exasperated look.

"Oh, right. Pet psychic. Well, I don't think Honey will want a cat called Don. She'll want to call it Mozart or Vivaldi, just like Martha Stewart's cats."

Chip said, "That's the dumbest thing I've ever heard."

"Be that as it may," I retorted, "'Don the Cat' will never make it in society."

But Gina reasoned that pedigreed pets always have long, agonizing names anyway. Couldn't we just shove *Don* within some name? We settled on "Tee Nee Romanini's The Don." I felt it had a quiet elegance.

I was left with almost $650 after getting The Don's shots, litter box, etc. That was a decent profit. That was a Sonia Rykiel pink check jacket.

Gina frowned. "That's a nice donation to an animal shelter."

Chip frowned. "That's a much-needed contribution to a fledgling indie publication."

The Don and I left for Honey's apartment. He was getting sick of the El, and so was I.

Salvation Army Santa at the Thirty-fifth Street train station rang his bell in his usual unrestrained manner, upsetting The Don. I asked him to please muffle his bell, and he said, "Muffle this," and made a rude gesture. I admired the bravado of the South Side Santas, but did they have to be so disgusting? I hated Christmas.

Snow fell on us as we walked the few blocks to the black glass building. The Don shivered in his transporter, but kept up a brave front. The doorman peeked inside the box and said, "Well! It's going to be a Merry Christmas for somebody." The Don obliged, lifting his little paw, a sort of return greeting. He had a lot of class; Tim Gideon's hideous Len could take a page from his book.

Honey had emerged from her bedroom and was seated writing at the Hearst table. Her eyes grew large and shiny when I walked over with the box. She clapped her hands together like a little girl.

"Honey Dietrich, may I present The Don." I opened the front of the carrier and lifted him out. He was very gentle and non-scratchy. She held him in her lap, where he settled in comfortably and began to purr.

"Delightful!" she cooed, and snapped her fingers for his pedigree.

She did seem a little put out at the name, but when I explained that he had originally come from a prominent Chicago mob family who had to give him up due to allergies, she seemed satisfied.

"I wonder who Romanini is?" she mused. Actually, Don Romanini is our cousin over in Armour Square. Although he has a successful roofing business, Honey would not be impressed. I said Romanini was a scandalous Italian viscount known for his love of beaujolais, three-card monte, and Parisian Hub kittens.

"Oh, my," said Honey Dietrich, and stroked The Don behind his ears.

At five o'clock, Honey handed me the list she had been compiling at the table. I was confused; she had already given me the names to whom I should send Christmas cards.

She stared at me and said, "This is a list of things I *want* for Christmas. My associates are always pleased to know in advance what they can get me. Send it to those with triple green stars in my address book." I looked down at the list. Items included perfume, silk nighties in size four (*please*), bee-motif jewelry, and, of course, "art in any form . . . I just adore artwork in shades of raspberry and ice blue."

On my way home, my cell rang. Eagerly, I checked the caller ID, but it wasn't Ray. I just knew he would never call me again; I would never see that FUCHET, RAY on my little LCD anymore. Instead, UPTOWN LIBRARY showed up. My stomach hurt.

"Hi," I said dejectedly.

"Fine, *don't* call me," huffed Tim. "Be that way. It's not like I sit around here at the reference desk awaiting calls from your highness anyway."

I tried to explain how hard my job had been lately, but he cut me off.

"*Your* job? How about mine? Libraries are a product of the Enlightenment! How would *you* hold up under that kind of pressure every day? Enlighten, enlighten, attempt to help your patrons triumph over mental darkness." He moved the receiver away from his mouth and shouted into the distance, "Hey! Put your pants back on! What do you think this *is*?"

I said, "Why are you yelling at me about the Enlightenment?"

Tim paused for a long time, then said, "You never call me anymore. Are you mad at me or something?"

I replied in the negative, but Chip's words about my shallow, hostile friendship with Tim had rung persistently in my ears those last few days. Tim would laugh at my remorse over the loss of my beloved junior janitor.

"I have to go," I said. "We're going through the tunnel now, and you're breaking up."

The day came for our scheduled psychic consultation with Gina. Honey was in a foul mood. Her Christmas-party invitations went out, and already three people had sent their regrets.

"I can't believe Cardinal George is not coming!" she fumed. "Yet he expects *me* to sit through a boring homily at Christmas Eve Mass and tithe ten percent, to boot!"

I said, "Maybe he has to administer to the sick that night."

Honey sneered. "The *sick*. He's blessing a new Porsche dealership on Irving Park Road."

The Don meowed once in his transporter. Perhaps he thought he was being taken back to the shelter. He had nothing to worry about: the moment he entered Honey's apartment, he belonged. Everyone liked him, his dignified kneading of the Empire loveseat cushions, the way he curled up on the rug in front of the gas fireplace, his little fights with the conservatory Christmas tree. Even Esmé didn't complain about having to attend to the litterbox duties. The cat fit in better than I did, which was depressing enough; the fact that I envied him was simply pathetic.

"Oh, no," said Esmé, as the car exited the freeway, "we're not going back to that terrible little neighborhood, are we?"

"Hush, Esmé," scolded Honey. "Bridgeport is . . . what is that phrase, Lisa?"

"The community of the future."

"Yes, the future. Maybe I'll buy some property out here." Then she confided, "You know, they say the mayor used to live here! Isn't that a scream?"

When we pulled up in front of my parents' lousy bungalow, I saw a different sort of scream building up within her, but she fought it.

She looked at the bungalow and said, "Psychics are rather fringe-type people, aren't they?"

I had hoped that Ma and Daddy, by some generous act of God, would be out of the house. But God was not feeling generous that day.

Ma opened the door and waved frantically. Gina must have primed her about the great socialite Honey Dietrich. She had replaced her shiny warm-up suit with a knee-length fuchsia sweater, threaded with gold, and black cigarette pants, though on Ma it was impossible not to see them as stogie pants.

"*Char*-ming," murmured Honey through clenched, wolfish teeth. Esmé asked if she might wait in the car.

"Mrs. Dietrich, it's nice to meet you," said Ma, as we came up the front walk.

"Ms.," said Honey.

"Miss?"

"Ms., Ma!" I shouted.

"Oh, Ms.," replied Ma, muttering as she turned, "*fancy*."

Ma welcomed Honey into her living room, where my father sat in his Barcalounger in a Bears sweater and ironed jeans. The house was spotless. Ma had dusted our senior photos in their wood-tone frames on the mantel. The Christmas-tree lights were on and Andy Williams crooned softly from the kitchen radio. The sofa looked like it had been cleaned, and even the red braided rug must have been shampooed, as its textured pattern had begun to emerge.

"Pleased to meet you, Mrs. Dietrich," said Daddy, rising from the chair.

"It's *Ms.*, Sal!" screamed Ma.

Honey clutched The Don's carrying case and flinched as though physically struck. She said, "Please call me Honey."

"Honey?" repeated Daddy. I willed him with my eyes to shut up, but he plowed on. "Why, that was the name of our dead dog."

Honey batted her eyelashes and said out of the corner of her mouth, "The words every woman longs to hear."

Ma said her daughter the animal communicator would be out shortly and made us sit on the sofa to await a tray of sandwiches. I began to understand what it was like being a guest in the Galisa home: excruciating.

My dad smiled politely. Honey smiled politely. I smiled like a nut job wandering the grounds of Happy Acres.

"That's a nice cat," commented Daddy.

"Thank you," replied Honey. "He's a Parisian Hub and I adore him."

"I guess I'm kind of a dog person myself," he said. "Our Honey was a great animal, fat and sassy, always wanted her belly scratched. Then she threw herself in front of a speeding tow truck—people around here still talk about it—well, that's a long story. But that Honey was one fine bitch."

Honey Dietrich's wind-tunnel face stretched into a baffled, frightened smile that threatened to undo years of expensive plastic surgery.

"And you, Lisa?" she asked in a strained voice. "Are you a dog person?"

I replied weakly, "Actually, I've always preferred koi."

Ma returned with a silver tray piled high with sandwiches: triple-decker cream cheese–and–deviled ham creations, white-bread rounds smeared with anchovy paste, and tiny mortadella subs. She poured out hot tea into chipped china cups. Honey accepted a teacup but refused the sandwiches.

"I absolutely couldn't," she said. "If I ate lunch I'd never fit into my new orange Versace gown."

"I love orange," said Daddy. I handed him two sandwiches, hoping to stave off future comments on the Bears and television and the garment industry, lest he ruin everything I had achieved with my employer. Once she heard his treatise on orange, she'd never believe it was the new black.

"I understand," said Ma, shoveling in a mini-sub. "Too much rich food and the next thing you know, you've got hips out to there." Everyone's eyes strayed to me.

Finally Gina came in and Ma and Daddy disappeared into the kitchen. They appreciate the privacy a pet psychic needs. My sister sat down on the sofa and held The Don in her lap. She avoided mention of his true origins, and concentrated on his present state of health and well-being. The Don, apparently, was quite healthy and enjoyed his new home. He liked sitting on the windowsill behind the couch best, but would like his very own pillow placed there.

Honey turned to me and snapped, "Get The Don a nice pillow today, would you?"

This continued for some time, with Honey cooing over trivial revelations such as The Don's favorite color (red), favorite treat (tuna), and preferred cat-box location (kitchen—disgusting). Then Gina paused for a few moments. Her eyes flickered warily back and forth from Honey to The Don.

Finally she said, "He doesn't want you to dress him up anymore."

The color rose in Honey's cheeks. "I don't know what you mean."

Gina tried again. "You put a little hat—no, no, a baby bonnet on him at night before bedtime. And wrap him in a blanket. He doesn't want you to do that. He says he gets too hot and the bonnet bothers him."

Honey laughed shrilly. "I don't do that! Ha-ha, a baby bonnet. *Really.*" She rolled her eyes unconvincingly. "Perhaps it's Esmé. I'll speak to her."

Just then Chip barged in the front door. He stomped through the living room, barely glancing at us, swearing under his breath. A second later he peeped around the kitchen doorway and beckoned me.

"I'm in the middle of something," I hissed.

He said, "I'm having a situation."

I looked at Honey, who said, "Go, go! You're interrupting our reading."

Chip motioned for me to follow him down into the *Prole* office. There he took a newspaper out of his bag and showed it to me. It was *Chicago Society,* and the page was turned to Babbington's column.

SLACKER MAG'S LACK OF STYLE BOTH SAD AND HORRIBLE

By Babbington Hawkes

I had such high hopes for *Prole* magazine. First, I was told it was published out of a secret underground location in Bridgeport, which is *the* place to be, as we all know. Second, they have connections to A-list celeb hangout Wysocki's Tavern and its ultracool Easy Hour. Third, the publisher is the brother of a certain shapely personal assistant I know who has a gift for tobacco appreciation. But, friends, it's no good. I'm sorry, but there it is.

The publisher, who goes by the moniker "Hard G," is an obvious newcomer to hip Bridgeport, and hopes its name will lend some cachet to his dreary political nightmare of a magazine. Hard G is no more than a vaguely disheveled Eugene Debs–

wanna-be with a trephination fixation. His staff of "reporters"—in truth, mewling chess players with typewriters—advocate "smashing the state" and "tearing down the pig system," all while living in their parents' basements. I was invited to come by the secret underground *Prole* headquarters (a rattan-furnished rec room, which was, Hard G pointed out, under the ground) last Sunday morning as they completed production on their maiden issue. Those of you who have visited the tasteful offices of *Chicago Society* no doubt recognize our commitment to serious, social journalism by the quiet good taste of our decor. By this same token, in viewing *Prole* HQ with streaming eyes, I can only surmise that the future of American journalism is in a sickening, squalid state indeed.

Articles are neither assigned, researched, nor, as far as I can tell, written by anyone with even a rudimentary grasp of basic spelling. Any wingnut can scribble a manifesto on a Hardee's menu and slide it under the *Prole* door; it will probably be published. The rantings of Jack Chick, Anton LaVey, and the Unabomber appear alongside reprinted interviews with Noam Chomsky and Bobby Seale. Their style editor, Bruce "Chairman" Tharr, predicts that holes in the skull will be the new look for the spring season. I am sure teenagers are digging in trash heaps for bone saws throughout the old South Side stockyards right now, all on the advice of this Algonquin Round Table of Idiots.

Hard G, here's some advice from one journalist to another: just because you're an anarchist doesn't mean you don't have to know the difference between *their* and *there*. Revolution? No. Revolting? *Yes*.

We sat there stunned for many minutes.
I asked, "Did you really call yourself Hard G?"

"No! He pronounced my name 'Chip Jalisa,' and I just said it was a hard *G*. Now no one will ever read *Prole*." He put his head down on the desk. He again resembled the unhappy little boy who used to go fetal under the chiffon scarves at Leisure Lady.

"Chip, you can't let this get you down. It's your first issue; of course it won't be easy right off the bat."

He said, "I don't think I can do it."

"Yes, you can. Remember what Daddy always said? That the time for foolish, go-nowhere enterprises was your twenties. You're not gonna want to be thirty-five and publishing a 'zine. The time to do it is now."

He lifted his head off the desk. "But I want to *get* him. That Babbington. I want a war, and I don't know how to get one."

There were very few people on this planet I could count on in my pre–Maria Callas days. This is not to say I liked them, or they liked me, but simply that they were *there*. There for my highest pinnacle as a personal assistant; there when my sixteenth minute arrived, as I knew it would. Home, as the saying goes, is where, when you go there, they have to take you in.

I said, "I'll help you."

Upstairs at the psychic fair, Ma and Daddy sat with Honey and Gina in the living room. Everyone was chatting warmly and laughing. Ma had brought out the bottle of Harveys Bristol Cream, and all refilled their teacups amply. Gina hugged The Don and fed him anchovy sandwiches. Honey fed herself the last of the deviled ham.

"Lisa, why didn't you tell me you had such charming parents?" she asked. "Your father has been telling me perfectly scandalous stories about his thirty years in the garment industry. Fascinating! Sal, tell me more about Leisure Lady."

I had not expected this scene and felt desperate for a Sobranie. I made do with a Parliament and a tumbler of Harveys.

"Those were the days," reminisced Daddy. "You should have seen the glamour, the gorgeous fabrics, the unequaled fit of double-knit. Everyone in Bridgeport seemed, at one time or another, to buy something from our store."

"Old-school Bridgeport," rhapsodized Honey. "How jealous I am! Now every Tom, Dick, and Harry has glommed on to the Bridgeport craze. I wish I could have seen it when it was pure and untouched."

I suffered a myocardial infarction, but masked it by choking on a mouthful of Harveys.

Ma said, "My Sal designed the most beautiful clothing for women. He really had a gift." Daddy shook his toupee self-deprecatingly.

Honey said, "We sure could use you now. Lisa has been searching for a dress for my Christmas party, but so far has found nothing."

Ma bummed a cig from me and sat on the sofa staring thoughtfully at Honey. A moment later, she rose and disappeared into her bedroom.

"What about a tartan ball gown?" asked Daddy. "I think I saw a picture of one not long ago that was very attractive."

Honey said kindly, "That was last season."

Ma entered the living room with a garment bag on a hanger. The moment I saw it, I knew.

"Ma! What are you doing?" I leapt up and tried to wrestle the bag out of her hands. We both held our cigs clamped between our lips as we struggled.

"Stell?" asked Daddy. He peered at the garment bag, and I could see he recognized it, too.

"What is it?" laughed Honey. "I must know! Lisa, sit down and let your mother show me what's in the bag." Miserably, I complied, and slumped on the sofa. Gina and Chip withdrew to the far corner of the room and whispered together.

Ma unzipped the bag slowly. "Honey, Sal designed the most wonderful, flattering, exotic piece of couture that Bridgeport had ever seen." She pronounced *couture* as "coocher."

Having got the zipper open, Ma slid the bag off the hanger and unveiled the garment in all its mothball glory.

She said, "My husband is a genius, that's all I can say. A little before his time, maybe, but a real genius. This was the rage of old Bridgeport, Honey. The one-legged pantsuit."

Honey's jaw dropped practically to her chest. She went over to Ma and felt the pantsuit, examined its fabric. I suppose it *was* a rage, in the common sense of the word. She said, "Stell, I have never seen anything like it in all my days."

Ma said, "Everyone around here was mad for it. It was our glamorous, South Side secret. You know, Lisa was her father's biggest supporter. She convinced him to go ahead with the design when others were too timid to voice their opinions." Pink spots appeared on her cheeks, and she dropped her gaze to the floor.

Honey said, "Lisa has wonderful taste; everything she suggests turns out to be a great success." She ran her finger along the flapping collar. "It's even in my colors: pink and orange. It matches my Christmas decor perfectly."

Had the cheddar-and-pink of the one-legged pantsuit inscribed itself that deeply upon my subconscious? It was the only way to explain my choosing those colors for Honey's decorations.

Honey took the hanger from my mother and held the pantsuit up to herself. The leg dangled a good eight inches above her ankle. "Oh, pooty! I wish I could try it on, but it's too small."

I wracked my brain so hard, I felt stress fractures develop on my skull. Then suddenly, I had it, I saw where all this could go. I saw an end to the selection of her blasted Christmas-party dress, but moreover, I saw a chance to validate thirty years in the garment industry, sixty-six years in Bridgeport.

I said, "Ms. Dietrich, I'm getting a sudden vision of your most fabulous Christmas party ever. Let me paint the picture for you. Your guests arrive adorned in the usual Armani tuxes, Calvin Klein basic black gowns, Valentino glitz. Some mink here, a Gucci minidress there. Everyone wearing the tripe they saw in the last *Vogue* or *Marie Claire*. Where is the originality? They don't know. They're afraid to try something new. But then you walk into the hub—I mean, the living room. At once, everyone converges around you . . . Honey Dietrich, the first proponent of Easy culture, the cutting-edge doyenne of Chicago society and haute couture, the owner of the only Parisian Hub cat in the Midwest. You are showered with presents, kisses, compliments. People are falling over each other to get a better look at your garment . . . handmade, exquisitely tailored, one of a kind. You are wearing the one-legged pantsuit, personally created for you by the House of Galisa."

All jaws in the room by now hung from their hinges like storm-cellar doors after a tornado. We came together as a single unit: the pet psychic, the indie 'zine publisher, the personal assistant, The Don, the socialite, the dressmaker, the mother of the clan. I climbed out of the trough and began the long ascent back to the summit. The House of Galisa was born. My father started to cry.

Chapter 25

Daddy enjoyed taking the many trips out to Honey's apartment for fittings and to some of his old fabric wholesalers from the Leisure Lady days. As for me, I was kept busy pulling together the final details of Easy Christmas.

My first order of business on Monday involved the writing of a letter. In the privacy of Honey's den (while Esmé scrubbed madam's feet with a pumice stone under the mermaid Christmas tree), I wrote down the words that would change my future. I signed Honey's name (easy—she has the block-letter penmanship of a first-grader), addressed it to Babbington, and included "secret instructions" for the Christmas party. I put it in my purse, though I didn't know how I was going to deliver it to the *Chicago Society* offices unnoticed. I'd think of something.

I stopped by Crump's with invitations to the party for Phranque, the eyebrow technician, and others. I heard people whispering, "She used to have a giant afro. Now she's with Honey Dietrich." In the spa world, logical inferences can be drawn from hairstyle changes. Next, I was to deliver invitations to Fishman's and other companies Honey patronized. I asked her if it wasn't rude to issue party invitations only five days in advance. She said, "Not for the tradespeople."

On my way into Fishman's, I stopped outside to enjoy a delicious cig. The snow fell lightly; buskers belted out Christmas tunes on the corners; and somebody just dropped a five-dollar bill on the sidewalk in front of me. Felt very Christmasy.

Honey had written out invitations only for Mrs. Lubbeth, Mrs. Consolo, Nan, Gulag Anna, Hui, and Mr. Fishman. Luckily, I had stolen some leftover blank ones and filled them in for all of Men's Wear, Women's Wear, Bernie, Jesus, and the cafeteria people. There would be so many people at the party, I figured Honey would not notice a few dozen extra.

When I got out of the elevator on the third floor, the first person I saw was Doris Mingle. She was folding irregular pajamas.

"Hi, Doris," I said. She looked up and smiled, sticking out her great paw for a handshake. I handed her an invitation.

She asked, "I'm invited?"

"Uh-huh."

She looked down at the invitation, turning it over and over in her hands. "How come?"

I said, "It's Christmas."

I asked her if she had any irregular wigs.

"Wigs? No. Why do you need a wig?"

I explained I had an errand to run, but I needed to be in disguise since everyone at *Chicago Society* would recognize me.

"What kind of errand?"

I said, "I need to right a wrong. I've made a mistake—all right, several; *many,* even—I thought my future lay in high society, Babbington Hawkes, Honey Dietrich, but that's not the future I want. I want my life Easy, but Easy is not just about mindless partying and clothes and South American hipsters. It's about having the courage, the frigging *optimism,* to move forward, to embrace the future by honoring the past. The elite will never understand how much I've grown to love my homely, freakish history, how I wish I appreciated what I had then. But if I could get this letter to Babbington without discovery, I might be able to help one man, and that would be a step in the right direction."

She looked surprised and sad as I poked through the irregular-hat bin. They were a sorrowful lot, the irregular hats. Some had no tops. My hair could not be restrained by such a thing, I would be recognized immediately.

"Lisa," said Doris, with her hand on my shoulder, "nobody knows *me* at *Chicago Society.* I could deliver your letter."

I hugged her suddenly. It was kind of awkward, hugging all those points and jagged edges, but she patted my back and smiled. I think I surprised her. To tell the truth, I think I surprised myself.

Back in my old department, Mrs. Lubbeth was herding old ladies into the dressing rooms with loads of sequined matronly gowns. As she shoved the last customer in, I saw her start to futz with her partial.

"Sesame seed?" I asked, putting my hands over her eyes.

She spun around and drowned me in a soft hug, no points or jagged edges for miles. "No, hon, I was just putting a little curse on one of our customers. She's tried on eighteen gowns today, and none of them are right. You remember how that is."

"Yeah," I sighed wistfully.

Mrs. Lubbeth peered at me over her bifocals. "What's wrong?"

"Nothing. Here's an invitation for Honey's Christmas party. It's this Friday, I hope you can come," I said. "I miss you."

"I miss you, too. We have a bunch of temp staff for the Christmas season, but none of them can sneak off to the handi-capped dressing room for a smoke like you could. You had a real gift, Lisa."

I went down to the boiler room to find the head janitor. After much cajoling on my part, he finally gave me the name and address of Ray's school. He wasn't really supposed to give out personal info like that.

"It's okay. I used to work here, remember? Maria Callas? I'm a good friend of Ray's."

"Oh, yeah, you. I scraped burnt feta off the floor of the cook-ware department for two hours."

I gulped, and copied down the address of Seward Academy. The janitor asked if I was such a good friend of Ray's, then why didn't I know where he worked.

"Because I'm stupid."

"Hey, when you see Ray, will ya ask him what combination of chemicals he used to dissolve dried vomit? He had a knack for that."

Science was so wonderful. Why had I never realized that before?

I reached Ray's school before classes let out, but I was not allowed to walk around inside to look for him. They have rules about that kind of thing now, you know, murder and mayhem and all that. But I handed the school receptionist the invitation, and she promised to put it in his mailbox.

I wrote on the inside of the card:

> Please, Ray, come to this party. After much con-
> sideration, I, too, oppose bumblebees, as they are
> aerodynamically unsound.
>
> *Love,*
> *Lisa*

I could see the wall of mailboxes from the receptionist's desk. Most of them were covered in fading, chipped blue paint, and the whole structure seemed to be held together with Elmer's glue and a buttress of stacked textbooks. Next to the mailboxes was a bulletin board. Cork had broken off all over it. But pinned to the board between leaflets and fliers were handwritten notes in colored ink: "You Can Make a Difference" and "One Child at a Time." Stickers of Charlie Brown and Snoopy framed the board. In the hallway, a child dabbed a tissue to his bloody nose and cried, while a teacher held his hand.

By the time I got back to Honey's, I had only a few minutes left to finalize the menu for the caterers. She wanted barbecue flown in from Memphis and salmon flown in from Alaska. She gave me enough money to cover it, but why fly in meat when there's a perfectly good grocery store around the corner? I put the leftover cash in my "Misery Fund," along with the $650 from the purchase of The Don. I dropped off FedEx boxes at the grocer's two blocks away, instructing him to deliver salmon and ribs packed inside on Friday.

"I don't understand," said the grocer, looking at the FedEx boxes.

I withdrew ten bucks from the Misery Fund and handed it over. "Don't ask," I said.

Finally I had finished my day's tasks. Honey was napping when I came back from the grocery store. Esmé was fixing a snack in the kitchen, for the second when madam awoke. Possibly at this very moment, Doris Mingle was delivering my letter to Babbington Hawkes. I stood for a while in the Parisian hub, holding The Don. I watched snow fall on the lake, turned on the Christmas tree. By Monday, I would be unemployed and would probably never know such luxury again. I kissed The Don and put him on his pillow, feeling weightless. The medicine ball was gone.

I went back down to the lobby. The doorman stood inside, reading a magazine. I looked inside the complimentary cigarette box, hoping for a policy change.

"You know what?" said the doorman. "I think I'm going to quit smoking. I never knew all the underhanded business that went along with big tobacco. I found all sorts of interesting material in this free magazine—there's a whole stack of them in the coffee shop next door."

He held up a copy of *Prole*.

Walking home from the subway station at Division Street, I passed the big futon store. Usually their front window exhibited a schizophrenic mishmash of color: neon sheets, life-size cutouts of *Star Trek* characters, lava lamps, pony skin rugs. But now it was blank and empty, and in the center of the display stood a black metal futon frame supporting a plain white futon. It looked like a prison cell or a going-out-of-business sale. Then I noticed a small card in the bottom corner of the window that read, "Dispose of the clutter in your life. Embrace the look of New Spare (as seen in the January *Elle Decor*)."

I opened the iron gate at the sidewalk in front of my building. On the front step sat Tim Gideon. It was still snowing, and he held an issue of *Prole* over his head.

"Hi," he said. "Thought I'd drop by."

We went upstairs and I put the tea kettle on. He sat on my tuxedo sofa, complaining about the lack of cushions.

"If you want cushy, go lie down on the bed," I suggested. He tried, but said my empty bedroom reminded him of his college dorm. He came into the kitchen and sat at the table.

After a minute he said, "I like those Ralph Lauren sheets." The now-familiar churn began in my stomach at the thought of all that had transpired under the embroidered *RL*. I poured us each a mug of tea. Tim thumbed through *Prole* while I chomped four Tums and washed them down with Earl Grey.

Tim said, "Your brother is a genius. This is the funniest thing I've ever read. Look on the masthead how they dedicated this issue." He showed me the page. It read, "This one goes out to all our dead homies."

I said, "Babbington Hawkes thinks his name is Hard G."

"Your brother? No! He's cuddly. He's Soft G. Or *Sof'* G. He's so soft, the *T* fell off."

"My brother, Sof' G. Chess-club president. Indie 'zine publisher. He's not really a bad sort, is he?"

I have a spare white apartment with nothing in it. I have an urge today to open up the closet doors and throw crap all over the floor.

I said, "Tim Gideon, you old sock, you, I have something to say." He waited expectantly while I breathed deeply and formed my thoughts. "Some of us are destined for poverty. Some are destined for celibacy—"

He groaned. "Not your commencement address again."

I said, "That's a good point, Tim. If I were to give a commencement address to, say, the eighth-graders at Seward Academy, I would say this: 'No man is a failure who has friends.'"

He stared at me. "You stole that from *It's a Wonderful Life*."

"Well, it's true. And you know what else? I really liked that junior janitor. The science teacher. Young Ari. I don't care who knows. I've probably blown it with him, but at least I know I can love someone besides Ralph Lauren."

Tim looked down into his teacup and swirled it around for a few moments. "Love?" he asked.

I nodded.

He looked me in the eye, then his features softened, and he smiled without the usual measure of ridicule. "Love is all right, if you go in for that sort of thing."

I slid Honey's Christmas-party invitation across the table and said I thought this would be my last society bash.

"Why?" he asked.

I considered this and answered, "I'm just not having it anymore." I popped another Tums and grinned.

Chapter 26

The day before the party, Daddy delivered Honey's pantsuit. It was marvelous—bright orange with pink satin collars. She had just the right Manolo Blahnik pink high heels to go with it. Esmé was beside herself. She detested the one-legged pantsuit and its origins (me), but was unable to badmouth it because Honey loved it.

She pulled me aside as Honey twirled in front of the mirror, and hissed, "Madam resembles an orange-jumpsuit felon."

I disagreed pleasantly. Madam paid my father seven hundred dollars for the outfit; those orange jumpsuits are free, courtesy of the state.

When Daddy had finished packing up his tailor's tapes and pins and fabric, I'd congratulated him on his success.

"Thanks!" he said. "Maybe it'll lead to other society ladies wanting one-legged pantsuits of their own."

"Maybe," I replied cautiously. "Or it could just be a one-shot deal, you know."

"That's okay," he said. "I just wanted to end on a high note."

I was glad Honey took me up on my suggestion to hire Fred as the official DJ for the party. He was going to bring go-go dancers in skimpy Santa suits. Honey was thrilled about this and decided she wanted a real Santa to hang out in the corner for her guests to sit on.

"You mean, sit on his lap like at a department store?" I asked.

She shrugged and bared her teeth devilishly. "Santa will be there for us to enjoy in whatever way we choose."

What kind of a Christmas party was this? I saw that I'd have to protect the Nativity crèche, so that it would not be manhandled by lusty guests or the swinging Santa. I'd dressed Baby Jesus in swaddling Armani, and He could not withstand multiple gropings.

I had to go out then and roam the streets in search of a Santa free for the following night. Who could I find? I knew I couldn't ask Ray to be Santa—even if he were speaking to me—and I was sure he wouldn't want to do the Queen Bee any favors. I walked to the El, and then I saw him. Salvation Army Santa! The kindly nonsmoker who had to muffle his bell. I explained the situation to him and begged for help.

"I don't know," he said doubtfully. "I usually serve at the soup kitchen Friday nights."

"Oh, please! You can bring your kettle, and we'll charge the guests to sit on your lap. You'll make much more for the Salvation Army in one night at a society bash than you would in a whole week of standing out here."

He relented, and I gave him the address and time.

"Thank you, you won't regret it. Plus there'll be tons of good food and free booze all night long."

He laughed, and said, "Oh, no, I gave up drinking a long time ago. I find that God gives me the strength to—"

"Listen, Santa," I interrupted, "don't start spouting that religious jazz at the party, okay? Do you want to ruin Christmas?"

Man, Christianity was like a wet blanket on my holiday fever.

That evening, I brought the red-and-white snowflake quilt sewn by Ma out from retirement in the basement. Red was kind of nice: warm, toasty. I called Chip, greeting him enthusiastically by his new name.

Through the phone lines, I heard the faint sound of gnashing teeth. "*Please* do not call me Sof' G."

"Well, I can't call you 'chess fag' anymore."

"You've called me chess fag and the president of the Sal Mineo fan club for fifteen years. Why stop now?"

I said, "Well, *you* know. It was one thing to call you chess fag when I thought you were straight. Now that I know you're gay, it seems mean."

He sighed and moved on to the topic at hand—Honey's party. "Will she let me in?" he asked. "She really only invited Ma and Daddy."

"Do you think Honey actually opens the door at her own parties? It'll be me or the scrubwoman; just make sure you have your fake press credentials hanging around your neck. Bring Bruce, a tape recorder, and at least two cameras. And afterward get the hell out. Honey always hires gargantuan Japanese bodyguards to patrol her parties and smash the cameras belonging to photographers who take unflattering pictures of her or her guests."

"Right, no problem. This is excellent, Lisa! I never said thanks, but let me say it now—"

"No need, Sof' G," I said happily.

I waited all week in vain for Ray to call. If he didn't show up at the party, then I'd know there was no chance for me. Ebes would be there, but I no longer cared. If these months had taught me anything, it was that it's wise to meet a man before you decide to love him. That meant the next four or five decades would probably be spent alone, until I moved back in with my family and died amidst pet fanciers and aging socialists. It would suck, but perhaps knowing that I'd done the right thing once would provide some comfort to me before I sank into my dotage.

Even with that prospect before me, there was no way I'd return to Luke, decent fellow that he is. He's nice to talk to, but now that I know what love is, I cannot doom myself to a passionless life of pleasant conversation.

On Friday, party day, Honey went to Crump's for a hot-waxing, eyebrow session, and dunk in the mud tub. She told me to call

Babbington and ask him to come along, but I said he told me he had other plans.

"That's so strange," she said. "Every time you've called him this week, he's been out or busy. I hope he's still coming to my party, that naughty little man."

"He'll be there," I promised, and shoved her out the door.

I hopped on the Michigan Avenue bus to Fishman's. Mrs. Lubbeth said I could borrow one of my old Maria Callas gowns for tonight's party. I chose the harlequin-patterned plum gown from *Lucia di Lammermoor*. Or the flaming-cheese dress, as it was known around Fishman's. The burns had been repaired, but it was not good enough for the irregular department. It was good enough for me.

"Try not to spill on it," cautioned Mrs. Lubbeth. "If you do, I won't be able to bail you out this time." It was Doris Mingle who bailed me out before, not that anyone remembers.

She told me that Hui had been so disappointed by the sluggish traffic in Clinton-inspired Men's Wear, that he called in sick three days in a row—an unprecedented turn of events. With a lame-duck administration and no supervisor, the Men's Wear employees surreptitiously pasted photocopies of Ralph Nader's face over Clinton's on their advertisements, in the hopes of boosting flagging sales. Rudderless, they'd begun to drift in a sea of identity politics.

I packed up my gown and prepared to say good-bye to Women's Wear, but I couldn't find anyone. Gulag Anna came in just then and said that everyone was watching a huge argument between Mr. Fishman and Jesus from Sporting Goods. Poor Jesus had been saddled with FDR as his department's presidential mascot, and the sight of the wheelchair dampened the sales of rowing machines and treadmills. Without asking, he changed his mascot to George W. Bush, who had not yet been inaugurated. Mr. Fishman had reportedly shouted that the store was only doing past presidents, not future, but everyone thinks he just objected to Sporting

Goods's fraternity-house decor and empty beer bottles everywhere. Jesus had hung signs on the bicycle rack that read, "He wouldn't have been given a DUI if he'd ridden one of these." Signs on the treadmills read, "You won't be getting health insurance or a living wage—might as well improve your cardiovascular endurance." Sales shot through the roof.

"I hate your democracy," said Gulag Anna.

Back at Honey's, I was supposed to brush The Don and put a red bow around his neck. But after I tied the ribbon, he tore it off and bit it and jumped up and down on it. I got the impression he disliked the bow, but then I'm no pet psychic.

Chef Molman arrived with an entourage of kitchen underlings, appetizers, and cooking sherry. Esmé stood by the stove and tried to order him around, but he just threw wooden spoons at her and threatened to storm off.

"Where are the meat and the salmon?" demanded Esmé. "They should have been here by now."

Luckily, the grocery-store delivery boy came by soon after and dumped off the goods in the FedEx boxes. The chef got to work, with Esmé hovering over him, and I began to slide furniture around the Parisian hub, making room for the DJ booth and dancing cages.

At seven o'clock exactly, Honey sank into her Empire love seat with a martini, awaiting her guests. Fred had set up his DJ equipment and began spinning some get-in-the-mood Easy (Herb Alpert and the Tijuana Brass's "Taste of Honey"). The Santa girls changed into their costumes in the bathroom. The Don sat placidly on his windowsill pillow, overseeing everything.

"How do I look, darling?" asked Honey. The one-legged pantsuit fit her like a dream. Daddy even managed to construct it in such a way that gave Honey the appearance of having a rear end, instead of just two legs going straight into her back.

"Divine," I said.

"Your *papa* is a genius. I shall have him do all my alterations from now on."

The guests began to arrive. I doubt Honey even missed the cardinal, as she was half in the bag by seven-thirty. It was amazing to watch the society folk react to the one-legged pantsuit. At first they staggered around horror-struck, until Honey opened her mouth and that smooth, sweet drawling voice of hers came oozing out, whispering about her private bespoke tailor and the fabric flown in from Milan. Frankly, Daddy *did* tell her he got all his fabric from Milan, but he meant Milan Feldman, the old wholesaler from Maxwell Street. Honey dragged Daddy from guest to guest, introducing him as Salvatore from the House of Galisa. I had to hand it to her: by the time she was done with him, she had people believing he was the black-sheep cousin of Prada's Patrizio Bertelli and the only reason he didn't design for Prada was that he was too visionary. Daddy smiled happily and said little. Everyone thought he was an eccentric Italian genius who understood no English. Ladies from the Creosote Club shouted, "Gorgeous pantsuit!" at him.

"Where is Babbington?" Honey hissed, taking me aside. "The invitation said seven on the dot, and he's never late." My postscript had suggested he arrive at nine, but I just looked innocently at her and shrugged.

Ma spent most of the evening in the kitchen, advising the chef. He tried to kick her out, but Ma is not one for taking hints. She said, "Chef, I see you have a little round steak left over. Why not let me pound it and make some nice braciole?"

The chef approached Ma with the meat tenderizer clutched in his fist, a situation about which I have often fantasized myself.

By eight, the whole crowd was swinging to the Easy sounds of Mantovani mixed with Stereolab. Fred paused while looking for new records to smile and wave me over.

"Guess what. Dennis Farina just hired me to spin at his New Year's Eve party!"

"Congrats, Fred. I knew you would be a success."

He held up an armload of Christmas records and CDs, beaming.

"Cover Duels?" I asked.

He nodded. "Bing Crosby versus the world."

Honey brought out a bottle of '97 cabernet sauvignon flown in from her family's West Coast vineyard, proclaiming it to be a very exciting little sauvignon. I poured myself a glass. It was not so exciting. Santa arrived and I installed him on Honey's Louis Quinze chair by the Christmas tree. We set his kettle on a sixteenth-century commode, and people lined up.

"Ten dollars for a Santa session," I informed the crowd.

"And five dollars for a picture," added Chip from behind me. He waved an Instamatic camera and smiled. Nice going, Chip. That would add a good sum to my Misery Fund.

Santa looked uncomfortable as adults threw themselves on his lap and asked for jewelry and cars. A diamond broker shouted out, "Hey, Santa, can you give my wife the ass of an eighteen-year-old?" Santa frowned.

A guy next to the broker said, "Your wife *does* have the ass of an eighteen-year-old, Jerry. A fat eighteen-year-old!" Everyone laughed except the wife. She put a hundred-dollar bill in Santa's kettle and quietly whispered there'd be more where that came from if he'd assault her husband in the alley after the party.

"Excuse me," I said, escorting her away, "Santa doesn't freelance."

I turned to let the next person in line step up to Santa. It was Luke. He said, "I've called you about a thousand times."

I said, "Santa will see you now."

Luke sighed and dropped ten dollars in the kettle. He sat on Santa's knee and said, "All I really want for Christmas is to go out with this girl I like, who won't return my calls. I don't know what I did, but I'm pretty bummed out."

Santa said, "We've all been there, son." Stomach churned again as I watched him shake Luke's hand and wish him luck. I hated myself. Where were my Tums?

Bruce took over my post while I went in search of Luke. I found him at the far end of the Hearst table, holding a Lenox Christmas plate full of food, staring out the window.

"Hi," I said.

He turned to me with his mouth full of braciole. "These are good," he said, stuffing another in. Suddenly I found myself unable to say anything else. He offered me the plate of skewered meat.

Relieved, I said, "Yeah, I'll have one of those." Fortified with meat, I made another stab at apologizing . . . for not calling, for not being truthful with him.

"What do you mean, not truthful?"

"Luke, I . . . I think I love someone. Else. Someone else. I'm sorry, I should have told you." Miserably, I ate more meat.

He didn't say much else. After all, what was there to say? I took the plate from him and finished it off. Poured myself an exciting little sauvignon. Then poured myself an exciting lot.

"At least you have your work," I said, moving over to the buffet and piling more braciole into a pyramid on my plate. Esmé was bringing out additional platters of food and watched me snarf with undisguised revulsion. Who cared what the scrubwoman thought? I slid one off its skewer whole with my teeth. Oops, gristly.

"Yeah."

"It must be satisfying to work for Roger Ebert."

He looked over his shoulder, as though I was talking to someone else. "I don't work for Roger Ebert."

I stopped, midsnarf. "Yes, you do. You're Roger Ebert's personal assistant. You said you worked at the *Sun-Times*."

He said, "Yeah, but I'm Phil Rosenthal's personal assistant."

I spit out the gristle. "Who?"

"Phil Rosenthal, the television critic." He pointed to a heavy-set man swing-dancing with Honey Dietrich.

I stared at him, thinking there must be some mistake. "But he's not even on TV!" I blurted out.

Luke asked, "What does that have to do with anything?"

What had I been doing in bed with Phil Rosenthal's personal assistant? I stood mute, in shock, as Ebert came up to the table then, trading old U of I stories with Dick Butkus while a nice-looking woman wearing a bemused expression followed behind.

"Hi, Mr. and Mrs. Ebert," said Luke.

Mrs. Ebert?

Luke whispered to me, "I hear she gives great Fourth-of-July parties."

I looked down at my empty plate and said, "I think I'm going to be sick." I turned to make a run for the bathroom—the crowd was impenetrable. I clamped my hand over my mouth, but it was too late. I horked braciole and cabernet sauvignon all over Esmé and her platter of salmon. Now *that* was exciting.

Tim Gideon helped clean me up in the bathroom while Honey stood outside the locked door and swore.

"Ignore her," said Tim as I blubbered and blubbered. "Thank God you didn't get any on your dress. That maid is in pretty sore shape, though. I can't believe your drunk did this to you. I thought you fired her."

I cried. "It wasn't her; it was *me*! I did all this. I'm a pig. I'm a pig and a bad person. I slept with the wrong personal assistant, and Ray's not coming to the party. Ebert saw me hurl and he already has a wife and who the hell is Phil Rosenthal?"

"It's my fault. I got the info wrong, Lisa. I really thought Luke was Ebert's whipping boy."

"Oh, I guess it doesn't matter either way," I sobbed. "I'm a failure and a disgusting individual; just throw me out the window into Lake Michigan."

"Don't be ridiculous," said Tim. "These windows don't even open."

After my scrub-down, I emerged from the bathroom into the shrieking face of Honey Dietrich. I apologized for hurling and started to cry again.

"She said she was sorry!" snapped Tim.

Honey looked at him in amazement. "And who the hell are you?"

Tim shot his cuffs and said, "I'm Alan Greenspan."

Honey narrowed her eyes at him, then said with recognition, "Ah, yes, the Bible salesman. Well, you get her out to the living room." She thrust a bucket of cleanser and a sponge at me and told me to clean it all up. I walked through the crowd with my scrubwoman accoutrements, face aflame, and knelt down by the mess. The Don had beat me to it and had already started to help in his own orderly, methodical way.

Thankfully, I was in the corner under the Hearst table, so nobody really saw me. I finished cleaning in fifteen minutes, though I thought, *Why bother coming out?* I sat a little distance from the site of my disgrace, still in safety. Part of me wanted to come out and find my dad and let him comfort me, or to go in search of the tender arms of Mrs. Lubbeth. But most of me was too ashamed to show my face. I watched legs walk by, listened to conversations about blue-chip stocks and Maui and hairstyles. I wished to see the hems of overalls, hear Gina talk about dogs and Saint Francis; I wanted Ma to stroll by in magenta warm-up pants and gush about her son, her son the newspaperman; I imagined Fred's silver bell-bottoms gonging away—perhaps he would kneel down, see me here, help me out from under everything. But he didn't. No one did.

I checked my watch. Babbington would be here any minute. I crossed my fingers, hoping Chip could deal with it. It was not fair for me to let him handle it all alone, but there you have it. I was selfish and cowardly; I was not Maria Callas or even a good personal assistant. I was just a person.

I heard Chip's voice. He was talking to red fun-fur pants.

"So, Santa," he said, "how's it going? I've made almost two hundred bucks just taking pictures."

"Yes, I've made a lot for the Salvation Army, too," said Santa, "but frankly, I don't know how much more of this I can take."

Santa shared some braciole with Chip, then went back to the Louis Quinze chair. Chip introduced himself to socialites as Sof' G.

Black Velvet Stirrup Pants ambled all around the table, followed by Chicken Legs in nude hose and sensible shoes. Chubby ankles swelled out around the stirrups.

"Our Lisa planned all this," remarked Black Velvet Stirrups.

"She's smart," said Chicken Legs. "I wish she still worked in the ladies' department."

"Me too, hon," sighed Black Velvet Stirrups. "Me too."

Red Silk Wide-legged Trousers came up to them. "We should have insisted Mr. Fishman give her a raise after her stunning performance as the diva and many successful fashion shows. I could have done more for her, but I was so worried about unloading all those Galliano tea dresses."

Black Velvet Stirrups seemed to murmur comforting words to Red Silk Trousers. Chicken Legs scratched her calf with the toe of a big Cobbie Cuddler. Then they all walked away.

Then Green Corduroys came up to the table and stood next to Single Orange Pant Leg.

Orange Pant Leg said, "Well, I just depend upon the stars, darling. My pet psychic says our destiny lies in the stars, don't you agree?"

Green Corduroys said, "I've always preferred the planets. Although Mercury is unstable due to its orbital-rotational resonance, as you might have guessed." Orange Pant Leg giggled.

Only one man I know can charm society hags with tales of science. I stood up quickly and bonked my head on the table.

"Ouch!" I cried. Green Corduroys crouched down and, as I'd hoped, became Ray Fuchet.

"Lisa! What are you doing under here?"

I said limply, "There was a situation. . . ."

Honey confided to Ray, "Poor dear had an eensy bit too much to eat and drink. Too sad. Sickie-poo all over my kilim!"

Ray immediately crawled under the table with me, which drove Honey mad. She stamped her foot and stalked off.

"I like it under here," said Ray.

"Ray, I've been such an idiot."

He grinned. "I like it even more now."

I said, "I can't believe you came. After everything I did, you really came."

He shrugged slightly.

I continued. "I have a confession to make."

"Uh-oh. Does this involve Roger Ebert's wardrobe again? Because he still isn't wearing that maroon sweater. Houndstooth sack suit, I think."

"No. I just wanted to say that . . . that you were right. I'm an optimist. I have hope for the future, and I don't care who hears me, as long as *you* hear me. Know what I mean?"

"Possibly," he said.

I swallowed uncomfortably and trudged on. "I, uh . . . I'm not really good at . . ." My voice trailed off.

"Being nice?" he suggested.

"No . . ."

"Apologizing?" He tried again.

I shook my head.

"Expressing yourself?"

"Right!" I sighed in relief. "Sharing, confiding. It's all hard. But I'm trying. The thing is, I made a mistake with that other guy, the nonboyfriend, and I'm . . . I'm truly . . ."

"Wretched?"

"Wretched? That's a little harsh. Well, all right, yes, I'm wretched. Really wretched. The most wretched person to walk the earth. But mostly, I'm sorry."

"Ah."

"Can I just have another chance? I've done everything wrong because I was trying to . . . to sabotage my own happiness."

"Sabotage your own happiness? What kind of excuse is that?"

Damn it. Never depend on Oprah.

"Ray, is it possible for us to rewrite history like you once said?"

"No, Lisa," he said. "I guess you really can't ever rewrite history."

My heart sank. *So I've done it,* I despaired, *I've ruined everything. I ruined myself and my chances with Ray. I'm a ruiner of things, a ruiner of people.*

Ray stroked his square chin thoughtfully. "But I suppose you can try to change the future. Want to try?"

I couldn't believe it: he wanted to forge ahead into the future with me? I was *not* a ruiner of things! At least not all things. I grabbed his pudgy earlobes and zeroed in to sensuous lips and dark eyes and magnatelike hairline. We fogged up his giant scientist spectacles.

Suddenly Orange Pant Leg reappeared. Its arm felt around under the table, caught hold of me, and dragged me out. She stood me up, leaned into my face, and growled, "What's with the chocolate Santa?"

"What?"

She pointed at Santa in the corner, who read aloud from a small, worn book. Fred had turned the music way down; it was Bing versus Esquivel, "White Christmas." Pretty. Ray crawled out and held my hand.

Santa said, "'For unto you is born this day in the city of David a Savior, who is Christ the Lord. And this shall be a sign unto you: Ye shall find the babe wrapped in swaddling clothes, lying in a manger. And suddenly there was with the angel a multitude of the heavenly host praising God, and saying Glory to God in the highest, and on earth peace, goodwill toward men.' My friends, that's what Christmas is all about."

With only Esquivel's soft melody playing in the background, the partygoers stood silent, looking at Santa. Then Phil Rosenthal said, "Hey, that's Linus's speech from *A Charlie Brown Christmas*!"

Everyone shouted with recognition and congratulated Santa. It was more agreeable for the guests to think of Santa reciting words from a television show than from the Bible.

Honey said, "I wanted a conventional Santa and you bring me this. A black, religious Santa—*really*, Lisa, what *were* you thinking?"

I found myself speechless. Ray had no such difficulty, and let loose with a string of invective that caused Honey to stagger backward theatrically and flutter her old claw to her throat. With a snort, she declared him char-*ming,* and turned on me like a wolverine. I backed away from her, hoping to disappear into the crowd, but ran into an immovable mountain.

"Mrs. Lubbeth!" I cried. But Honey had already advanced, pushing me aside.

"How nice to see you, Mrs. Lubbeth," she cooed. "There are simply too, too many awful people here. It's wonderful to see a friendly face." I felt exactly the same way. Waiting in the Santa line were Nan, Bernie, and the underwear salesman, who was waving at me. Mr. Fishman danced with the shoe people near the DJ booth. Mrs. Consolo admired the cut of Honey's pantsuit, and Doris Mingle came up to the two of them shyly and said hello. Honey stopped chattering and her face froze.

"Pardon me, missy," she said to Doris. "But what are you doing here?"

Blood drained away from Doris's face, leaving her ashen and wobbly. "I was . . . invited."

Honey opened her eyes wide in mockery. "*Were* you? How is that possible, since this is my party and I did not invite you?"

I said, "I invited Doris, Ms. Dietrich."

She wheeled about and stared at me. "You! After I told you how I felt about her, you expressly disobeyed me."

The guests directly around us stopped talking and turned to watch the spectacle. Doris tried to melt into the background—I knew all about that. I said, "Doris is a nice person, and I thought it was mean to exclude her. Goodwill toward people and all that. Besides, I like her."

Honey sputtered, "Don't tell *me* about goodwill! I've been standing here listening to your Goodwill Santa ram his religion down our throats."

"Salvation Army," corrected Santa, but no one paid attention.

I protested, "Ms. Dietrich, just think of all that Doris has done for you in terms of finding *discount designer irregulars!*" The crowd gasped. The secret was out.

I felt fantastic.

Honey lurched at me, talons extended. She screeched, "You're fired!"

I replied, "You can't fire me. I quit." Just like that little dentist-elf on *Rudolph the Red-Nosed Reindeer.*

At that moment, Honey's front door swung open. Without me or vomit-splattered Esmé to welcome in guests, they had to let themselves in. I'll always remember the music that was playing when the figure stepped through the door: Rick James versus Mantovani, "Super Freak (Part 1)."

"Hello, friends, and Happy New Year!" shouted the figure, a nearly naked man dressed only in top hat, cotton diaper with large gold kilt-pin (thank God for the diaper, which spared us complete trauma), and hateful mustache.

Chip and Bruce snapped photos. *"Sic semper tyrannis!"* they shouted, then dashed out the door.

"Where's everyone's costumes?" squeaked Babbington Hawkes.

Chapter 27

The day after the party, I went to Fishman's to try and apologize to Doris Mingle. I didn't mind being a barfing laughingstock as much as I minded her humiliation at the hands of high society. She and Mrs. Lubbeth were marking up irregulars. It was comforting, being in the midst of Women's Wear and irregular underpants again.

"Hi," I said humbly. I expected censure, but Mrs. Lubbeth squashed me warmly and Doris smiled.

I said, "Sorry about the party. Sorry about everything."

Doris said, "Thanks for inviting me."

"What are you thanking me for? What good came of it?"

She said, "You invited me."

I felt myself coloring. I cleared my throat and said, "Thanks for delivering that letter. Did you see the hideous man-baby rush in? I couldn't have done it without your help, Doris."

She looked both pleased and somewhat alarmed.

Mrs. Lubbeth handed me some underwear to fold. She said, "You know, these temp clerks don't appreciate the kind of camaraderie we permanent salesladies have. They can't get into the spirit of the thing."

I glanced enviously at the temps. How could they not see the joys of lifelong Fishman employment? They didn't know what lurked out there beyond our store's limestone walls, that's the only explanation. *I've* been out there, *I* knew. I've lived through the *war,* sugar.

I handed Mrs. Lubbeth a pair of underwear with only one leg opening. It brought instant tears to my eyes.

• • •

Two days later, Mrs. Lubbeth did the kindest thing imaginable. She called me and pretended she couldn't cope with the ineptitude of the temps, and asked if I'd come back to Fishman's.

"I don't deserve to," I sniveled. "I abandoned you after you made a success out of me."

"Hon, I heard you tell Ms. Dietrich that you quit. I heard you defend Doris. You belong here with us, in our little Fishman family."

I thought for a moment and said, "You know, Mrs. Lubbeth, I really had a wonderful life."

She said after all my experience with high society and couture, I was ready to move up to senior saleslady. Additional duties would include overseeing theme management and handling negotiations with Hui.

She said, "I'm afraid it doesn't pay much more than junior saleslady, but don't forget the perks."

"What perks?" I asked.

She said, "Brown name tags."

Chapter 28

Christmas Eve brought chilling temperatures, but the snow had stopped. Bridgeport was quiet, the shops had closed for the holiday, people stayed indoors. Nana DeRosa puttered around our kitchen, pounding salmon scaloppini and preparing sweet-and-sour meatballs, a favorite of her grandson, her grandson. Grandma and I sat in the living room with Daddy, looking through fashion magazines.

"I like this one," said Daddy, pointing to a blue beaded chiffon gown.

"Ick, it's so grandma," I said. Grandma scowled.

"Not you, Grandma," I said. "Other grandmas."

Daddy said, "I could make this," and dog-eared the page.

"Why bother? I thought Honey told you, 'Get out, get out, and never come back,' after the party?" Again I had brought about the destruction of his livelihood.

He said, "Oh, who cares? I told you I didn't like the way she screamed at you and Santa and the tall skinny girl with the big nose." He pulled a card out of his wallet. "I got a real nice letter in the mail yesterday from a gal who'd like a gown for a Valentine's Day ball. I'm bringing samples and drawings to her next month."

He handed me the card that was enclosed in the letter. It was engraved with a tiny old-fashioned teapot and sugar bowl. The name on it—Sugar Rautbord.

Gina stood in her bedroom, hands on hips, surveying. She had moved in a computer and a bigger desk, file cabinets, a library of animal-health books, and several volumes on starting your own business.

She said, "There's not enough room in here anymore."

I asked, "What will you do?"

She smiled at me hopefully.

I said firmly, "Fine. But there's no room in my apartment for the miniature working farm."

We shook on it.

My sister and I barged into Chip's room. It was time for Midnight Mass, also time for a little hit of Acapulco Gold. Chip sat at his desk, outlining the contents for the next *Prole*. Naturally, the photo of Baby New Year Babbington would go on the cover, along with a scathing exposé of the slice of socialite life as witnessed by Chip and Bruce. They planned to launch an Internet protest as well. They are all about sending scurrilous e-mails these days under the name Sof' G. Until the next alderman scandal, they're looking forward to turning their attention from the Republicrats at City Hall to the jackbooted thugs at *Chicago Society*. I told Chip I hoped he didn't mind the nasty column that appeared in today's issue.

"No, I don't care," he said. "Do you?"

CHRISTMAS RUINED
BY DEGENERATES

By Babbington Hawkes

It's sad when a joyous holiday is destroyed by malicious interlopers. As you know, Honey Dietrich threw her annual Christmas party last Friday at her lovely apartment. Usually, we quietly celebrate the Yuletide at Honey's with friends, enjoying simple food, simple decorations, simple carols, and simple presents from Bailey, Banks, and Biddle. Not so, this year. We will probably not celebrate the holiday ever again, so traumatic was the evening.

Blame former personality Lisa Galisa. I am told she had planned what started out as a chic Easy Christmas party for Honey, complete with the sexy musical stylings of DJ Fred and the Caged Heat Dancers. The decor was au courant, the music divine, the food tasty (especially those skewered meat things, thanks Chef Molman), the trees festive. New addition, Tee Nee Romanini's The Don (a rare Parisian Hub Cat), watched the goings-on from his windowsill pillow. I sincerely hope he does not think *all* of our parties end the way this one did.

Galisa, society's most ardent gate-crasher and longtime abuser of hair products, decided to have a little fun at old Babbington's expense. Why go into details? Suffice to say I missed half the party and arrived underdressed. Also crashing the party were publishing's newest poseurs and anarchists-with-a-bar-code, *Prole* magazine. No doubt they will document the sordidness in their pathetic little rag—thankfully no one reads it.

Those of you familiar with Galisa's modus operandi will not be surprised to hear that, again, she used a public arena as her own private vomitorium. Society breathed a sigh of relief when it heard that Honey fired her. Scuttlebutt has it that she's going to be flogging sportswear again, after the January white sales.

Honey is recuperating in seclusion, venturing out only to take counsel with the cardinal, attend her family's Christmas celebration, and welcome in the new year with close friends. January 2 will find Honey in Boca with The Don, trying to put all this depravity behind them. . . .

I put the paper down and said, "No, it doesn't bother me, either." I went from person, to personal assistant, to former personality in a few short months. I'm back to person again.

. . . .

At Midnight Mass, Daddy cried as usual, hugging us all. Nana and Grandma stayed behind to fight in the kitchen. We rode home from St. Barbara's together in the station wagon. Ma turned around and looked at her three mildly stoned adult children in the backseat.

"Sal, look at our kids."

"I can't," he said. "I'm trying to make this light."

"I'll tell you what I see: I see a beautiful and successful animal telemarketer—"

Gina said, "Animal communicator."

"—and a brilliant newspaperman, and a senior saleslady/ adviser to socialites. We're damned lucky."

Daddy said, "See, Lisa? I always said there was nothing more satisfying than selling a decent garment." No mention was made of retail hell.

He continued. "By the way, Chip, I need to revamp the basement into a sewing room, so you're gonna have to think about relocating your newspaper."

Chip cried, "Where are we gonna go? Where will we find rent-free digs?"

Slowly, all eyes turned to me, even Daddy's, who nearly drove us into Mikolajczak's front window. "Oh, no," I said. "I live in a studio apartment, and Gina's already moving in. There's no room for chess tournaments."

Chip said, "Fred's parents are renting out that big apartment over their bar. It has three bedrooms and together the three of us could afford it. I could run *Prole* out of the dining room."

I debated this for a few minutes. North Side versus South. Wrigley versus Comiskey. Sushi and latte versus Polish and Old Style. Would I be sliding backward or moving forward?

"The South Side's cool," pleaded Chip. "Get with it."

"Get Easy," corrected Daddy.

I decided to go with it. Bridgeport is the community of the future.

At home in our kitchen we found Grandma and Nana dancing to the groovy sounds of Andre Kostelanetz. A third figure, a man, stepped in between them and dipped Nana. She kicked her Dearfoam slipper up in the air.

"Wheeeee!" she squealed, squeezing the boxy behind of Ray Fuchet.

"You came," I said.

"Of course. Who in his right mind would skip Christmas Eve with the Galisas?"

Ray. Ray, with black-and-silver hair falling over his brow, and tough lantern jaw, and square head, and janitorial mischief dancing in his dark eyes. Ray, inventor of ultra-absorbent sick sand and teacher of astronomy at the sixth-grade level.

He spun Grandma around. "I stopped by to have a beer with Fred first. I felt like celebrating. Yesterday, we found out that someone had anonymously donated over seven hundred dollars to Seward Academy. The accompanying note suggested we could use it to start our own science fair and buy new mailboxes. It was signed, 'the Chairman of the Misery Fund.'"

Nana shoved Grandma aside and wriggled into Ray's grasp. Grandma refused to let go. The three of them twirled around together, accomplishing a rather heartbreaking waltz. I felt my face stretching into the demented smile of a perfectly happy person.

Nana said, "I like the cut of your jib, Ray Fuchet."

He said, "What's this I hear about a bonfire?"

The grandmothers and Ma set to work in the kitchen, bringing out shrimp fritters with roasted-garlic sauce. Daddy turned on the TV, aghast at the broadcast biography of Alan Alda. He recounted to Ray the long list of annoying men on earth as well as the career paths of various *Love Boat*–reunion stars.

Chip got the bonfire going. It crackled loudly from the space-ship-wok firepit. Mr. Krespi watched us from behind his kitchen curtains.

"I hate this ritual," grumbled Grandma. "And the fritters are cold."

"*Ice* cold," added Nana.

"So don't eat 'em," said Ma.

Nana threw her hands up in the air and screamed, "Forget I said anything!"

Grandma sniffed, "All this shouting is giving me a headache, not to mention that cigarette smoke." She glared at me and pro-ceeded to choke and sputter, waving her hands frantically in front of her nose. I popped a few Tums and lit a new Parliament with the butt end of the old one.

Gina and I sat on the wooden picnic bench, huddling under an afghan. The night sky was clear, velvet black studded with dia-monds. Ursa Minor, Orion's Belt. I breathed in my cig, comforted amid the swirling maelstrom of Galisa lunacy.

Gina asked what I was going to burn. I said I couldn't think of anything. That my many failures this year had unpredictably transformed themselves into successes. Ma threw her lottery tickets into the fire as Daddy renewed a previous conversation with Ray on William Shatner's role in the history of television annoyance.

Gina watched the exchange, giggling. She whispered to me, "Can you believe someone likes you enough to sit through all this?"

I said, "No, I cannot." But I looked up at the stars and tried to.

ACKNOWLEDGMENTS

I would like to thank the following people for their support and guid-
ance: Caroline Sincerbeaux, Noah Lukeman, Amye Dyer, "Easy" Ed
Marszewski, Joe Collier, and especially my husband, Chris.